YOUNG MISTLEY

BY

HENRY SETON MERRIMAN

AUTHOR OF "THE SOWERS," "RODEN'S CORNER," ETC.

NEW YORK

A. MACKEL & COMPANY, Publishers

1899

YOUNG MISTLEY

CHAPTER I

" MONSIEUR JACOBI—the Baroness de Nantille! "

Monsieur Jacobi bowed with grave courtesy—the Baroness de Nantille inclined her head without raising her eyes, and the introduction was complete. The introducer, Mrs. Wright, turned away with a little sigh of relief to continue her duties of hostess. Monsieur Jacobi and the Baroness had never been to her house before, and the astute little Englishwoman was not prepossessed in favor of the foreign lady. Monsieur Jacobi, of course, was irreproachable. Everyone knew the name of the new musician whose violin had insinuated him into every circle in London where the fine arts came under unprofitable discussion. Mrs. Wright rather prided herself upon being particularly English, however. She avoided Continental celebrities who, like prophets and other self-made folk, are entirely unknown in their own land. She was, no doubt, terribly prejudiced, after the manner of her countrymen and women; but the fact remains that Bohemianism, long hair, and sallow faces received a scanty welcome in her drawing-room. Affectation in

1

any form or manner was singularly distasteful to her, and she was not afraid of showing her feelings in this matter.

The most regular frequenters of her cheerful little entertainments were not, as a rule, celebrated in any way. There was a sprinkling of young military men, a carefully-selected assortment of active politicians, and some waifs and strays who followed various crafts and professions. It is to be feared that Mrs. Wright found her friends among a circle of very cheery idlers. Men without lofty aspirations—women without ambition. Maidens who danced, and sang, and loved, and laughed—youths who rowed, and rode, and roamed, and smoked wooden pipes in the streets.

Of such the small rooms were full this evening, and Madame la Baronne de Nantille was hanging heavily upon her hostess's hands. The stalwart youths at that moment dancing in the other room had, by some strange mishap, one and all discovered that their programmes were full when Mrs. Wright proposed to introduce them to the distinguished stranger. Every hostess knows the difficulty attached to allowing their guests to bring friends, and if Mrs. Wright had thought it worth her while she would have borne some ill-will toward the ladies who had been the means of introducing two such "unlikely" people as the Baroness and Monsieur Jacobi into her house. But, as was her cheery habit, the little lady took things and guests as they came, making the best of everything. And now a weight was removed from her mind. The sudden inspiration had passed through her brain to introduce these two to each other, and trouble little more about them. Monsieur Jacobi, as already mentioned, was a most presentable person. Clean-

2

shaven, dark and sleek, his manners were suave and courtly; his medium-sized, graceful figure was an ornament to any room. Such minute peculiarities of dress as he indulged in were offensive to none, and most allowable in a musician somewhat above the average. In Kensington he was much run after by damsels who mistook, in themselves, bodily weakness for mental woe, dressing in sombre misshapen garments in order to pass on the belief to others. But in Mrs. Wright's house Monsieur Jacobi had not as yet succeeded in creating in any fair young bosom the least thrill of interest. The hostess herself, who it is to be feared was somewhat cynical, persisted in looking upon him as a violinist and nothing else. She accorded to him no greater attention—and indeed not so much—as she did to young Sparkle, who had just scraped his way into Woolwich Academy and his first dress-coat.

With the Baroness, however, it was a different matter. Mrs. Wright honored her with a good deal of attention of an unobtrusive order. In fact, she took every opportunity of glancing unobserved in her direction, noting with her quick gray eyes every detail of the Baroness's dress, every tiny movement, many of which betrayed to the woman of the world that this stranger was out of her element.

The introduction took place in the smaller drawing-room, which was almost deserted at the moment. Indeed, there was only one other person present. This was a man with hair and pointed beard, mustache and overhanging eyebrows as white as snow. The head was that of an old man—such as one pictures the ancient patriarchs to have been—but the body was straight, and the movements, without being lithe, were far from denoting

3

infirmity. This was Laurance Lowe—a mossless stone whose rolling-days were done. People whispered to each other that in days gone by Laurance Lowe would fain have ceased his rolling ways, but that Providence had willed it otherwise, sending a courageous and fairly intelligent young soldier—one Lieutenant Wright—to set the stone once more agoing, and to gather for himself the moss. Whatever may have passed between the white-haired man and the cheery little matron (still comely and hearty) in those forgotten days was only known to themselves, and neither ever referred to it. People wondered why Mrs. Wright should trouble herself with this silent old man, who contributed in no way to the entertainment of her guests. They considered him an old bore, though he never displayed the least anxiety to be honored with their attention—never yawned, never confessed to fatigue, and never partook in a general conversation.

It was to him that Mrs. Wright turned with her ready smile, which, however, had something different in it when her eyes met his. She raised her eyebrows and made an almost imperceptible movement with her lips, which plainly said, "I do not like those people." Lowe gazed at her solemnly beneath his shaggy white eyebrows as she crossed the room, but his face betrayed no sign of having read aright the expression of hers. His eyes never returned the little flash of mutual understanding: the light from the candles on the delicately tinted wall glimmered on the surface of the small single eyeglass he carried perpetually and without an effort. It was well that his face was thus expressionless and habitually somewhat stony, for Monsieur Jacobi was watching from out of the corners of his eyes.

Laurance Lowe inclined his head with an old-world courtesy as Mrs. Wright approached him.

"Coffee?" he said interrogatively, without moving mustache or beard, and offered her his arm.

"Thanks, Laurance, I will!" replied the little lady, with a grateful smile. During the last twenty years these two had gone through that little ceremony many hundreds of times.

They passed together into another room, and the Baroness was left alone with Monsieur Jacobi. He had possessed himself of her engagement-card, and was now studying it, pencil in hand. Every curve of his body, the very manner in which he held his pencil, his eagerly bowed head, were expressive of the utmost deference and respect.

The Baroness had not yet raised her eyes from the polished floor. Her strong white hands, beautifully shaped and encased only in open-work mittens, lay idly upon her lap. There was something in her whole attitude, in the repose of her fair face, in her downcast eyes, which was forced and unnatural. Hers was indeed a beautiful face, sculptured on rather a smaller scale than Englishmen admire, pale and very calm, with red level lips and close-set eyes. Her soft colorless hair, almost white in its exquisite fairness, was arranged with extreme simplicity, but she wore it parted upon one side, in accordance with a fashion now obsolete in England. She could not have been more than twenty-five years of age, despite her repose of manner, which was almost that of a matron.

When Monsieur Jacobi had made sure that they were alone, the expression of his keen face underwent a remarkable change, though his attitude remained unaltered.

"Who," he asked in a low-pitched voice, and with an unpleasant smile—"who is the old fossil who wears an eyeglass in one eye and sees with the other?" The Baroness raised her calm blue eyes, and met Jacobi's sardonic smile with a contemptuous stare.

"Your conscience must indeed be an evil one, Jacobi," she said slowly. "You are forever suspecting the most innocent and harmless of treachery and double-dealing."

"Nevertheless, Baroness, who is that man?"

"That man, my friend, is one Laurance Lowe—an English radical, which means nothing. He has by this time completely forgotten the existence of both of us. I should imagine that his whole attention and time are given to the management of his own affairs."

"You know him, then?" said Jacobi, seating himself lightly and gracefully near to the Baroness.

"By reputation only."

"You know someone who knows him well?" persisted the violinist calmly.

"I do!"

"Ah! May I inquire——"

The Baroness suddenly cast down her eyes, and the white lids closed over them. A faint pink tinge appeared on either cheek.

"I obtained my information from Mr. Charles Mistley," she said in an indifferent voice.

"Brother of *the* Mistley?"

"Brother of *the* Mistley."

"Who is daily expected in England, with his chief, Colonel Wright?"

The Baroness bowed her head in acquiescence. Her red lips were pressed close together, her colorless eye-

6

brows slightly raised. Monsieur Jacobi prided himself upon his deep discernment in matters connected with the female heart and mind. He therefore changed the subject somewhat abruptly.

"You did not expect to meet me here to-night," he said with exaggerated coolness.

"No." Her voice was totally without expression.

"I am here on business."

"Indeed."

"And you?" inquired Jacobi insolently.

The Baroness looked up with slightly raised eyebrows.

"That is my affair!"

Jacobi smiled again with a singularly unpleasant curl of the lip.

"Yes, Baroness," he said; "I am here on business connected with the Brotherhood, and I call upon you to assist me."

The Baroness looked somewhat sullen, and remained silent.

"Miss Lena Wright," continued Jacobi, "the daughter of our amiable hostess, is, I have reason to believe, likely, and more than likely, to come in for a considerable fortune on the death of . . . Mr. Laurance Lowe, whom I have seen to-night for the first time. She is, I am led to suppose, singularly amiable, somewhat romantic, and with no more strength of mind or purpose than is considered desirable in a young English lady. The Brotherhood, as you know, is desperately in need of funds. You begin to see, fair Baroness!"

"You wish to enrol her?" asked the Baroness in her emotionless manner. "You wish to enrol her, and for the sake of her money!"

"I think," replied Jacobi, gazing sadly at the floor, "I think it would benefit the cause."

"What do you wish me to do?" asked she abruptly.

"Nothing much—to-night!" was the reply. "Tell me what Miss Wright is dressed in, so that I may recognize her. I will manage to get an introduction somehow. That will be enough for to-night."

"She is dressed in white," replied the Baroness, in the concise manner of one who observes everything and forgets nothing. "Tall and slight, with hair a little darker than mine, rather badly dressed and somewhat untidy. I suppose she is considered beautiful!"

"You do not know her?"

"No!"

Monsieur Jacobi now became absorbed in the re-arrangement of the delicate flower in his buttonhole, and took the opportunity of glancing keenly at his companion's face, which, however, was motionless and devoid of expression.

Presently the Baroness looked up, and caught his side-long gaze fixed upon her.

"I think, Jacobi," she said, "that you make a great mistake in attempting to be too diplomatic—too mysterious. There is, in fact, about you too much of the stage conspirator. You may of course, as far as I know, be a member of a thousand secret societies, whose mission it is to reorganize the world and society by means of crime and bloodshed; but I would have you remember that you are connected with me only as a joint member of the Brotherhood of Liberty, which is no secret society at all. With me you need observe no mystery, no precautions. I am not to be impressed, like a weak girl, by your stagey little surprises and deceptions. Why, for instance, you

8

should have allowed, or asked perhaps, Mrs. Wright to introduce you to me to-night—I do not know. No good can possibly come of it, and I distinctly prefer to take no part in such small farces in the future. Your authority over me ceases as soon as our meetings are adjourned. It extends in nowise to my own life; and unless we are in meeting, I must beg of you to treat me as a stranger, or at least a distant acquaintance. So long as I pay my subscription and attend such meetings as you may think proper to call, I am free to live how I like and where I like—with whom and among such as I may think fit ! ''

The Baroness had been speaking in French with a slight accent such as Germans never overcome in that language. Her voice had not been raised above its calm pitch, and she had never taken the trouble to look into Jacobi's face in order to see the effect of her speech. This was no half-hysterical effort of a weak nature to throw off the influence of a stronger mind; it was mere calm self-assertion, and Jacobi drew back before it. The Baroness had been daintily arranging the lace at her wrist, and now she crossed her hands upon her lap and gazed quietly at the dancers, whose movements could be followed through the open door of the inner room.

Jacobi smiled his saddest, most deprecating smile, and replied :

'' I am sorry, Madame la Baronne, that you should take exception to my conduct; but to-night, as in most cases, I had important reasons for doing as I did. As you observed just now, I am a bit of a politician, and, I trust—a patriot. Those, madame, who are suspected cannot be too suspicious! ''

With these words Monsieur Jacobi rose, and gracefully

9

tendered the assistance of his arm to the Baroness, who accepted it.

"I have taken the liberty of placing my name against the dance about to commence," said he. "It is a waltz. Shall we go into the other room?"

CHAPTER II

WHEN Mrs. Wright and Laurance Lowe left the smaller drawing-room, they turned their steps toward a diminutive apartment, where some late arrivals were yet partaking of tea and coffee. For some moments neither spoke. Laurance Lowe was a singularly silent man, and Mrs. Wright was by no means an excessive talker. They understood each other thoroughly, and both enjoyed these long spells of silence. Lowe found a seat for Mrs. Wright in the dimly-lighted corridor, just outside the small coffee-room, and left her there while he went in quest of the coffee. Presently he returned and sat down beside her.

"Dark horse!" he murmured, within the white recesses of his mustache and beard.

Mrs. Wright was fanning herself gently, for it was June, and she closed her fan slowly as she looked up and met his solemn eyes.

"I think they form a good pair," she said, smiling a little. She had rightly divined that her companion was referring to Monsieur Jacobi.

Lowe reflected deeply for a minute.

"No," he said at length, with senile deliberation. "No; I think the girl is all right, but I do not like the man. He reminds me of a dentist I once had cause to visit, and I hate dentists."

11

At this moment the servant appeared with the coffee. Lowe selected the fuller cup, and handed it to Mrs. Wright. He dropped one piece of sugar nimbly into it without causing a drop to splash up, and then he began a deliberate search for a second piece of smaller dimensions. He knew to a drachm how much sugar Mrs. Wright liked. There was no lump of the desired size, so he broke a piece in his gloved fingers, and daintily holding one half in the sugar-tongs, he proceeded to scrape with the other half the particular angle that had come into contact with his glove. The tray in the servant's hand shook in a suspicious manner, but his face was perfectly stolid. Mrs. Wright smiled a little pathetically, but made no attempt to intimate to her companion that his labors were unnecessary. At length the task was complete, and the servant was allowed to turn his face away and grin his fill.

"Lena," said Lowe pensively, as he stirred his coffee, "is looking lovely to-night."

Through the curtained doors the cadence of a slow soft waltz reached their ears, rising and falling on the heavy atmosphere. Mrs. Wright was anxious this evening, and a little restless. She had that morning received a telegram from her husband, announcing his arrival at Brindisi on the homeward voyage from India, and she had not seen him for two anxious, weary years. She sipped her coffee, and glanced over her cup toward Laurance Lowe. His great eyebrows were drawn forward, so that his eyes were in impenetrable shadow. He looked very old and somewhat worn, but he had looked so for many years.

"Yes, Laurance," said she softly; "I am a little proud of my daughter."

12

He made no reply, but continued to stir his coffee absently. Presently he moved slightly and looked up, drawing in a deep breath.

"Thursday morning?" he said, in a slightly interrogative tone. This was the time mentioned by Colonel Wright in his telegram for the arrival of himself and Winyard Mistley at Victoria Station.

"Yes; Thursday morning at half-past seven. Will you come with us to meet him?"

Lowe shook his head slowly and with much deliberation.

"Better not," he said gravely. "Would only be in the way. You and Mrs. Mistley go alone; that will be best."

"Well, then, come in to breakfast at nine o'clock," urged Mrs. Wright.

Again Lowe shook his head, his white thin beard waving from side to side.

"Thanks," he said. "I will look in during the morning."

Mrs. Wright paused a moment as if choosing her words to say something difficult.

"Willy,"—she said at length—"Willy will want to thank you . . . for . . . for everything; for your kindness to us during his absence. It has been a great comfort to him, I know, to feel that you were always near to us, and . . . and it has been a great comfort to us, Laurance, to have you. I do not exactly know what we should have done, Lena and I, without you."

The little lady actually blushed. It was rather difficult for her to thank this impassive man. The thought of gratitude stirred up smouldering memories, best left to smoulder in the depths of her womanly heart. It made

13

the practical woman of the world look back over the perspective of full years to the days of heedless girlhood.
Perhaps it made her recognize the great change that had come over her own being since those days, and compare it reproachfully with the steadfastness of the man at her side.

She had more to say—much more, and she was going on to say it; but Lowe stopped her.

"No thanks," he said, "are wanted. I have done nothing but 'stand by,' as Charlie would say, to be there when wanted."

"Yes," said Mrs. Wright; "but 'standing by' is sometimes weary work."

Laurance Lowe glanced sharply at her. His light-blue eyes suddenly acquired an unwonted brilliancy. It almost seemed as if Mrs. Wright's remark might have had a second meaning; but nothing was farther from her thoughts. If any man could know the undeniable truth of the assertion just made, that man was Laurance Lowe. He had "stood by" all his life.

Instantly his eyes became dull and vague again. It was merely a passing flash of life upon marble features.

"He will find Lena changed," said Lowe, knowing that he was broaching a pleasing subject.

"Yes, he will find her grown. She is a young lady now, and quite—quite——"

"Quite able to take care of herself," suggested Lowe. Mrs. Wright turned, and their eyes met. Lowe's were grave; but there was about the lines of his face a faint suggestion of a smile. That was the best he could do in the way of smiles, by reason of the long white mustache that hid his lips.

"Yes, I hope so," said Mrs. Wright seriously. She

14

knew that her daughter was fair, and also that it is the fairest who find the saddest lives here. She knew the thousand temptations that beset the path of a beautiful woman, the thousand little slips so easily made, the thousand hands ever ready to push the stumbler down the hill. But her faith in Lena was very great. There was no tangible, no possible cause for fear; but with all her worldliness, all her merriment, and all her apparent carelessness, Mrs. Wright was a true mother; that is to say, she was weak with all the sublime weakness of her kind. It was merely a natural misgiving that came over her at the thought that her daughter's life was now an individual thing—a separate and distinct vessel floating upon the great waters, and truly obedient to only one tiller— the tiller of her own heart.

Lena had her mother, her father, and Laurance Lowe to watch over her, to guard and keep her, to fend off the blows that fall upon us all, rich and poor; but Mrs. Wright—weak woman—was pleased to believe that father, mother, and friend were alike powerless to shield their darling from certain small arrows with an exceedingly sharp sting and a bitter barb—arrows which fly about at random, sometimes with the speed of forked lightning, sometimes slowly and very surely, sometimes glancing off and leaving but a scratch, sometimes burying their barbed heads so deep that to extricate them would mean death. But the shooting is never good, never reliable, and never sportsmanlike.

While these two old travellers were worrying themselves over the roughness of the road they had long since left behind, the object of their solicitous thoughts made her appearance at the end of the corridor—a dainty vision of soft white muslin, with a broad yellow sash round a slender waist. Lena was attended by a huge cavalier of peaceful but distinguished appearance. As she came lightly along the corridor, she was busily engaged in putting back over her ears sundry little stray wisps and tendrils of hair. These particular little curls were almost golden, while above them the heavier coils darkened into living brown. She was smiling and breathless, and just a little flushed. Lena's eyes were in striking contrast to her hair and fair complexion, for they were hazel—a dark, deep hazel—full of ready laughter, capable of sparkling with unbounded mischief; but in repose they were as demure and illegible as those of a nun. At the present moment they were soft and glistening with excitement and weariness: dangerous eyes for a man to look into, especially amid the surroundings of odorous flowers, within the sound of slow dance-music, for the next waltz had begun.

The big man, upon whose arm she was leaning, was fanning her with great sweeping strokes, so that the lace upon her dress fluttered in the breeze.

"Oh, Charlie," she was saying, "that *was* lovely! I do not think that I ever danced like that before. The music seemed to stop suddenly, to die away into nothing, and then we came to earth. Why was it so lovely—why was it so lovely?"

The big man continued fanning. He looked down at her with a slow, grave smile, such as one expects to see on a Saxon face.

"And why," he said, "did we come down to earth again?"

They had both seen Mrs. Wright and Laurance Lowe, and they both knew that they were within earshot; but that appeared in no way to interfere with or restrain their conversation. They advanced slowly along the corridor, Charles Mistley taking one stride to every two of Lena's.

Occasionally the young man glanced down at his companion as young men do glance at maidens. Although Lena was tall and straight as some young tree, the coils of sweet brown hair came no farther up than his shoulder. A very observant person would have noticed two singularities about this young man. First, he was clean-shaven; and secondly, he walked with peculiar firmness, as if there were some power of holding to the floor in the soles of his boots. These, added to the manner of carrying his hands half-closed (as if there should have been a rope within them), and his very brown face, demonstrated satisfactorily that Charles Mistley was a sailor. In the good old times, he would have been a worthy lieutenant to some hardy old sea-dog, all fight and energy—a true sailor and a brave fighter—but Providence had been pleased to place his lot in later times, so Charles Mistley took things as he found them, and was a very good sailor as they make them now; that is to say, half-sailor and half-engineer. He was not considered to be brilliant, like his young brother Winyard; but his reputation for cool, reliable pluck was firmly established, and his shipmates loved him one and all.

As the two young people advanced, Laurance Lowe slowly raised his head, and his emotionless eyes met Mrs. Wright's, fixed upon his face. They looked at each other, thus, for some seconds, and then turned aside without a word. Lowe's wrinkled hand, burnt brown by many a scorching wind, shook a little, so that the spoon rattled in the saucer. The expression in that elderly lady's eyes resembled so remarkably that which

he had discovered in those of a lovely and happy girl,
twenty years ago, when she had told him gently and
wistfully that his life must henceforth be hopeless, aimless, and objectless, that he could not meet them, though
his own were illegible in the deep shadow of his brows.
It was, perhaps, no coincidence that when Lena and her
partner approached the two older folks looked up, not
at her, but at Charles Mistley. Something, some vague
and doubting wonder, must have prompted Mrs. Wright
to do this, for every mother looks ten times at her own
daughter in a ball-room for every once that her eyes rest
on some other person's offspring. They can no more
help it than an artist can resist the magnetic attraction
which draws him to the contemplation of his own picture in a gallery full of superior works. But this good
lady looked at Charles Mistley, her eyes resting on his
strong, clean-cut face with a wistful, questioning expression which seemed almost to savor of foreboding. Laurance Lowe gazed at the young fellow with those keen
blue eyes of his, and his face bore absolutely no expression whatever. It was merely the calm impassive contemplation of an indifferent looker-on.

The young sailor looked down upon them from his exceptional height and smiled quietly. Charlie Mistley's
smile was a pleasant one to meet. It seemed, somehow,
to bring him down to a lower level; and smaller, plainer
men felt less inferior. It was a ready smile, too, and
women liked it for its sincerity.

"I have," he said, "danced Lena into a state of senti-
mentality. She requires bringing down to an every-day
level, so I brought her to her mother."

"Mother," said Lena breathlessly, "being an every-day
level?"

18

Mistley laughed, but made no reply. He seldom indulged in the dangerous game of repartee, which is like boxing "just to get warm," inasmuch as a blow may be dealt with unintentional force in the heat of strife.

"Look at him!" continued the girl gayly. "He is as cool as—as——"

"His native element," suggested Lowe, without looking up.

"Yes, thank you. As cool as his native element, and I am perfectly breathless! But it was lovely, was it not, Charlie?"

"Yes—lovely," he said, looking gravely at her. Then he brought forward a low chair. "Sit down," he said, "and I will get you an ice."

"I will sit down," she replied, "but I do not want an ice, thank you. You are so terribly practical and earthly —n'est-ce pas, mother?"

"He is very useful, at all events," said Mrs. Wright, favoring Mistley with a smile. "I am very grateful to you, Charlie," she continued, "for dancing with that Baroness de Something. I have had great difficulty in finding partners for her; the young men nowadays are so hard to please, and I find a growing tendency among them to divide the programme among four or five partners at the most."

Charles Mistley smiled. That smile of his came in frequently, very profitably, in place of words.

"Yes," said Lena musingly, with all the wisdom of her first season, "I am afraid that is a characteristic of the rising generation."

And she looked demurely and innocently up at Mistley, whose initials appeared five times upon her engagement-card.

He, however, did not appear to notice her glance; he was looking at his programme.

"Yes," he said presently, "I have had two with the Baroness; I should not be surprised if she dances beautifully. There is something about the way she holds herself which leads one to think so."

"I suppose she is very lovely," said Lena, smoothing her gloves.

"Yes, she is a beautiful woman," replied her mother indifferently.

"Who is she?" asked Mistley quietly.

It was an innocent little question, innocently asked, but it received no reply. Mrs. Wright shrugged her shoulders and sipped her coffee. Laurance Lowe slowly raised his head, and his solemn blue eyes rested inquiringly upon the young sailor's face. Lena continued to smooth her gloves. The question obviously possessed no interest for any of them except Mistley, and his was only the passing thought of a young man upon the possible history of a beautiful woman.

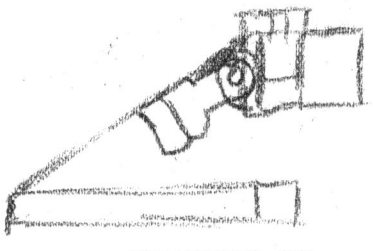

CHAPTER III

"By George, Mistley, this is splendid! Listen to this from the Cologne paper:

"'We learn from our London Correspondent that the Mayor of Dover, in his robes of office, awaited, yesterday, the arrival of the Calais boat, despite the heavy rain to which he was fully exposed on the pier, for the purpose of an address to Colonel Wright and his able young coadjutor Mr. Winyard Mistley, to deliver' (the translation here is somewhat literal). 'On the arrival of the boat, it was, however, discovered that Colonel Wright and Mr. Mistley were not on board. They parted from the other Indian passengers at Brindisi, and no one appears to have learnt by what route they purposed returning to England. It will be remembered that these gentlemen have been engaged upon an arduous diplomatic service on the Indian frontier, and their daring firmness and resolute defence of the acknowledged rights of their country in the midst of treacherous friends and unscrupulous foes'—et cetera, et cetera—*et cetera!*"

The speaker, or reader, was a tall, gray-haired man of military aspect. His mustache was almost white, and cut rather close to his lip. His features showed signs of having once been fine, but wrinkles and hardship had

21

changed all that. His nose was long and aquiline, a true military feature, but it was peculiarly thin; and the skin, though brown, was transparent and entirely free from that suggestive ruddiness which is somewhat frequently found upon the features of elderly military men. He laid aside the German newspaper, and looked at his companion with a twinkle of amusement in his gray eyes.

"No, no," said the younger man gayly. "Go on— let us have it all—I like it;" and he returned gravely to the discussion of a piece of chocolate.

"'And unscrupulous foes,'" continued Colonel Wright, reading from the paper as it lay—"'and unscrupulous foes'—oh yes; here it is—'undoubtedly saved the Indian Empire endless trouble and strife upon the frontier, while a graver mishap has perhaps been averted, and the peace of Europe preserved, by the prompt and consistent action of these two soldier-statesmen.'"

Winyard Mistley wagged his head very sapiently, and, addressing himself to the piece of chocolate in his hand, he observed:

"Oh yes! Rather disappointing for the Mayor of Dover, eh, Colonel?"

"Rather," replied the old soldier, folding the newspaper.

"You will be pleased to remember that this brilliant idea of dodging the Mayor of Dover and the rest of his kind emanated from my fertile brain."

This remark called for no reply, and for some time the two men were silent. They were seated opposite to each other in a first-class railway-carriage, an airy broad compartment lined with brown linen. A fine dust floated in the air and lay on every available space, for the train was rushing over the bare plains of the Netherlands. All

around lay vast tracts of yellow sand, varied here and
there by glassy sheets of motionless water. In these
pools stood, here and there, a long-legged solemn heron.
On a raised embankment the train ran smoothly through
the deserted land. The sun had long since set, and a
faint blue haze was stealing inland across the sand from
the distant sea. Winyard Mistley lay back in his corner,
and gazed out of the dust-covered window over the monotonous plains. It was a peaceful, dreary outlook—one
calculated to call up sweet memories of the past, to make
one dream vague day-dreams fraught with impossibility.
The faint light of dying day in the western sky lay over
the native land of these two men, the land to which they
were returning after two years of arduous work, of constant danger grown wearisome from very monotony.
That pearly light spoke to them of home, of rest, and
love; all three rendered marvellously precious by absence
in the past years. To the younger man this home-coming must have been doubly moving. Four years before,
he had left England an insignificant young soldier with
no great prospects, encouraged and sustained by no great
influence at headquarters. Now he was about to set foot
on England's shores again, a man with a name among
her greater sons, with a definite object and aim in life,
and that aim the greatest of all that man craves for—the
glorification of his own country.

It is assuredly no great wonder that Winyard Mistley
should be silent under these circumstances. The very
movement of the train in its smooth rapidity, the be-
witching hour, the happy days in store—all could not
fail to appeal to a youthful heart and a young imagination. But in the man's eyes there was no far-away look,
no dreamy wistfulness. Ah! would I were a lady-novel-

ist! How infinitely romantic, how yearningly interesting could this youth be rendered! This duller pen, however, has a humble pride in truthfulness.

Winyard Mistley was an eminently practical young man. He was an adept at mending his own clothes, cooking his own dinner, and grooming his own horse. Practical people, however, are not necessarily devoid of sentiment. They hide it—that is all. What dreaming they may indulge in is done in private.

His was a striking face, whether in animation or repose, with dark gray eyes of singular penetration; eyes that seldom smiled, despite the readiness of the lips which smiled perhaps too easily. A great charm about him was his peculiar unaffectedness. Whatever he did, or said, was to all appearance perfectly spontaneous and without after-thought. Never at a loss in the most trying emergency, no one ever saw a look of embarrassment or self-consciousness on Winyard Mistley's face. He was simply without vanity, and therefore was fortunate enough to be unafflicted by jealousy.

At this moment his face wore an expression of calm reflectiveness. He was thinking, but not deeply. Perhaps he never had thought very deeply over anything. His thoughtfulness was characterized by an extraordinary readiness. It was not deep, but it was very quick, and therefore likely to make its mark in this shallow age. Such mental work as this never shows itself upon a man's face, and Winyard Mistley looked younger than he was, despite a few lines about his mouth which were the result of physical hardship, and therefore in no way permanent.

Coming from a military stock, Mistley had himself been in the army; but the authorities having been pleased to place difficulties in the way of his accepting Colonel Wright's pressing offer to accompany him on a difficult frontier mission, he had calmly laid aside his sword to take up the sharp pen of a diplomatist.

This, though rapidly carried out, had been no hasty conclusion. The young fellow knew that the Indian army was no field for an active-minded man endowed with more than his due share of brains and ambition, such as, without the least conceit, he suspected himself to be.

Such was Winyard Mistley: a man who at the age of twenty-eight had been not only fortunate enough to find his speciality, but had gone so far as to get his feet well planted upon the rungs of his own particular ladder. It is true that his name was always coupled with that of Colonel Wright, and invariably came second in such mention; but there were whispers in more than one diplomatic circle that in this happy partnership, one gave the larger experience and more patient attention to details, while the other supplied the brilliant conception and rapid execution.

Colonel Wright was a diplomatist in one great and important matter, if in nothing else. He could, with unfailing discrimination, gather round him the men he required. At a glance he recognized the fighting-man, a mere thoughtless creature of courage, whose ambition lay in the two letters "V.C."; whose soft heart was the most vulnerable portion of his anatomy, his head being the least so when hard knocks were flying. The thinker, also, could the Colonel select from the crowded ranks of human workers. He had no need for, and took but small interest in, the slow and deliberate thinker of such material as produces essay-writers and specialists; but he

25

knew full well the value of a brilliant and rapid man whose thoughts are almost instinctive—one who, as a plot unfolds itself before him, can at once, and with light touch, lay his finger upon the motive and say, "This is what he is leading up to"—"That is what he will do next;" and who, like a skilful chess-player, can execute a counter-move of apparently trifling importance, which, when the crisis comes, carries everything before it.

Of this latter type was Winyard Mistley, and the Colonel was fully aware that the best step he ever took in his life was to persuade that young officer, then fretting under the command of a man somewhat his inferior in many ways, to leave the army and join him, since he could not retain his commission and accept the offer. Two years of constant intercourse, of days spent in the performance of a common task, and nights passed together in various degrees of discomfort often amounting to danger, will do much to obliterate the barrier that invariably stands between men belonging to a different generation. It had been so with Colonel Wright and Winyard Mistley. The friendship commenced at a mess-table, and based upon letters from the wife of one and the mother of the other, had grown into something stronger; and gradually the two men (though thirty years lay like a wall between them) had become necessary to each other. Of course there were mutual debts. Had it not been owing to Colonel Wright that Mistley had found his mission in life? But for him the young officer might still have been idling his life away in semi-indifference. On the other hand, without his brilliant assistant Colonel Wright would undoubtedly have failed to carry out the difficult mission intrusted to him. Without this aid he would not now have been returning in triumph to his home, and certainly the honor which they were both so anxious to avoid—that which had awaited them on the pier at Dover—would not have been tendered by the self-constituted representative of a spasmodically grateful country.

It was assuredly something more than mere chance that had brought these two men together, so perfectly suited were they to each other. What the Colonel lacked Mistley supplied, and such slower qualities as were wanting in the younger man were to be found in his chief. Many good qualities, however, had these men in common, qualities necessary to the traveller and sailor, such as independence, readiness of resource, rapidity of execution. They were travelling with very little luggage, and no encumbrances whatever. Each clad in a simple tweed suit, they might have been beginning some trivial local journey, instead of being at the end of a rush across half the world.

Two small black boxes, lost in a chaos of huge trunks somewhere in the van, were all they could claim, and there was something characteristic even in these small receptacles. Identical in form, size, and color, they appeared to cling, as if from long habitude, to each other. The same labels and enticing hotel placards were to be found on both; and in particular there was around each a slight indented mark as if from chafe or friction, such as one sees round a river-side post. This betrayed the hardships they had passed through, one on each side of a weary pack-horse, balancing and supporting each other, lashed together, though separated by the body of their bearer. Many of us, methinks, go through our travels like these road-worn trunks, with a mark of friction upon us, showing what we have come through.   A grocer, for instance, though he be clad in purple and fine linen, seems to me to have a slight indentation round the centre of his person, where the apron-string was wont to press. It is his mark, his trade-mark as it were, worn and chafed · into his soul as into his body.

Winyard Mistley lay back in his corner, serenely unconscious of his senior's steady gaze.   Colonel Wright was absently looking at him, merely because, perhaps, that clear-cut intelligent face was the most interesting object in sight.   At length he spoke with the determined air of one who has weighed his words carefully, having something rather difficult to say.

"In twenty-four hours," he said in a speculative tone, "our official relationship ceases."

"Alas!" observed Mistley with ready cheerfulness.

"I do not wish you, Mistley," continued the Colonel gravely, "to go away without knowing how fully I appreciate and have appreciated all your unfailing patience, your skill, and your happy power of being ever cheerful and good-humored under the most trying circumstances. As for my own personal feelings in the matter, I have never ceased to congratulate myself upon my action two years ago in asking you to join me, and I only hope that you will never have cause to regret it."

"For me," replied Mistley, looking out of the window, and purposely avoiding the Colonel's eyes, "these two years have simply been a holiday.   That soldiering in India was not the work for me at all—there is too much unavoidable routine—too little to do, and too much time to do it in.   Besides, there is always the feeling that the first fool who comes along with his head full of theory could do the work as well, if not better, than one's self. There is absolutely no individuality in the army. We are like so many brass buttons on a tunic; if two come off they can be put back in reversed order, or two new ones can be sewn on, and no one is the wiser— the tunic is neither better nor worse. Thanks to you, I am no longer a button. Thanks to you, I have got my foot on the ladder which to me has been the only one worth climbing since I was old enough to know that my life was my own. The gratitude should be on my side, I think, Colonel.''

This was unsatisfactory, and in no manner helped Colonel Wright in his little speech. So the old gentleman went straight to the point at once, and somewhat surprised his junior by the unexpected powers of observation which his remarks betrayed.

"I think," he said, "that it is of no use mincing matters between us, Mistley. We know each other too well for that. You have got beyond the lower rungs of the ladder, for you are half-way up it already; and in climbing you have found time to give a helping push to an old slow-coach above you, who bid fair to stick where he was. I am not blind, nor am I ashamed to acknowledge that you are a sharper fellow than I. You are my superior in the work we have had to do together, and there is no reason why it should be concealed. The difference lies in the fact that you were born to it, and I had it forced upon me by circumstances. Everything in you points to what Providence designed you for; with me rests only the honor of finding out the intention of Providence. Your gift of languages points to it, your restless love of travel, your very face even. Why, look at me—I say something very diplomatic, and the best I can do in the way of disguising my feelings is to look blank and vacant;

whereas you can think one thing and make your face express the very opposite!"

Mistley was intensely relieved at this moment to catch sight of the distant spires of Flushing, which enabled him to change the subject. Like many of his countrymen, he could not bear being thanked.

CHAPTER IV

VICTORIA STATION is not a favorite resort of the fashionable world between the hours of seven and eight in the morning. In fact, that sweetest, freshest, most entrancing hour is rather apt, in London, to be dull and somewhat dismal; therefore better spent in bed. The early porters were busy sweeping up with long brushes the dust shaken from the feet of many a weary traveller, and sprinkling water in strange circular patterns upon the pavement of the station, when the first hansom-cab of the day made its appearance with much clatter of hoofs.

From it there alighted a brisk little lady, who instantly glanced up at the clock. Her movements were very quick without being in the least fussy. She paid the cabman with an air of quiet confidence, which did not fail to impress upon that most uncivil of public servants (which is saying much) that she was perfectly aware of the fact that he was receiving sixpence more than his legal fare. Then she turned to a porter, and said in a silvery voice, with the faintest suspicion of a foreign accent:

"The Queenborough train, porter. Which platform, please?"

"The far platform, ma'am. Due in ten minutes," was the reply, given with a politeness which seemed always to be this little lady's due. With a quick nod of thanks, she went in the direction indicated. A light, almost girlish form, with a firm elastic step, such as is of more service to a girl in a ball-room than the most enticing beauty. Many a man in passing that girlish form in the street had turned his head, to be met by a pair of calm gray eyes, and to see with a shock of surprise that the pretty energetic face was surmounted by a mass of silvery hair. Mrs. Mistley's white hair was an inherited peculiarity. Long, thick, and silky, it was gray at the temples when she married Major Mistley. It did not change much for two years after that, but at the end of the third year, when she returned from India, a widow of twenty-two, it was white. She wore it piled up high upon her graceful head, after a fashion which vaguely suggested Madame de Lamballe, or some other gracious lady of the old French Court. This mode of coiffure harmonized with the faint accent which was hardly that of a foreigner, but rather of one who had for many years spoken in an acquired tongue. Such, indeed, was the case with Mrs. Mistley, who had spent the greater portion of her life in France. For her, this was the land of the blessed, the home of sunshine and flowers, of sweet and calm country life. It was not the country known to the majority of us—the France of Paris, of broad pavements and lofty buildings, of outward brilliancy and gaudy vice, of dust and reckless merry lives. Her France was a land of smiling meadows and quaint, crumbling family palaces, far from the restless city; where loyalty is still to be found among a quiet, self-contained people, living out their lives of voluntary exile from the haunts of man with a strange, restful patience. A race bearing names dangerously historical, and carrying their heads above the petty strifes of Republican office-seekers with a dignified pride intensely galling to the people. They talked sometimes, though rarely, of these same people, and always with a smile, half pitying and half contemptuous, as one speaks of a wayward, headstrong child.

Mrs. Mistley walked as far as the platform, and finding no one there, returned to the entrance of the station. Presently a small victoria arrived, and from it Mrs. Wright alighted. The two ladies kissed each other warmly, and both remembered later that that form of salutation had not passed between them since the caressingly affectionate days of their girlhood. Mrs. Wright was somewhat pale, but she returned her friend's smile bravely, and they turned toward the platform indicated by the porter. The train was late, and the two ladies walked up and down the deserted platform in silent impatience. The circumstances of their meeting that morning seemed to have swept away the barrier of years. A coincidence of memory took their thoughts back to the days when they had walked side by side beneath the great silent trees of a vast French forest—a pair of thoughtfully happy girls, and the necessity of speech was no more.

They were now essentially women of the world, well dressed and brisk, hurrying through life, and gathering much enjoyment from it, practical, cheerful, and universally liked. They had met again in a whirl of London gayety, after having lost sight of each other for almost twenty years; and each having come through the whirring mill of Youth, with its loves and fears, trials and delirious joys, found the other, as in the olden days, a very counterpart of herself. The two young girls whose friendship had found birth under the trees of Melun, as they walked side by side beneath the gently watchful eyes of the nuns who educated them, had each left upon the character of the other her individual influence, which had never died away. And so it came about that these two women of the world, walking side by side upon the deserted platform of a London railway-station, found again in each other that little germ of human love which we call sympathy, and wondered over it, each in her own mind, as we *do* wonder over human kindness when we meet with it. They hardly spoke at all, but each little movement, each word, and the manner of saying it, recalled those bygone days. It was like the recollection, note by note, of some forgotten air—new, yet subtly familiar.

Presently they sat down upon a highly polished seat, and, hidden in the folds of their dresses, their hands met and clasped each other.

"Do you remember," said Mrs. Mistley, with a pathetic little smile, "all the nonsense we talked in the old Melun days? How we were never going to cease corresponding; how, if we married, we were to be constant companions; how our children were to grow up together as brothers and sisters; how . . . our husbands were to be friends."

"I am afraid," replied Mrs. Wright, "that we were very foolish and romantic in those days!"

The brisk little lady stopped short. She was at a loss for something to say—a very rare occurrence. Mrs. Mistley had touched upon a page of her life which was closed to her friend. Those three years of married life were as a sacred memory, and Mrs. Wright thought that the pages were better left unread.

Young Mistley

"Who would have thought," said Mrs. Mistley presently, "that we should have one day to be waiting here for your husband and my son—waiting together for them to arrive together? It almost seems as if Providence had heard all our girlish vows; for we have come together again after all those years, and our children will be friends!"

"Yes," said Mrs. Wright absently. "Yes, our children will be friends!"

Then they relapsed into silence. Mrs. Wright betrayed a greater impatience than her companion. It had been promised that after this expedition her husband should leave her no more, and she was terribly afraid that something would yet come in the way of this pleasant arrangement. As the time wore on, she began to picture to herself a thousand-and-one dangers which in reality never existed. Now she knew that he was in a civilized land where travelling was a pleasure, unattended by hardship or danger; but he was not home yet.

It was only natural that Mrs. Mistley should be thinking of her son at that moment, and the thoughts were apparently pleasant, for occasionally she smiled with a passing gleam of pride in her eyes. Her two sons appeared to her maternal vision such as any mother might reasonably be proud of. In accordance with an old tradition of her husband's family, she had made one a soldier and the other a sailor. Soldiers and sailors the Mistleys had been from one generation to another, rising as high as hard blows could bring them, but caring nothing for honors or titles. Ambition was not infused into the Mistley blood—at least, it had never shown itself until Winyard laid aside his idle sword to wield the mightier pen. And the astute little lady recognized in this action the handiwork of a certain restless energy which had been inherited from herself, along with other characteristics more or less Gallic in their vivacity and quickness. At first, Mrs. Mistley had not approved of this sudden change in her son's life; but by the time the letter announcing it had reached her, things had gone too far to make objection of any use; so, like a wise woman, she held her tongue. Now, she recognized and frankly acknowledged that Winyard had been right.

Her feelings as she waited for the train that morning were strange. After a four years' absence her son was coming back, and the day when he had left was as fresh in her mind as ever. She could recall the very expression of his face as the train moved away—a handsome boyish countenance, with a peculiar rigid purity of outline, expressive of too great a degree of refinement for comfort in this world. He had left England a merry, reckless boy, with no great sense of responsibility in life; and now he was coming back a man, with a name among his contemporaries, with a definite purpose in life. She wondered vaguely whether he would be much changed, whether she would now find him thoughtful and serious.

It was hard for Mrs. Mistley to realize that this was really her son—her youngest born, over whose tiny crib she had stood so many years ago, with staring dry eyes and a breaking heart, while in the next room lay the still form of his dead father. Could this man, with the burden of life already upon his shoulders, be that same helpless piece of infantine humanity? Woman-like, she began to think of his appearance, and pictured herself walking by the side of a squarely-built bronzed man, with a heavy mustache, and that queer *Indian* look in his eyes that she knew so well. Nor was this mental portrait so very far from the truth. It was a modification of the memory of her husband, but Winyard Mistley was a cleverer man and more intellectual than his father. His face was cut upon a keener mould, the features were lighter in their modelling, and expressive of a refinement almost amounting to nervousness. Charles Mistley was in reality more after the type of his father, with the same tranquil Saxon strength visible in his eyes.

At last there was a bustle in the station, and a troop of porters assailed the platform, arriving in the most astonishing manner from all sides. Then the great locomotive came clanking in, with a mighty sense of its own importance and general superiority over the mere local engines around it.

A moment later Mrs. Mistley was looking into the face she had so longed to see. Even amid the confusion and excitement of the greeting, she found time to marvel that there was so little change in it—a little browner perhaps, with a hard dry look which spoke of great hardships borne manfully, and testified to exceptional powers of endurance.

"Where is Charlie?" were Winyard's first words. While his mother was explaining that her younger son would be detained at Greenwich until later in the day, the Colonel approached with Mrs. Wright at his side. No form of introduction was attempted; the old soldier came forward with outstretched hand, and as he took Mrs. Mistley's fingers within his, he bowed with a peculiar old-fashioned courtesy, which conveyed a wondrous amount of admiration and respect.

"Mrs. Mistley!" he said; "I should have known you anywhere. We carried a photograph of you in our de-

spatch-case for many months. I think Winyard considered it the most precious document there.''

"And which,'' added that respectful youth gayly,
"the Colonel left lying about one night in the rainy season, the consequence being that it all came ungummed,
and nothing was left next morning to the eyes of a be-
reaved son but two sticky rolls of wrinkled paper, one of
which was found adhering to the person of a native dog.
How do you do—Mrs. Wright? . . .''

The young fellow became suddenly silent, and turned
rather hastily to find the luggage. There were unshed
tears in Mrs. Wright's eyes, and perhaps he was not
quite sure of himself; at all events, he was by no means
sure of the Colonel, who, like many brave men, was
afflicted with a soft heart.

Presently the two small boxes were found and placed
under the care of a porter, who shouldered them both
at once with much zeal. He saw how the land lay, and
knew that his reward would be greater than his deserts.

There were now many travellers upon the platform,
and the usual bustle attendant on the arrival of non-
phlegmatic foreigners on these tranquil shores supervened. It therefore occurred that no one except Winyard Mistley observed a tall fair-haired youth who had
evidently been awaiting the arrival of the train. In
appearance this young man was distinctly Germanic,
although his face was of a more refined type than one
usually meets with in the Rhineland. Although his
presence on the platform appeared to be other than the
mere result of accident, he did not give one the impression that he was there to meet a friend. The thought
passed through Winyard Mistley's mind that this man
was watching the Colonel and himself, but at the

moment he did not attach much importance to the suspicion, though he remembered it later.

After having arranged that Mrs. Mistley and her two sons should dine with them in Seymour Street that evening, the Wrights drove away, and mother and son were left alone together.

CHAPTER V

THERE is in the lamentably uninteresting parish of Lewisham a long street where the numbers of the houses attain to three figures. Standing at the end of this street, one has before one's eyes a lesson in perspective, from which it could be easily imagined that Mr. Vere Foster had taken those strange diverging lines by the help of which he undertakes to instil the rudiments of perspective into the densest minds.

As a rule, there is no object to spoil the purity of line from end to end: the grass-grown road knows the pressure of a daily milk-cart and a rare cab; otherwise nothing.

From number one to number one hundred and forty-nine on the one side, and from number two to number one hundred and fifty on the other, the houses bear such a deadly resemblance to each other that the oldest inhabitant of Prout Street, a bank-clerk of regular habits and mechanical mind, is compelled to look at the number on his own door before trying the latch-key, and his house is opposite the fourth lamp-post on the left-hand side. For those who live between the lamp-posts the difficulty is naturally greater, and it is on that account that Mr. Sellerar (who is in some manner connected with the City dinners, though his name never appears in the list of guests), occupying number forty-eight, invariably spends a portion of the night, or, to be more correct, early morning, in trying the effect of his latch-key upon the lock of number fifty, which house is inhabited by the two Miss Parks, of an uncertain age.

Number fifty-one is occupied by Mrs. Gredge, a lady who, like the blind beggar, has seen better days. After the manner of elderly females of a brilliant past, Mrs. Gredge lets lodgings, and it is with her lodger that we have to do.

The yellow rays of sunset shone in the sky over the roof-line from number forty-eight to fifty, and lighted up the bare parlor of number fifty-one, Prout Street, Lewisham. The hideous wall-paper, representing innumerable baskets of impossible flowers hanging from festoons of blue ribbon attached to nothing, was shown up in all its brilliant crudity by the searching light.

Small portions of this flowery abomination were hidden by framed prints, of which the poor workmanship and general vulgarity prepared one for the information in the corner of each, to the effect that they were specimens of German enterprise.

In strange contrast to the brilliant wall-paper and repulsive prints, there was suspended in one corner of the room a small but beautifully worked representation of the Virgin and Child. It was an emblem of the Greek Church, and before it hung a tiny oil-lamp of red glass with a floating wick forever burning.

The workmanship was rather finer than that of the ordinary Russian "ikon" or shrine, suspended in every house and homestead of the great Empire. The body and raiment of the Virgin and Child were of stamped silver, and small spaces were left in the metal where the faces and hands appeared, beautifully painted on wood behind the silver. The painting itself was of the simple, smooth style which reminds one of the work of Botticelli, and seems to lend itself particularly to religious subjects.

At the table in the centre of the room sat a young girl. She did not look more than twenty years of age, though at times the expression of her face was almost that of a woman of forty. From a low white forehead, her dull flaxen hair rose in a soft curve before it yielded to the black ribbon that bound it in a loop low down on her neck. The light rested softly on it, but failed to draw from its smooth bands any gleam of life. She wore it parted at the side and brushed well back. Her delicately cut face was pale, and there was a peculiar drawn look about her lips, which were very red. Mrs. Gredge knew her lodger by the name of Miss Marie Bakovitch; to many lovers of music in London she was known as the Baroness de Nantille.

The whole life of her being seemed to be centred in her eyes. They were intensely blue, with an almost metallic gleam.

Before her on the table was a newspaper which she was slowly scanning, column by column. She followed the line of columns with a pencil; not like one who is reading word for word, but as if she were searching for some particular news, the rest of the printed matter being indifferent to her.

The fingers that held the pencil were singularly white and beautiful, but they trembled painfully as if from inward excitement.

The girl's pale and striking face, more beautiful than pleasing; her painfully searching eyes, her small trembling hand, and the softly rounded active figure, all seemed to imply an unusually nervous and impetuous temperament.

Young Misley

She appeared to be very ignorant as to the system followed out in the formation of an English newspaper, as she read through the leading articles with the same anxious haste as she devoted to the advertisement columns.

Suddenly she laid down her pencil, and looked toward the window with expectation visible in every feature. She had not been mistaken. From below came the sounds of hurried footsteps on the deserted pavement, then the creaking of an iron gate.

She could hear the distant tinkle of a bell, and a few moments later someone knocked hurriedly at her door.

"Come in!" she said in a quiet voice, and she leant back in her chair without looking toward the door.

A tall graceful man entered the room.

"Marie," he said, "he has come. He is in London!"

The girl did not move nor look toward him; her eyes were fixed on the yellow sky over the roof of number forty-eight.

"He has come . . . he is in London!" she repeated after him, as if to force the news into her own brain.

One white hand was lying idly on the table, extended toward the young man.

He took a step forward, and raised her fingers to his lips. Then he seemed to remember the shrine in the corner of the room, for he bowed toward it, and crossed himself rapidly but with reverence.

For some moments he looked at the fair girl in silence; she was slowly pressing the hair back from her temples. Then he suddenly fell on his knees at her side, and seized her two hands in his. He forced her passionately to look at him.

"Marie, Marie!" he exclaimed in Russian; "for the love of Heaven give this up! It is madness; his life will make no difference; you can do no good by the sacrifice of yours. Think of your mother, your sister; think of me! You cannot love me, or you would not hold to this mad purpose!"

She looked down at his pale miserable face with an expression which any but a lover would have read as fatally kind and affectionate.

"Yes, Ivan dear," she said in a faint weary voice, "I love you. But I love my country first; O Ivan, will you never understand what this love of one's country is? I reproach myself again and again for filling your brave heart, so that there is no room in it for patriotism. No, no, a thousand times no! I cannot give it up. Think you that I travelled to the South, then home to holy Moscow again, only to leave it in a few days for this doomed land, to give up my inspired purpose after all? No, it cannot be. Let me think what must be done. I am dazed, like the hunter who suddenly finds himself face to face with his quarry. Where is he?"

"He is living with his mother in Bedford Place, London. Marie, I will warn him if you do not listen to me. It is my duty. I must save you at all risks."

"Ivan," said the girl with a passionate thrill in her calm voice, "if I thought you would warn him I should kill you now as you kneel there! God who gave me this work to do will help me to execute it! Besides, has he not been warned, more than a year ago, and he simply ignores it?"

"Then threaten him," said the young man, rising and walking toward the window.

"Threaten him!" retorted the girl, shrugging her shoulders. "You do not know these Englishmen, Ivan. Threats are to them what oil is to a smouldering cinder—it brings out the fire that no one thought to be there.''

For some moments there was silence in the room. The young man stood with his back toward his companion. He was exceptionally tall, with a slight droop in the shoulders, which suggested a man of thought more than of action.

His slim white hands rested on the centre woodwork of the window, and he was gazing abstractedly at the deserted road, parched and grass-grown. Gradually there came life into his eyes, the inward light reflected from an alleviating thought within his brain.

He turned slowly, and his eyes rested thoughtfully on the young girl's bent head for some moments.

"Marie," he said at length, "if I swear to kill him, will you marry me to-morrow? Let me call you wife for one day, and I will be willing to take the risk of getting away when . . . when it is done. We can go to America; my art will keep us comfortably there. See, I have only been in England a few days, and I have already sold many sketches. It is a strange way to win a wife, by assassinating a man whom I cannot but admire!''

"Admire!" echoed the girl. "The man, the individual, does not come into my thoughts at all. It is the work he has done and will carry on, unless he is stopped; the harm he has done to our country. What care I if he be a scoundrel or a patriot, young or old, beloved or alone in the world? It is the same to me, Ivan. It is the power within him I aim at, not the man himself. You cannot realize what harm this man can yet do. You are half a Nihilist, and think that our country's ruin will be brought on by a succession of emperors; they at least are patriots. No, no; if you men would

only combine, the whole world could do no harm to us!
It is the inward rottenness of the people's patriotism that
drags down Holy Russia."

"Will you let me do it?"

"No, Ivan; I cannot. God gave me the work to do,
and I must not shirk it. If He intends me to escape
when it is done, He will help me; if not, I will take . . .
what comes!"

Her blue eyes flashed with the fire of religious fervor,
but she leant across the table and laid her hand on his,
as if to soften the cruelty of her own decision.

The girl looked very frail and nervous as she sat in the
fading light. There was, however, a strange set look
about her mouth; her level red lips were pressed together
with a firmness betokening a marvellous determination
for a girl of her physique.

The young man rose from his seat and walked to the
window, pressing the soft straight hair back from his
forehead.

"If you forget your own mother," he threw back
sharply over his shoulder, "you cannot overlook his.
What has she done that you should punish her? She is
no doubt proud of her son, who, after all, has done nothing but his duty, though God knows he has done that
well!"

"I think of nothing, Ivan—I think of no one. All
must be sacrificed to the good of the country! Am I not
willing and ready to risk my own life——"

"And throw aside my love," interrupted the young
man.

"For the holy cause? Can you not give up something, Ivan? Though I married you, I could not make
you happy. It is not in me to be content with the trivial

occupations of a wife and . . . a mother. I cannot rest now; I often think, Ivan, that there will be no rest for me on earth."

She spoke in a cold, weary voice, as though the words were forced from her by some superior will, not emanating from her own being at all.

Then he came toward her with both hands outstretched.

"Only marry me, Marie," he urged in a voice hoarse with suppressed passion. "Marry me, and all will come right. Rest will come, and peace—ah! and love, Marie; for you do not love me now. I can see it in your eyes. We will go away, and find a new home in a new land. There we can watch things from afar, for we can do no good; the sacrifice of our happiness to the cause can do nothing. It is not thus that the fate of an empire is ruled. It is in higher Hands than ours; or, as some say, it will work itself out despite emperors and statesmen, despite lives thrown away and homes made desolate. If there were work to do, I should be among the first, and you know that, Marie. It is weary work to pass one's life in idle waiting for a crisis that never comes; but it is written, and we cannot but obey. When the time comes, there will be no call for statesmen and politicians; the people will do the work, the people will find the leaders. Ah, Marie! if you would only listen when I tell you that this is no work for women, these are no thoughts for a woman's mind! Everything in the past points to it, everything in the present confirms that God will *not* have such work done by a woman's hand. He will never bless such an undertaking."

Mental resistance in women is usually totally without respect to physical force. The man might have argued and persuaded till dawn, but it would have been of no avail. The frail girl was as intent on her purpose as the most determined man, and with the additional incentive of a woman's unreasoning belief in her own convictions, which will not listen to the most direct and convincing argument, while it laughs at milder measures.

The man knew this, and yet, with the stubborn calmness of his Northern blood, he still sought to appeal to her reason. At the same time, he attempted to rouse in her some faint reflex of the passion within his own heart. He took her two hands again; he drew her toward him, and, stooping till the soft wavy curls about her temple touched his lips, he spoke fervently and with flashing eyes that vainly sought hers.

But she, forgetting that her two hands were prisoners, that his arm was round her, and that his hungering lips were close to her own, still clung to her argument merely as an argument, and not with the feeble resistance of one who has the faintest idea of yielding.

"And Charlotte Corday," she said—"her life was not thrown away."

The man's patience was almost sublime, but he relinquished her fingers suddenly with a little movement, as if to cast her hands away from him.

"She!" he said bitterly—"Charlotte Corday—what good did she do? Think you that France would have been different now had she never existed? No, no; events were moving on slowly and irresistibly, she neither accelerated nor retarded them; and she has left a lasting example of violence behind her for other women to follow. Think, Marie—think what you are doing! It is murder, the most vile of human crimes; not even murder with the extenuation of hot blood, but a calm and unflinching thirst for the life of a fellow-creature, and he a

man who has served his country as few men have. He
has fought an open fight, dealing with the most treacherous and unreliable miscreants; he has ever been the soul
of honor; no mean subterfuge has stained the brilliancy
of his diplomatic skill. Would that I could say the same
of our own countrymen!"

By dint of praising this man, the passionate young
Russian student had gradually grown into the habit of
attributing to him virtues which he perhaps did not possess. Nevertheless, he was a true champion, though he
had taken up the sword from purely selfish motives.

"He may be doing his duty toward his country," said
the girl, with the cool, cruel judgment of an Inquisitor,
"but from what motives? These Englishmen are no
patriots; they do not possess that burning love for their
native land that lies in our Russian hearts, Ivan. Think
you they would go cheerfully to the horrors of Siberia,
content that they had made one attempt, failure though
it may have been, to loosen one stone of the structure
they pit their helpless strength against, as flies against
a gravestone? These English fight for the love of fighting, whether it be with sword or pen; and then, when it
is over, they are quite content to go home and spend
their lives in profitless leisure. No, Ivan; do not speak
to me of duty to country and of patriotism. It may or
it may not influence this man—this . . . Winyard Mistley, for we do not know him; but if it is the case, he is
not like the rest of his countrymen. Ah! if I could only
meet someone who knows him, who could give me some
opinion as to his motives! He never speaks; he never
shows himself; you never hear his opinion quoted. He
seems to laugh at fame, and yet he is the most powerful
of them all. He works silently, like a mole; but when

the work is done he seems to forget it all, and is almost
a boy. What did Marloff, the cleverest of the Government agents, find out on the voyage home to Suez?
Nothing—nothing at all. He wrote to me of a light-
hearted, recklessly merry boy, whom he could not believe
to be identical with the man he was told to watch. He
spoke of one who was ever the foremost in organizing
amusements on board—think of that, Ivan, organizing
amusements, and keeping the whole ship merry and joy-
ful! Ah, it is maddening! This man, who can find
time between the rounds of his amusements to outwit our
cleverest diplomatists, and then laughingly resume his
pleasure. I tell you he is laughing at us, laughing at
our best statesmen; and you speak to me of threatening
such a man as this! It is strange . . . it is strange—
that he can be the brother . . . of the sailor!"

The girl stood by the window in the rapidly fading
light, twining and intertwining her slim white fingers,
while her lips quivered with an almost childish passion.

"Marie," said the young man, in a slow, cold tone,
"has it never struck you, has the idea never passed
through your brain, that someone else is laughing at
you? Have you never thought that the Government—
our own Government—whose duty it is to watch over all
its people, is making a tool of you? They fear this man,
and with good reason; therefore they would not be sorry
if he were removed from their path. They dare not suggest such an action, but they dare to forward it indirectly,
so long as they are themselves safe from suspicion. They
pretend to know nothing of you, and to be ignorant of
your motive in coming to England; but why was it made
so easy for you to leave Russia? and why was I, the son
of a Nihilist, and myself a suspected Nihilist, allowed to

come to England with you? Can you not see that they do not wish to make inquiries? They allowed Marloff to write to you, because you pleaded a personal interest in this man. For all they know, this Englishman may have wronged you personally; doubtless they will say it was so. 'Give the girl the information she requires,' they would say; and the letter would be drafted from the Vasili Ostrov for Marloff to copy out in his own handwriting. If you carry out this scheme—this mad scheme of yours, Marie—think you that the Government will say a word for you? No! they will express to the English Government their sincere regret that this dastardly assassination should have been perpetrated by a Russian; an attaché will attend his funeral, and the English newspapers will by some means get hold of the information that there has always been madness in your family!"

"I have thought of that," replied the girl, "and it only confirms my inward conviction that I am working for the good of my country. Ah, if I only knew his motives—if I only knew him!"

The girl was much more influenced by her own doubts than by the young man's arguments, though perhaps these were indirectly fostering her doubts.

He was not slow to see this, and take advantage of it.

"Well, then," he urged, "wait; wait and watch him; we may even get to know him. They are different from us, these Englishmen, for they can throw aside their work entirely for a time, and take it up again where they dropped it when the moment comes. He will probably be doing nothing now for some time, and then who knows what his next mission may be? They are a universal people these, and try many things; they have no discrimination in their judgment of men. Do they not make statesmen of their generals, and naval lords of their men of letters? Mistley may go into Parliament, and do nothing more in the world."

"If he went into Parliament," said the girl forebodingly, "he would be more dangerous still."

"Well," urged the young man with pleading eyes, "but at all events give him a week or a fortnight."

"Then I must leave this forsaken place, and live in London," said the girl with determination.

"Yes; I will take lodgings in Bedford Place, and you will join me there. You will be my sister again, Marie."

"Yes, Ivan," she said with a little weary ring in her voice, as she laid her hand on his; "I will be your sister again!"

He raised the cool, lifeless fingers to his lips, and left her alone in the darkened room, where the light of the sacred lamp cast its ruddy gleams upon the calm faces of the Holy Virgin and her Child.

CHAPTER VI

To Colonel Wright this home-coming was full of delight and sweet anticipation. His life had been broken up by many wanderings, many campaigns, and many separations. All that was now to be left behind, and before him lay a prospect of active leisure, a life of intellectual ease, of pleasure and loving companionship. He had passed so many years in the East that he brought home with him an Anglo-Indian freshness and energy for home-pleasures. He was young enough to be still of an active mind, and leisure with him by no means meant idleness.

That first breakfast was an event to be remembered. So clean, so bright, so homelike was everything. Surely there never was a cloth so white, no silver ever shone so brilliantly as those forks and spoons. And never had happy father so fair, so dainty, so sweet a daughter to pour out his coffee, with just a little movement of shyness in the curve of her rounded arm.

"Then they are coming this evening?" remarked Lena when they were seated, looking across the table toward her father without ceasing her occupation of filling a coffee-cup, which manœuvre successfully directed the nourishing beverage into the saucer.

Mrs. Wright noted this result, and immediately gazed intently at the ceiling with a marvellous expression in

her face, which distinctly gave one to understand that
she saw the coffee in the saucer, knew how it came there,
and from the entire proceeding deduced that it is always
well to look before one pours.

"Yes," replied the Colonel. "They are coming this
evening, the sailor being included."

"Mother," said Lena presently, "have you told papa
about the invitation to Broomhaugh?"

"Yes, and he is quite ready to go."

"Oh, I am so glad! Papa, it will be simply lovely.
Charlie has told me all about it. It is a melancholy old
house, built by some remote Mistley, who was a cattle-
lifter, or a borderer, or something romantic. The Mistleys have lived there ever since—in the intervals between
their wanderings. Great bare hills all round, and a little
colony of pine-trees round the house, which is bleak and
gray, like an old fortress. Below the house, at the foot
of a sort of cliff, there is a trout-stream, where you can
fish all day; Charlie knows every inch of the stream, and
talks very wisely about flies, 'March-Browns,' 'Pro-
fessors,' and all sorts of imposing names. Then we are
going to get up some theatricals; we have arranged it
all, and chosen the piece. Charlie says that his brother
acts splendidly."

"Oh yes! He can do that!" replied the Colonel,
sapiently wagging his head. "He is always acting. In
fact, it is very hard to say when he is and when he is not.
I have watched him listening to a long story, which he
knew to be a fabrication from beginning to end, and the
childlike innocence of his expression was a perfect study.
He is the very man for theatricals; he was always stage-
managing something or other out in India."

"Perhaps he will be too good for us," suggested Lena;

"but it would be very nice to have a really good actor for the principal part, because the whole piece depends upon it."

"Charlie?" suggested the Colonel, with the ghost of a twinkle in his eye as he looked at his wife.

"Charlie won't take it," replied Lena, with perfect innocence. "He insists upon having a minor part, as he is to be stage-manager."

"What part do you act?" asked Mrs. Wright.

"Well, we have not quite decided yet. Charlie wants me to be the heroine, and a Miss Sandford, who lives close to Broomhaugh, to take the part of a sprightly widow. Now I think I would do for a sprightly widow much better than for a devoted heroine; but Mrs. Mistley says no. Let me see . . . if I were the widow, Winyard Mistley would be my son—a source of endless woe to his relations; if I were the heroine . . . oh . . . he would have to make love to me!"

"Ah! he would do that," said Colonel Wright, with conviction. "He would do that well!"

"I think I would rather be his mother," said Lena.

"Nonsense!" exclaimed Mrs. Wright incredulously.

"I once saw him making love," began the Colonel, in a tone somewhat suggestive of a long story.

"Indeed," said Lena indifferently, and she extended her hand toward the morning paper.

"Yes," continued the Colonel. "It was one of the funniest sights I have ever seen, and yet Mistley was as grave as a judge. She was a Russian; her complexion was of a dull yellow; she appeared to be ignorant of the primary use of water, and she smoked very bad cigars. Added to that, she was somewhat older than his mother!"

"Why did he do it?" asked Lena, smiling. She was more interested now in the little story, and had laid aside the newspaper.

"He wanted some information which we knew her to possess."

"Are you sure you did not make love to her too?" asked Mrs. Wright with a smile, which the old soldier fully appreciated.

"I tried," was the candid reply, "but could not get on at all. The best of it was that she half suspected what he was about; but she was so anxious to get some information out of him, that she encouraged his love-making. In fact, it was a game of cross-purposes."

"And who won?" asked Lena.

"Oh, he did," replied the Colonel, and he returned to his toast as if there could only have been one answer to that question.

Presently, after some moments spent in deep thought, Lena looked up with a twinkle of merriment hovering in her eyes.

"I think, papa," she said, "that he will do very well for the part we wish him to take. Your description of him sounds dark and mysterious, and that is what we want."

"Excuse me, little one. I never said he was dark and mysterious. As it happens, he is rather fair and the very reverse of mysterious, for he is open and almost boyish; though, indeed, his manner changes so much and so suddenly, that it is nearly impossible to say when he is in earnest or in fun. Generally the latter, I think."

"Because," continued the girl, "it is a villain's part —a very nice villain, though!"

"The part he takes in life is that of the light comedian, I think," said the Colonel, thoughtfully stirring his coffee. "He usually plays the light comedian to my heavy schemer, if I may put it thus; but then it is only because he has found it convenient to do so. People consider him a frivolous light-hearted boy, and he is content that they should do so; but I know him to be different. The fellow is a born organizer, foreseeing everything, ready for every emergency, which he meets with that imperturbable smile of his, as if he were enjoying himself immensely."

"I am rather afraid of this paragon," said Mrs. Wright, rising from the table.

"My dear," replied the Colonel, who was occupied in selecting a cigarette from a very highly-polished leather case, "if it were not for this paragon, I should very probably not be sitting here now. You must not let my praises prejudice you against him, as praise is very apt to do. Winyard Mistley is a clever fellow, and what is better still, he is sincere. He does his work well, and he does it because he loves it. It is such men as he who get on in the world—provided they do not marry."

"Why should the poor man not marry, papa?" asked Lena, who was busy with some flowers at a side-table.

"Simply because marriage would completely spoil his career. You see, a man cannot go roaming about in disguise in the heart of Central Asia, when he has a young wife fretting her life away at home."

Lena looked round, and then turned again to her flowers, which she continued to arrange thoughtfully for some moments. This was a new phase in man's existence which her father presented. She had hitherto (with some excuse, for she was young and fair) considered that love and marriage were the two crowning events of a man's life, around which all those dreary years of early youth and late old age circled like planets round the sun, gaining their light, their very being, therefrom. And now her father, who was no cynic, calmly laid the fact before her that a man may find a life's happiness in the building up of a career, in imprinting upon the sands of time his own particular footstep. And (alas, poor Cupid!) what was still more lamentable, there was on the face of it a certain reason in the argument that love and a wife could, on occasion, be nothing less than encumbrances.

She was not by any means convinced, however, and smiled a little to herself. You and I, fellow-traveller, can smile a little too. *We* know what a fell destroyer of man's career that tiny-winged god can be, when once he gets his range and settles to his aim. We know that ambition crumbles away before love, as a sandheap before the rising tide. But Lena knew none of this. She only felt that there was something wrong, or that there *should* be, in this argument; and her next question was of some weight.

"Is that his view of the case, or yours?" she asked demurely.

"Mine, but Mistley knows it to be true."

"And," continued Lena very indifferently, "will it be his mission to roam about in Central Asia in disguise?"

"Probably," replied the Colonel, who promptly seized this little opening to launch forth upon his favorite topic. "Probably. You see, he is the only living man who knows his way about those parts. There is no doubt about it that the movements of our white-coated friends must be watched closely, and the Government are beginning to recognize it. Mistley is the man to do it, and if they send anyone they will send him. It will be a difficult mission and a dangerous one; what we have been doing is mere child's play compared to it. I am getting too old for it now. The old folks have to make way for the young ones sooner than they quite bargain for; but I make way for Mistley with pleasure, for I know that he will do the work better than ever I could! And it will need the best men we have; there is more going on out there than people think. It is a strangely overlooked land; people here think of it only by fits and starts, once in every six months or so, while all the time those fellows are working and scheming; plotting with native potentates, learning the resources of the country, and generally forwarding the cause of Holy Russia. One day Central Asia will be opened out, suddenly and completely, by the biggest fight the world has ever seen. It has not come in my time, it may not come in Mistley's; but come it will, as sure as fate."

Lena remembered these remarks later, when she could compare with them Winyard Mistley's views upon the subject, of which he was accredited with so great a knowledge. The younger man took a less alarming view of the case; but while exercising a greater reservation, he spoke with a certain confidence, which, however, might or might not have been sincere. Winyard Mistley had a peculiar aversion to the subject of his travels, past or future, being discussed in the presence of ladies, and by some instinct the Colonel avoided any such mention when he was there. It is to be feared that, beyond a mere objection to talking "shop," Mistley had rather a poor opinion of a lady's discretion. Like many a wiser and more experienced man, he was of the opinion that politics are no woman's study. Even in his limited diplomatic experience, he had found means of discovering that in any phase or walk of life a woman has not the power of sinking her individuality. Her own personality is uncrushable; those strange unreasoning opinions, instinctive hatreds, and unaccountable loves which we men can never understand and never be too thankful for, clearly demonstrate that she was not constructed or intended for that cold, selfish science we call politics.

"I know," said Lena, partly to herself and partly to her mother, when the Colonel had left the room—"I know I shall be disappointed in him."

Mrs. Wright said nothing. She was standing near the window with the newspaper in her hand; but she was looking over it into the sunlit street. She was thinking of the lives of two women who had married soldiers—lives that had not been quite a success—lives made up of weary waiting and anxious watching; and running through these thoughts was a vague desire that this visit to Broomhaugh might yet be avoided.

CHAPTER VII

THE language of conversation is woefully limited. Whatever our feelings or our nature may be, we say what we wish to say by usage in precisely the terms that usage may dictate, and in the self-same words as are employed by thousands of other mortals to express the passing thought. Thus we may pass hours in the presence of a fellow-creature—hours made pleasant by the flow of easy conversation, and yet at the end we know no more of that fellow-creature's inward soul than we did at the beginning. Opinions may have been exchanged, but doubtless they were nothing more than mechanical phrases expressing a stereotype idea. Views of men and things may have been asked and given; but these views are as original and individual as the colorless photographs of a lovely scene with which enterprising manufacturers of useless little wooden boxes love to disfigure their wares, and which cannot fail to impress upon every observer the fact that they are turned out by the dozen. The truth is, that our thoughts are the slaves of the tongue. They may conceive wondrous ideas and opinions, but the tongue refuses to speak them—it prefers the well-trodden paths of easy and ready-made phrases. When, however, we take up a pen, our thoughts often gain the upper hand. Old conceits, long overlooked, wake up in the silent pigeon-hole of the brain where they were hidden; and lo!—set down in black and white, to be read by the world and sacred to none, are the secret thoughts we would not dare to speak to any living being. It seems that the pen has the power of making men forget their vain individuality.

But, thank Heaven, it is not vouchsafed to all, this outlet of the pen! Many put their thoughts into music; many into pictures; and some into song. Of these, the musicians are the more numerous. Not that they compose music, and thus express what in them lies; but, in playing on whatsoever instrument, the music of whatsoever composer, their whole soul goes into their fingers, and they forget their audience, they forget everything. For them the *allegro*'s and *piano*'s and *pppp*'s have no meaning. The composer's intention comes to them instinctively, and all they know is that the harmony in some manner fits into the train of their own unexpressed thoughts. Perhaps this is why we may hear sweeter, truer music from a girl practising in an empty room than has ever thrilled out from a platform, over the heads of an appreciative audience.

Lena singing and Lena in every-day life were two very different persons. To the ordinary world she was merry and light-hearted, rather frivolous perhaps, totally without romance, and probably heartless. So thought such people as had never heard her sing, or had not attended while she was singing; or again, whom she did not consider worth singing to. Combined with a sweet, clear voice and a true ear, she had the rare power of imparting a meaning to the words she sang. No song of hers ever seemed trivial or senseless. In wandering through the world, it has usually been the experience of the present writer to hear a drawing-room audience burst into rapturous " Thank you's " and " Who is that by's ? " the

very instant that the last note of the singer's voice had
died away. When Lena Wright ceased singing, there
was generally a little pause before anyone expressed their
thanks. It is of no great importance perhaps, this momentary silence, but yet it may be worth mentioning.
Sometimes Lena noticed it, and then a passing look of
embarrassment came into her eyes as she turned from the
piano.

Most people had known the Lena of every-day life first,
and first impressions hold to the memory like a woman to
her argument—through contradiction and undeniable
evidence, through ridicule and sober reasoning. Those
obstinate first impressions never die; and we look back
through the greater events and crises of a friendship to
them, and believe in them still. Thus it was that Lena
Wright had, among certain of her friends, the reputation
of being somewhat worldly, a little frivolous, and not
entirely averse to mild flirtation. No one accredited her
with any share of that shy romance which, to a girl, is as
the dewdrop to the tender bud. There were, it may be
mentioned in passing, two notable exceptions to this rule
—an old and a young man, both of whom were gifted
with a singularly reliable power of observation. Laurance
Lowe looked upon Lena as a fair replica of the fairest
human picture he had ever studied; and he could not
well make a mistake, as he himself had blended the colors
for both. It does not often occur that a man influences
the life of mother and daughter in the same way; but
when such does happen, the two women will be very similar in character. Charles Mistley was the second exception; he had only known Lena for three years; but that
dangerous intimacy which springs up between the children of old friends had grown rapidly with these two, and

he knew the girl's character and nature as her own mother did not know them. A dangerous study for a young man, you will say—these inner depths of a maiden's heart! Alas! perhaps it is so; but fire is a mighty pleasant plaything, and has been found so since man existed, and maidens smiled upon him!

It happened that Winyard Mistley heard Lena sing before he spoke with her; and in after years that first impression remained uppermost in his mind. He never afterward doubted the presence of a deep true woman's heart beneath the gay and almost frivolous manner she chose to assume before the world. Perhaps he was judging in some degree from himself. He knew that the gay and somewhat shallow youth, known to the generality as Winyard Mistley, was not the true inner *thinking* man, whose ambition was fortunately tempered with a whole-hearted sense of patriotism rarely met with in these self-seeking times.

When Winyard arrived at the door of Colonel Wright's house in Seymour Street, the postman was just turning away from it, having dropped a letter into the box and given his recognized rap. Thus Jarvis, the old soldier-servant, saw the shadow of a visitor upon the ground-glass of the door when he came for the letters, and did not wait for a second knock. The old warrior knew who this brown-faced stranger was at once, and stepped back, holding the door wide open.

Lena was singing in a small room immediately opposite the entrance, and the door of this room was wide open. The old soldier's movements were quick and noiseless, as a soldier's movements should be; but Winyard was quicker, and, with a touch of his hand, he stopped Jarvis from going forward to announce him.

Young Mistley

"Wait a moment!" he whispered.

Lena sang on unconsciously. She had heard the postman's knock, and recognized it; but was not expecting any particular letter, and therefore did not interrupt her song.

The two men stood outside the door and listened in silence—the old soldier, whose fighting-days were done, and the young man, whose time was yet to come. One a sturdy, powerful figure, very straight, with a peculiarly flat back and a square honest face; the other somewhat taller, of lighter build, lean and wiry, active as a cat. They could just see Lena's shoulder, and the play of her white hand and wrist. Occasionally, as she swayed a little to one side with the rhythm of her music, they caught sight of her dainty head, with the soft dry hair drawn well up and clustering down again.

It was a strange song that this light-hearted maiden was singing to herself, while awaiting the arrival of her mother's guests. A "Farewell," sweet and low as the sound of the sea at night when the sunset breeze is dying. There was a mournful, almost hopeless swing in the old-fashioned air; but the words were brave and strong. The words of a true woman to the lover she was sending away forever; for a woman is always the braver where love has no earthly hope. It was a song written and composed by a woman who was white-haired and a grandmother when Lena sang it; the only musical work of her life—the one sad song of her heart. Never having been printed, it was little known, and Lena had copied it from the manuscript-book of a school-friend. It happened that the girl was in the humor for singing on that particular evening. The day had been an eventful one, and she was looking forward to the evening. All this made her sing as she had rarely sung before.

Young Mistley

When the last note of the accompaniment had died away, Lena swung rather suddenly round upon the music-stool, and found herself face to face with Winyard. He was standing with his overcoat still upon his arm, and at first Lena thought that it was Charles Mistley. So quick was her movement that she caught Winyard looking grave—a luxury he rarely indulged in.

Instantly Lena rose, and although she blushed, she smiled with perfect self-possession.

"Mr. Mistley," she said, extending her hand, "I never heard you come in."

Then they shook hands, and Jarvis vanished with Winyard's coat.

"I am afraid," said Mistley, looking a trifle guilty, "that I have been standing outside since the end of the first verse."

Lena gave a little laugh, which was not quite free from embarrassment.

"That was rather mean," she said.

"I am afraid it was impertinent," said Winyard quickly, "now that I come to think of it; but at the moment I hardly thought of what I was doing. You see, I came in with the letters, and then, as soon as I stepped inside the door, I heard . . . you singing. I am afraid I prevented the man from interrupting you. I could not help it. You must make some allowance for a wanderer whose manners have suffered, Miss Wright. You see, I have not heard anything . . . like that for three years, and I could not resist hearing it all. Do you think I should have said 'Ahem!' or banged my umbrella into the stand, so as to let you know that someone was listening?"

"No doubt," replied Lena, "that would have been

the proper course to pursue; but it does not matter much, I suppose. If you like to listen to people practising, there is no actual harm in it. Let us go upstairs to the drawing-room. Our respective mothers are there. Papa is dressing, and Charlie has not come yet."

Lena stopped rather abruptly, and led the way upstairs. It suddenly struck her that the Charlie whose name came so naturally from her lips was this man's brother, and that her easy manner of speaking of him must sound objectionably familiar.

Winyard gave her no time to think of it, however. He saw the passing embarrassment, and came to her relief at once.

"I have not seen Charlie," he said quietly, as he followed her, "since he went to sea. He could not get away from Greenwich till this evening, and of course the Colonel and I have been spending a happy day at the Foreign Office. I suppose he is a great big fellow now; he was rather weedy when I went to India, but there was a promise of great strength about him."

"I think," said the girl softly, "he is the strongest man I have ever seen."

Winyard looked up quickly into her face, which he could now see, as she had turned at the top of the stairs to wait for him.

"In every sense of the word?" he asked; for he thought he detected a deeper meaning in the tone of her voice than the mere words conveyed. But he never received his answer, for at that moment the drawing-room door opened, and Mrs. Wright came forward to receive him.

"It is striking seven," she said, with a smile. "You are here to the minute. I know now how it is that you never hurry, and always have time for everything, as the

Colonel tells me you have. I need not introduce you
two, apparently.''

" No, it is not necessary, thank you," replied Mistley,
standing aside to allow Lena to pass into the room.
" We have settled all that, and I have got myself into
trouble already.''

" How so ? ''

" By listening.''

" Did you hear any good of yourself ? '' asked Mrs. Mistley, who was waiting for them in the inner drawing-room.

" I heard the most pathetic song I have ever heard,''
returned Winyard, glancing at Lena.

" Pathos being so very much in my line!'' laughed
Lena, as she dropped into a low seat.

" And in Winyard's!'' added that youth's mother
merrily. " You are neither of you very likely subjects,
I am afraid!''

Winyard Mistley laughed a clear, practical, ready
laugh, as he sat down in obedience to Mrs. Wright's gesture, and then quietly changed the subject.

" The mariner is late," he said.

" The mariner," observed Mrs. Wright, with a mock
severity which betrayed a kindly feeling toward its
object, " has a gentle way of lounging serenely in about
ten minutes late upon most occasions. Never more than
ten minutes, mind; and he does it so unobtrusively, so
calmly, and so good-naturedly that one cannot be angry
with him. By the by, Winyard—I suppose I may call
you Winyard—when I said that we would be a family
party this evening, in case you should be tired with your
journey——''

" Mistley is never tired," said Colonel Wright paren-
thetically, as he entered the room; and after carefully

raising his trousers, so as to avoid dragging them at the knees, he sat down.

Mrs. Wright nodded in acquiescence, and continued:

"When I said we would be a family party, I forgot that it would be necessary to explain that Laurance Lowe would be here. To your mother such an explanation was unnecessary, as she knows our ways. Mr. Lowe is such an old friend that we consider him one of the family, you understand."

"I think," said Colonel Wright, in his peculiarly slow and somewhat hesitating manner—"I think that Mistley knows a good deal about Laurance Lowe. You see, we had a large amount of spare time upon our hands out there—morning papers were not readily procurable, Mudie's was some way off, and altogether we were thrown a good deal upon each other's society, so we talked of home. Eh, Mistley?"

"Yes," chimed in Winyard cheerfully; "we got quite learned in each other's family affairs, and, by dint of hearing extracts from letters, began to take an absorbing interest in the doings of people we knew nothing whatever about. I shall be glad to meet Mr. Lowe."

"Laurance Lowe," said the Colonel sturdily, "is the most silent man and the truest friend I have ever known."

Winyard Mistley nodded with a peculiar little acquiescent smile, which meant that he was not thinking very much about the subject under discussion.

"A silent friend," he said presently, with a great show of gravity, "is as rare as he is valuable—— I think I hear Mr. Lowe upon the stairs."

The next moment the door opened, and Laurance Lowe entered the room, closely followed by Charles Mistley.

CHAPTER VIII

THE old man entered in his usual slow and deliberate manner. The Colonel advanced to meet him with out-stretched hand and a hearty word of greeting.

"Ah, Laurance, I am glad to see you! There's life in the old dogs yet, although the young ones are growing so big around us!"

Lowe answered never a word. He took the outstretched hand in his thin, strong fingers, and bowed as he pressed it with a quaint, old-fashioned courtesy.

In the meantime the two brothers had met.

"Hallo, Charlie!"

"Well, Win!"

They were close to Lena when they shook hands, and she heard the characteristic greeting. She also saw the long slow glance of their eyes, as each noted the work of the last three years in the development, bodily and mental, of the other's forces.

As they stood thus together before her, she saw, with feminine rapidity of thought, that there was not such a marked resemblance between the brothers as she had at first imagined. What likeness there was lay rather in manner and carriage than in feature. She saw now that Charlie was a much bigger man than his brother; also that he was fairer and with blue eyes, while Winyard's were gray and quick in their glance. In one, the slow, sure characteristics of a Saxon predominated; in the other, the quicker organization of a Dane.

Lena's comparisons were at this moment interrupted by her father, who came up and shook hands with Charles Mistley, dispensing with an introduction.

"Ah," he said genially, "you should have been a soldier instead of a sailor! You are too big a fellow to be cramped up in a torpedo-boat. I am afraid we old soldiers think that every man should be a redcoat, and perhaps we're right, after all. I know that every time I hear the roll of the drum or the tread of trained feet I look down for the gold lace on my arm, and think that if I had another life to live I would try soldiering again."

Winyard Mistley had turned away, and across the room his eyes met Laurance Lowe's calm gaze. Mrs. Wright had been watching them in anticipation of that moment, and now she hastened to introduce them formally. One great secret in Winyard Mistley's success was his ready adaptability to the circumstances in which he was placed as to social surroundings. With the merry he could be merry, and silent with the silent. This was no *tour de force* with him, but a happy gift of which he was not fully conscious. Without devoting even a passing thought to the matter, he shook hands with Laurance Lowe without saying a word. The strength of the grip he received caused him some little surprise; but this was not betrayed in the genial gravity of his eyes as he met Lowe's solemn gaze.

To the young fellow, who, like all born travellers, was a keen observer of human nature, this unobtrusive old man was intensely interesting. He was too intelligent to fall into the common error of considering Laurance Lowe a mere cipher in Mrs. Wright's circle of friends.

Young Mistley

His silence was not the natural reserve of a self-absorbed man, nor did it emanate from the simple fact that his brain was fallow, and that he had nothing to say. Before the evening was far advanced, Winyard had established these two discoveries to his own satisfaction, without betraying to anyone that he was watching Laurance Lowe. He observed that the old man followed the conversation, which, among such closely-allied friends, was perforce general; that no remark passed unheard, no sally was missed; but that he never spoke unless he was directly addressed, which occurred frequently on Lena's part, occasionally with the Colonel, and rarely with Mrs. Wright. Winyard also observed that whenever Lowe met Lena's eyes the lines of his face, which were deeply drawn, especially immediately over his mustache, relaxed somewhat, and that a faint motion of his lips beneath the silky white hair took place. These phenomena constituted a smile.

There was in Lowe no desire to pose as a man with a story—a blighted being who lived in a hopeless past, whose interest in life was dead. Indeed, nothing gave him so much pleasure as to sit as he was sitting this evening, among intelligent women and travelled, genial men; to listen to their views on men and things, however frivolous, however ridiculous, and to add that shadowy smile of his to the general merriment. And when he was referred to he invariably proved that his humor consisted of more than the mere appreciation of humor in others, which is like the reflection of a candle in a mirror, inasmuch as it is light, but not original light. Many of us are capital mirrors, but without the candle we are woefully dull.

Strange to say, it was these little flashes of humor that

Young Mistley

caused Winyard to realize the living pathos of this old man's existence. They came as a suggestion of wasted capabilities, of powers unheeded, of opportunities wilfully ignored. There is pathos in the sight of a man who, having tried, has failed; but infinitely greater sadness is there in the contemplation of him who will not try because he is indifferent. Winyard Mistley was just at that age when a young man is perhaps a little too self-confident—a fault which soon wears itself away. He was full of energy and life, and quite ready to try his capabilities upon any task—not with the blind self-reliance of conceit, but with a brave knowledge that he was ready to do his best, which might, after all, prove as good as the same commodity from the hands of any other man. If the situation of Prime Minister had at that time been offered to him, it is possible that he would cheerfully have expressed his willingness to try. To him, therefore, the sight of Laurance Lowe, a man whom he instinctively recognized as clever and capable—the sight of him, aimless, hopeless, indifferent, was not only pathetic, but it was disheartening and disquieting. Could it be that this energy, this restless desire to be pressing forward in the great race, this qualified ambition, was only a momentary incentive? Could it be that there are, after all, other things in life worth striving for than fame, and the glory of placing one's chiselled stone in the great structure of an empire? Winyard Mistley's love of his country was exceedingly great; but, after all, it was only human, and we all know that in the flower of every human love there is a gnawing worm called Self, which, though often unseen, is sufficient to render it but a poor misshapen shadow of that other love of which we talk so much and know so little.

Young Mistley

The young diplomatist knew well enough that the poorest in the land, the very humblest cripple of a shoeblack, may be a loyal and true patriot; but he also knew that for all the good such loyalty and patriotism could do, the man might as well be a black-hearted traitor. Therefore his ambition ran very smoothly with his sense of patriotism, upon the principle that the higher he climbed the farther could his voice be heard.

It was not until after the ladies had left the room that the conversation turned upon the subject dearest to the Colonel's heart; and then Mistley learnt with some surprise that upon this, as on every other question that had been raised, Laurance Lowe knew something. This tongue-tied, callous Englishman was one of the few who from the enervating security of peaceful Britain could look afar with watchful eyes and note the rising of that tiny cloud in the East, which at times seems about to rend the heavens with the fury of its lightning, and then again will dwindle away to mere vapor, floating over the blue ether of time. Winyard, being of a colder, less enthusiastic nature than the Colonel, was more correct in his reading of the public opinion in England upon matters Indian and Colonial. He was well aware that a fresh and daring encroachment upon the frontier of our Indian Empire would rivet the gaze of every Englishman upon the sullen movements of the aggressor for the whole space of a week, provided some fresh excitement, some thrilling murder in Paris, or a shipwreck attended with graphic details, did not usurp its place in the public interest. But beyond that he was too wise to expect anything. He recognized, therefore, that Laurance Lowe was more learned on this question than the majority of Englishmen. But in this, as in everything, Winyard found that strange lack of enthusiasm, and even of interest. He found that Lowe's observations, keen and far-sighted as they were, confined themselves to the mere indifferent criticism of a looker-on, whose life or happiness could in no way be affected by future events.

Thus it came about that Laurance Lowe, who was no favorite with young men, added that evening to his scanty circle of admirers. The attraction, also, was naturally in some degree mutual, as such friendships invariably are. Lowe was prejudiced greatly in Winyard's favor from the mere fact that he had proved such a valuable assistant to Colonel Wright, and also as the brother of Charles Mistley.

Lena, also, had that evening cast a little seed upon the broad earth by the mere singing of a plaintive song. It had fallen upon a spot where other seeds had taken root, and grew in strength already; but within that little germ lay power and life to outgrow them all in strength and height and splendor.

CHAPTER IX

AWAY up in the gently undulating land that rolls northward from the Cheviots to the Lammermuir and Pentland Hills lies the little town of Walso. Indeed, it lies upon the downward slope of Cheviot; and the clean streets, now grass-grown and silent, have many a grim tale to tell of the warm blood trickling down their gutters into the glancing river, if stones could only speak. Walso is a town with a past history such as few can boast of—a history full of brave deeds and fierce horror, for it stood in the very midst of Border warfare when the Cheviot burns ran blood, and the great silent hills echoed the ring of steel.

But now all that is past, and from it has grown up a prim, clean little town, paved throughout with spotless stone. No brick in all the burgh can be found—stone, stone everywhere, as strong, and clean, and sturdy as any Walso man. Side by side the gray houses are set down, shoulder to shoulder, as the brave old burghers were wont to stand when the Borderers were out. Up and down these narrow streets pass to-day a race of grave-faced men and tall women. Men with long, slow limbs and broad shoulders, brown faces, golden hair, and gray eyes. These same gray eyes are strangely direct in their gaze, looking into one as if they were looking into the sea-fret—as, indeed, they do during half the year. Up the broad valley from the North Sea this fret comes stealing like a gray veil all moist with tears, and envelops Walso, with its attendant hills, in mystery. And so the men possess a peculiar contraction of the eyelids, which makes shifty eyes feel shiftier—and so the women are blessed with complexions as purely pink and white as sunset over snow.

Life up here is conducted upon a slower principle than in the bustling South. Slow of movement, slow of speech, but wondrous sure, is this tall race of men and women. Taciturn about themselves, and not too genial to strangers, the men are reputed to be very shrewd and farsighted, especially in matters pertaining to pasture, wool, and "beasteses." In fact, they, one and all, appear entirely capable of managing their own affairs. The women in Walso, as also (I am led to understand) in other parts of the world, must necessarily be of superior intellect to their spouses, as they find time not only to manage their own affairs, but also those of every other woman in and around their native town. One worthy woman there was, however, who by experience had learnt discretion in its closest sense. This was Mrs. Armstrong, who let lodgings in the High Street. Her lodgers were mostly of the same habits and inclinations—in fact, they were all trout fishermen. The pavement of the High Street, which had rung beneath many an armed heel, now knew again the touch of steel, but of a more peaceful metal. Day after day these patient anglers slouched down the street toward the river, taking long, ungainly steps, and swinging their heavily clad feet and legs with a slow rhythm which indicated powers of long endurance. These same anglers were no ornaments to Walso society, for it must be confessed that their appearance was uniformly disgraceful. One and all affected a very loose tweed

coat, much dragged and misshapen by the creel-strap, a
tweed cap of a different pattern, embellished with the
gleam of gut and gaudy fly, a short pipe and a long stride,
stained waders and greasy brogues.   In the morning they
tramped heavily over the stones, with many a screech of
polished nail and heel-plate; in the evening they slouched
along, leaving little trails of water after them.   All wore
the same calmly contemplative expression; for your trout
fisherman, whatever he may be in ordinary life, is a med-
itative being when he gets within sound of running water
—loving solitude and seeking it, yet ready with a genial
nod or word of greeting.

But now it happened that the busy tongues had really
something tangible to thresh out between them, for Mrs.
Armstrong had let her lodgings to a stranger much more
interesting than an unobtrusive, indifferent fisherman.
This was no other than a young lady, "a furrineer," as
was generally supposed.   The worst of it was that no one
in Walso could put forward, for the general benefit and
information, a single fact concerning her.   Mrs. Currie,
the station-master's wife, had seen her descend from the
train, and was at first inclined to consider her a "likely
enough" young lady—whatever that distinction might
be worth—but on overhearing an inquiry as to whether
lodgings were obtainable in the village, the worthy matron
at once withdrew her mental observation.   She had
naturally expected that this was another visitor for Broomhaugh, as she understood that Mrs. Mistley had many
"furrineering" acquaintances; but that a young woman
—"ay, an' wi' good looks, too"—should arrive alone—
that is to say, with no other companion than a diminutive maid, who spoke no word of honest English—why,
the thing was "pre-e-posterous."

Young Mistley

This event, following close upon the arrival at Broom-haugh of Mrs. Mistley, young Mr. Winyard, and several guests, among whom was a real "cornel," proved almost too much for Walso. This sudden influx of other folk's affairs in want of management was unprecedented, and it is to be feared that, in their zeal for the good of others, many prominent ladies of Walso neglected sadly their own interests. Several tins of embryo bread, set before the fire on baking-day for the purpose of "rising," were allowed to rise and fall again by reason of evaporation; and the two Misses Currie were disappointed of their new white dresses on Wednesday evening, because Miss Eghye allowed her tongue to overrule her needle. Their first dressmaker-made dresses, too!

As it was more or less generally understood that Mrs. Mistley was in some degree capable of managing her own affairs (though the advice of an experienced woman such as Mrs. Currie could surely never come amiss), the greater share of public criticism and assistance was kindly accorded to the young lady of foreign proclivities who enjoyed the hospitality of Mrs. Armstrong's roof. Now, this young lady was no other than Miss Marie Bakovitch, or, as she was pleased to call herself upon occasions, the Baroness de Nantille—a title enjoyed by her mother before that lady married the Odessa merchant, Peter Bako-vitch, her second matrimonial venture.

With a gentle wonder at the glibness of her own tongue, the girl had told Mrs. Armstrong on arriving that she expected her brother Ivan in a few days. The old woman knew the responsibility of her position too well to abuse it by retailing to her neighbors incidents that might be injurious to her lodgers; but the ways of this vague, fair-haired girl were not her ways, and Mrs. Armstrong positively ached to confide the fruits of her observations to the ear of some sympathetic soul. According to her simple code of honor, she was bound by the laws of hospitality to protect and defend any person temporarily under her roof; and, although there were many facts sorely troublesome to her mind—such as the affixing to her walls of a small picture of the Virgin and Child, and the constant illumination of the same by an uncouth and uncanny little oil-lamp—Mrs. Armstrong succeeded in containing herself until the arrival of Ivan Meyer at Walso.

This took place two days later than the advent of Marie Bakovitch herself, and before the wonder of her coming had been fully discussed or exhausted.

Meyer soon discovered that the silence of the absorbed and dreamy girl was more likely to do harm than a discreet straightforwardness of speech. He therefore informed Mrs. Armstrong of sundry particulars concerning himself and his sister Marie. Without ill-treating the truth, he slipped round about it by that same path which at first looks so broad and easy, but soon becomes tortuous and hard to trace with reliant clearness.

Himself he described as an artist desirous of immortalizing some of the charming hillside stream-beds hitherto familiar to fishermen alone. His sister Marie was delicate, of a nervous temperament, which could not fail to benefit by contact with folk of such well-known self-reliance and sturdiness of character. He was afraid that London, in which restless city they had been sojourning, was not by any means the proper habitation for Marie; but Mrs. Armstrong would understand that a needy artist was compelled to live where there was a demand for pictures.

" Ay, dootless, dootless," replied Mrs. Armstrong. " I

dinna ha'ad much by pictures mysel', but there's folks that likes them ! ''

'' Ye-es, Mrs. Armstrong,'' responded Meyer, without having the faintest conception of the good lady's meaning; but he knew the value of agreeing with a woman, especially if she be from the North country.

This and more he told her, for the purpose of having it spread through Walso, even as the seeds are spread over the earth by windy impulse ; but the tongue of a Walso woman could ever beat the wind.

Ivan Meyer was young, and therefore full of hope, which is essentially a flower of springtide growth. To have constant intercourse with Marie Bakovitch was to this patient lover a source of happiness. His cold Northern blood allowed his mind such thorough control over his heart, and those latent passions which exist deep down in the soul of every man, be his eyes of calm blue or fiery black, that he could, at her bidding, in very truth cast away the lover and become a brother.

He still hoped to persuade the girl, whom he in his simplicity looked upon as possessed for the time being by a mental disease—though he did not suspect that the doctors had already commenced to give it a name—to give up her mad project of serving her country by a useless murder. Also he hoped, by the constant influence of his presence, to turn her thoughts to other things, and to bring back the sweet and merry little Marie of his boyhood. Yet behind the sublime light of Hope he vaguely felt the presence of a cloud. A dull misgiving was ever at the portals of his heart, awaiting the night hour, or the aid of some passing untoward circumstance, to effect an entrance.

He rather dreaded the first mention of the subject

which occupied the girl's mind, and, though he did his best to talk of other topics, she took the very earliest opportunity of bringing it forward.

Mrs. Armstrong had just cleared away the remains of their simple evening meal, and set the lamp on the table. Meyer produced his portfolio and spoke of his latest sketches; but the girl quietly placed her hand upon it so as to keep it closed, and looking across the table, she forced him to meet her eyes, and said slowly:

"Ivan, what news have you?"

"He is here," replied the young artist reluctantly.

"At Broomhaugh?"

"At Broomhaugh. His mother is there also; Colonel Wright, his wife and daughter as well."

Marie Bakovitch sat for some moments in silence. Her hands, very white and beautifully formed, were lying upon the green tablecloth, with a peculiar stillness which was characteristic of the girl. It was a stillness without peace. Without raising her eyes, she said presently:

"And the other—the sailor?" Her voice was singularly calm and indifferent.

"He comes in a fortnight. At present he is detained by his duties at Chatham or Greenwich, my informant could not say which."

"When did the Mistleys come?"

"On Monday, the same day as you, Marie."

The girl nodded her head, as if in silent confirmation of Meyer's statement.

"Have you seen Marloff?" she asked suddenly.

"I have."

"And you have the photograph, Ivan?"

"No," replied Meyer, shaking his head slowly. "The photograph has been destroyed—such were his orders!"

" But you have the verbal description ? "

" Yes . . ."

" What is it ? "

" ' Of medium height, square shoulders. Looks military, walks lightly, is agile in his movements.' . . ."

" Yes—yes," interrupted the girl impatiently. She had been following the description as if it were familiar to her. " And his face ? "

" ' Face, intelligent and much sunburnt; eyes gray, of some penetration, though usually wearing a smile. Light mustache, somewhat fairer than the hair, which is brown. Profile good, and expressive of determination.' "

Meyer stopped. He had been reciting in the monotone of a schoolboy who knows his lesson well, but he had been watching his companion's face steadily, and now he saw her change color. The faint pink flush left her cheeks, while the shadow beneath her eyes deepened. The brilliant redness of her lips was startling in comparison with her pallid face.

" Marie—Marie! " he exclaimed, taking her cold hands within his. " You are killing yourself with all this excitement! For God's sake listen to reason! This man . . ."

Marie Bakovitch rose suddenly and walked to the window, which was open, though the thick curtain was drawn across it. She jerked it back, and looked through the branches of a geranium plant out into the deserted street.

" I travelled from London with him," she said presently.

" In the same compartment ? " inquired Meyer anxiously; he had risen and was standing beside her, looking down upon her fair head.

"No, in the same train."

"Thank the Holy Virgin you did not know him!" exclaimed he fervently.

"I did know him," the girl replied softly; "I knew him by his resemblance to—to his brother."

"Marie!" exclaimed Meyer suddenly, "Marie! You *must* wait. As long as he is here, he can be doing no harm. The moment he stirs from here, instead of placing difficulties in your way, I will help you."

"So you *have* placed difficulties in my way?" she said wonderingly, as she looked up into his sensitive, feeble face; but he did not meet her gaze.

"You will never understand my love for you," he said by way of reply, and his voice was wonderfully soft and patient.

As she looked at him, her blue eyes slowly filled with tears, and it was a proof of her ignorance of love that she did not hide them from her lover.

"Good-night, brother," she said gently, holding out her hand.

"Good-night, Marie." He took her fingers, and was about to raise them to his lips, when his eyes met hers. Something he saw there made him drop her hand, and cross the room to open the door for her to pass out.

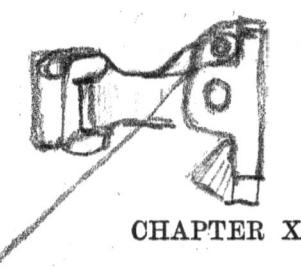

CHAPTER X

THERE is always something pathetic in a friendship between men of widely different ages. However great a tact the younger may display, he cannot always conceal the fact that there are resources of vitality and reserves of energy within him that the elder man has lost. He may slacken his pace upon the curve of a hill with infinite cunning, but it is probable that the elder man will detect the movement, perhaps saying nothing about it; but that makes it only sadder, for silence can express greater pathos than any spoken language.

Mrs. Wright was not a sentimental woman; her heart was filled with that infectious joyousness which is as sunshine on a gray and barren land; but when she saw her husband and Winyard Mistley together an unaccustomed obstruction rose in her throat, and, always a busy woman, she became busier than ever. This sight made her think more than was desirable of a little mound far away in an Indian churchyard, whereon the turf had thickened with the growth of twenty years. It took her back over that dim road which narrowed and finally vanished in the blessed perspective of time, and in her heart this brave lady wondered at her own cheerfulness.

One morning, soon after their arrival at Broomhaugh, this sudden glimpse of the past came to Mrs. Wright with unusual force. The Colonel was anxious to begin fishing

without delay, and there was consequently a great display
of fly-books and rods on the table near the window. Over
these the two men were bending their heads, absorbed in
the disentanglement of dry and curling gut. Their
brown hands occasionally touched as they cleared the
loops and freed the spiteful hooks; and Mrs. Wright,
glancing over the morning paper, noted the slight trembling of one pair of hands and the deft steadiness of the
slighter fingers. She saw the close brown curls almost
touching the older head of gray verging on to white, and
thought again of the infinite possibilities buried in that
little churchyard far away, within sound of the roaring
Indian surf.

"I must get accustomed to seeing them together,"
thought the unsentimental woman, turning resolutely to
the Parliamentary news.

Upon a chair near at hand was seated Adonis, a lamentably plain Irish terrier. Grave and expectant, he was
watching with intelligent interest every movement, every
preparation, doubtless thinking the while of the pleasant
day he was going to have among green hedges and soft
grass, with here and there a succulent blade over which
to perform strange labial contortions, to the detriment of
his personal appearance, but infinite benefit of his inner
dog. In connection also with the last-named matter, he
glanced occasionally toward Lena, who was helping Mrs.
Wright to prepare sandwiches for the fishermen; and
when he looked that way he slightly lowered his ears and
smiled a little, for Adonis was woefully impressionable,
and loved a pretty maid.

At last the lines were ready and the casts made up with
cunning combination of parti-colored flies, tempting and
gay, but not fulsome. At hand were also two gray

flannel bags, with close neat seams of Lena's work, containing in cool moss a crawling, restless Gordian-knot of red worms, in case the fishy appetite should be too coarse for daintier fare.

Then Lena approached with a bright smile, and two dainty packets neatly tied with a knot which would have brought a smile to Charlie's face had he been there to see. One she stuffed into her father's jacket-pocket, and held the other out to Mistley. But he unaccountably became clumsy at that moment, and all his fingers were employed with his rod. Somehow the joints would not re-enter the narrow bag constructed for their reception. So the ingenuous youth murmured "Thank you," and glanced audaciously at the pocket of his rough fishing-jacket, which hung conveniently open. The rod showed no signs of approaching submission, so Lena was compelled to drop the small parcel into the open pocket, which she did with much exercise of care, in order to avoid touching any part or portion of the coat.

"Then," said Winyard, with a great show of innocence, "we are to be home by three o'clock, to ride over to Sandoe."

Lena had walked toward the window, and was now standing just inside. She turned her head, after a little pause, and said indifferently:

"That was what you arranged; but of course, if the fish are taking well, it would be a shame to drag you away from them."

Winyard bowed low, and opened the large, old-fashioned window for her to pass out on to the terrace.

"You are very considerate," he said in a low voice, as he followed her.

This terrace was a charming feature of Broomhaugh.

Young Mistley

It was formed by an old wall built up sheer from the
sloping bank of the Broomwater, and was paved by huge
slabs of rough stone, now worn smooth by the tread of
many feet. The house itself was low and gray, being
built of the same stone. Grim and sturdy, it harmonized
with the bare hills around and above it. Signs there
were still of the old fortifications, notably the wall forming the terrace, which had rendered Broomhaugh practically impregnable from the river-side in the olden times.
Below it, amid the whispering leaves of silver birch and
mountain-ash, ran the little river—a trout-stream, such
as one finds only within the shadow of the Cheviots—and
on this fair morning its gentle ripple scarcely reached the
ears of those upon the terrace, for rain was sadly wanted.
A downpour of two hours would convert the clear brown
water into a yellow torrent rushing down to the sea, as if
ashamed of its own impurity. Then would the air at
Broomhaugh grow heavy with a dull roar rising from
the tree-clad valley beneath, and old Lee, the gardener,
would peer down through the branches and mutter:
" Eh, but she's a big watter! " As the waters gradually
subsided, the old fellow was wont to hobble away to his
little cottage, and there, with trembling, clumsy fingers,
would adjust his rod and laboriously disentangle his cast,
in readiness for Mrs. Mistley's suggestion that he should
go down to the burn and catch a basket of fish for breakfast.

As Lena and Winyard paced slowly backward and forward on the terrace awaiting the Colonel, the ripple of
the stream awakened within the young fellow's heart a
fisherman's longing for the sight of running water. Only
fishermen can understand this love of nature, for only
they know the delight of wandering rod in hand up the

bed of a stream with legs encased in waders, and the heavy swing of brogues at their ankles. Their sport, with its quiet concentration, gives time for a passing admiration of the solitary beauty around them, and the murmur of the glancing water is to their ears as the voice of one they love.

Men born among these hills may go to dwell in cities, they may change their mode of life again and again, until the days of their youth lie away back in the perspective of the past; but the sound of running water, and the smell of it, will bring a message back to them unaltered by the years that lie between, and the old love of solitude, disturbed only by the peaceful rill of water or the curlew's weird cry, will rise within their weary breasts again. The hand cramped with holding a pen will long to grasp the quivering rod, and the ears weary with city din will ache for the sound of the whistling line.

Presently Lena stopped at the corner of the terrace, and stood motionless, gazing down the narrow valley where, like a silver thread, the Broomwater ran its tortuous course.

"I have never understood before," she said slowly, "what the love of one's native country is. You see, I have never had a native country. We have always been wanderers upon the face of the earth. But when one can call a place like this one's home, it is very different —the most heartless person could not help being a patriot."

"And yet," said Winyard, "what wanderers we are! It has even come to my being a professional wanderer, you see; while Charlie is a sailor, which means that he will never be quite happy anywhere upon dry land."

"But still, it is something to think of in your wander-

ings that you have a home like this to come back to; that
these hills will be the same—the house, the stream, this
old gray wall, everything. Adonis knows what I mean
—do you not, you solemn old thing?"

Hereupon followed an embrace which Adonis bore with
good grace, but failed somewhat to appreciate.

"I understand what you mean as well as Adonis," observed Winyard, with grave humility. "Although, perhaps, I do not look so solemn about it as he pretends to
be. I understand it, and I suppose I feel it all; but the
spirit of the tramp is very strong in the family, I am
afraid. After all, it would never do to sit here all one's
life, as we are sitting now upon this wall in the sunshine,
admiring the scenery! If you were a man, I know you
would not do it."

"I wish I were," she said softly.

"Thank goodness you are not!" he exclaimed fervently in a low tone.

And then they sat there and said never a word, while
Adonis watched them with his left ear slightly raised.

Presently the Colonel appeared at the open window
equipped for the fray, and eager to begin it. Instantly
Winyard became the polite host, and, raising his hand to
point down the valley, he said to Lena:

"Do you see that round hill with the steep incline on
the south side? Follow that incline down to where the
slope of the next hill cuts it, and just there you will see
a faint blue line across the gap."

"Yes, I see it; and that blue line is . . ."

"The sea. That is called Mistley's Gap. The sea is
twenty-six miles from here; and you can never see that
blue line after ten o'clock in the morning. The people
about here think that at that time the sea subsides, and

falls below the level of the valley, on the principle that there is more water in the streams early in the morning than at any other time. In reality, it is of course a mere atmospheric peculiarity. There is a tale told by the shepherds that in olden times a band of Borderers hanged a Mistley in that gap. He was a sailor, and as he was returning home, after a long absence, they caught him and hanged him upon a rough sort of gibbet, in sight of his home and the sea."

"So that you know that at least one of your ancestors was hanged," said the Colonel, with his hearty laugh.

"Yes," returned Mistley; "and history tells of others as well who came to grief in the same way, owing to some slight error of judgment regarding other people's sheep. We are an eminently respectable family. But if you are ready we had better go."

The two fishermen then arranged that Winyard should walk two miles down-stream before commencing to fish up, while the Colonel appropriated the water immediately below Broomhaugh. So they parted at the gate, and Winyard went swinging along the road at a pace that promised to make short work of the two miles.

The bright promise of early morning had received a cloudy check from the west, and now a gray day, if not worse, seemed a safe prognostication. In little more than half an hour the younger angler was at work, rejoicing in the familiar whiz of the flying line.

There are occupations wherein a certain mechanical portion of the brain is sufficient to guide and inspire the hand, leaving the remainder free for other work. The steering of a ship is one of these; hence sailors are a thoughtful race of men, holding quaint and original notions on the way and manner of living through a human

life. Give a sailor the spokes of a wheel within the span
of his arms—allow to pass unnoticed an unsightly bulge
in one cheek—and during two hours, his "trick" at the
wheel, he will think you out as many solid thoughts as
any philosopher of inky inclinations. The swaying compass, the pulse of the restless wheel, and the shivering of
the topmost sail that curves its white breast to the horizon, are all well within the grasp of his mechanical brain;
that is, of the outer office, where the mere clerks are
capable of dealing with the case, only knocking at the
door of the sanctum occasionally, and asking advice
when mechanism fails and authoritative decision is required.

It is a mistake to imagine that trout-fishing belongs to
the above order of things. The man who seeks to catch
this dainty fish mechanically will probably catch little
beyond the lower branches of a willow across the water.
Now this shows and fully establishes the mental superiority of trout over the rest of the finny tribe—their business must needs be transacted in the inner office.

Winyard Mistley possessed the happy power of giving
his whole mind to whatever work or pleasure he might
for the moment have in hand, and his entire attention
was therefore accorded this morning to the slaying of
harmless fish. When youth and a certain activity of
brain, combined with a lifeless heart and a lively diges-
tion, work in unison, there are few deeds within human
reach that are not feasible, and none that are not worth
trying. With practised eye and an untiring wrist the
young fellow cast his cunning flies on to the rippling surface of every likely pool. The fish were inclined to en-
courage duplicity and cold murder, for they invariably
answered the call made upon them; not only the young

and foolish, but large and burly fellows with misshapen mouths and stout hearts for an uphill fight.

While his master was engaged in studies piscatorial, Adonis was gravely employed in botanical research. With one vigilant eye devoted to the inward swing of the silvery line (his fly-catching days being over), he did not forget for one moment the pleasant chain of slavery that hung around his neck, and the spirit of sniffing inquiry was held in check by a stern sense of duty which forbade any straying away. Occasionally, also, Adonis considered it only polite and respectful to take an interest in and inspect the vanquished foe as he lay panting on the turf, if only in consideration of his master's feelings as a sportsman.

At first the stream ran through a level meadow, where the grass was rich and green compared with the scanty brown covering of the hill. It was the widening of the valley, and the hills stood far apart, as if drawing back to make their farewell bow to the pleasant laughing water which did not despise their aged company, and brightened for a while with its smiles and glancing merriment their grave and time-worn melancholy.

As Winyard progressed up-stream, from pool to pool, by rippling shallows and stony runs, the vale narrowed in, and the great bare slopes began to dictate to the yielding water, and measure out its path. The voice of the stream grew louder as its existence became more eventful, and the difficulties thereof greater. There were big rocks to be circumvented, and to be laughed at when passed and gleefully avoided. Soon there were little leaps to be taken with smooth curve and snowy froth, whereunder lay the wise trout awaiting a chance worm torn from the broken bank a little higher up. In and about these variations of flow lay deep and tranquil pools, where the water recovered its bright purity after the disturbing influence of eddy and fall.   Here dwelt the larger trout —fish of a certain standing in life, with rights of way and habitation, originally acquired by strength of tail or fin, and now held by reputation and rights of long possession.

With gentle turn of wrist, and clever calculation of strength, duly allowing for the cool breeze hurrying down the valley, Winyard searched each pool and corner for the feeding fish; and already the weight of his creel was of some consideration upon his back, with every now and then a thrill of life as some brave trout gave his last convulsive kick.

Presently Adonis, who, having conceived the idea that there might be water-rats about, had turned his attention to the river's edge, looked up and broke the silence.

" Woff! " he said—an internal interlabial bark, the sound of which appeared to strike the gleaming barricade of teeth, and travel down again to the inward parts of his muscular person.

" I beg your pardon," observed his master absently, being at that moment absorbed in the deft placing of his flies beneath an overhanging branch across the stream.

" Woff! " repeated Adonis, showing all his ribs with a sudden drawing-in of breath.

" Indeed! " said Winyard with kindly interest, and following the direction of the dog's eyes, he saw the cause of his annoyance.

This was the form of a young artist, who, seated upon a humble camp-stool, was transferring to his tiny paper a very pretty glimpse of the Broomwater.

As the fisherman passed, the artist slightly raised his

hat with foreign politeness, which salutation was immediately returned, and Mistley continued on his way. When he had passed out of sight, the artist promptly rose from his seat and packed his materials away into a portfolio.

"He does not remember me—assuredly!" he murmured in Russian, as he turned and walked rapidly downstream toward Walso. But in this Ivan Meyer was mistaken.

CHAPTER XI

WINYARD reached Broomhaugh before the Colonel, and as he climbed the narrow stone steps cut in the solid wall, he saw Lena on the terrace. She was sitting reading in the corner whence the view of Mistley's Gap was obtainable.

"Back already!" she said, looking up with a smile.

"Yes," he said slowly. "Back already."

He seated himself on the low wall beside her, and swinging his creel round, he opened it for her inspection.

Mrs. Wright happened to be in her bedroom, and from the window she could see these two young folks. She had no desire to watch their movements—no wish to spy upon anyone—but she could not help noting that the two young heads were very close together over the open basket; it almost seemed as if Lena's soft dry hair were touching Winyard's lips.

"I wish," whispered Mrs. Wright, as she turned away from the window—"I wish I knew what to do. I wish Laurance Lowe were here—he knows Lena better than anyone; and Willy is enjoying his stay here so much that I do not like to trouble him with my misgivings."

In the meantime Winyard had closed the creel, and having laid it down in a shady corner, he returned and sat down beside Lena again. The water was slowly dripping from his waders, forming two little pools upon the stone pavement. With his foot Winyard gravely constructed a little canal connecting these two pools, while Lena watched him in silence. Presently, without looking up, he said:

"I must write to Charlie to-day about the theatricals—what am I to say, Miss Wright?"

His eyes were quite grave, but his lips were twitching with suppressed laughter as he gravely awaited her reply.

"You are to say, Mr. Mistley . . ."

"Excuse me, you appear to find a little difficulty in saying Mr. Mistley," he interrupted. "It *is* awkward, I know—people have remarked upon it often. Mistley is one of those names with which 'Mr.' goes badly. You will find 'Winyard' much easier to say . . . I think!"

"You are to say," continued Lena, carefully omitting any name whatever, "that Miss Sandford will take the heroine's part, and that I will have much pleasure in doing my best as the sprightly widow."

"And that I will commence at once to study the part of the domestic servant who comes in once and says 'The carriage is at the door.'"

"No—we settled that you should take the principal part."

"*You* did."

"Yes!" said Lena, with a decisive nod.

"And I settled that you should be the heroine," observed Winyard meekly.

"But I cannot act it."

"Why?"

"Because there is too much pathos in it, and I cannot do pathos; it is not in my nature, I am afraid."

"You forget," said Mistley, "that I have heard you sing."

"Oh, that is a mere matter of tuition!"

Winyard slowly shook his head. "You never learnt to sing that song as you sang it the evening I listened behind you in the hall."

Lena shrugged her shoulders and laughed. "Tuition," she said again.

"Then," said Winyard, turning toward her suddenly, "let me be your tutor. If you would act that part, I know we could make it a success. With Mabel Sandford I simply could not do it; she has no conception of the character, and would spoil it. When you see her, you will acknowledge that I am right. She is very nice, of course, but absolutely without the least power or individuality. If she had only remained in the country she would have been all right; but two seasons in town with a scheming old aunt have, according to all accounts, completely spoilt her!"

"Do you think that your arrangement will suit Charlie?" asked Lena.

"I am certain of it. In fact, it is not my arrangement, but his. He maintains that he could not take a larger *rôle* and be stage-manager as well; and we must have him as manager, because no one else can do it so well."

At last Lena consented, on condition that it should not be mentioned until after she had made Mabel Sandford's acquaintance; and with this Winyard was forced to be content.

While they were still talking over this matter, the Colonel arrived with a very heavy basket of fish, and a separate tale to tell of each individual captive of his rod.

It was nearly three o'clock before they were mounted and on the road to Sandoe; and as they rode along the

Colonel continued to regale the two young people with his experiences during the morning.

Presently, however, they left the road and turned into a narrow lane, Lena leading, the Colonel next, and Mistley last. Winyard was quite convinced in his own mind that there was ample room between the hedges for two to ride abreast, but Lena kept in the centre pathway, and the Colonel squarely followed. Such lanes are common enough about Walso. A mere strip of grass between two hedges, worn, like you and me, in proportion to the traffic passing over them, and to the friction of wind and weather. Some have only one worn track, and that but shallow, like the late wrinkle cn a smooth face; and again, some have as many as three rugged furrows, like the lines on a scantily thatched head, which has remained stationary while others passed over it.

The Sandoe road, however, was well-to-do, and of evident prosperity and luxuriance. At the foot of either hedge the nettle and gentle dock grew together in harmony; while overhead the wanton brier-roses, not content with the place assigned to them, spread long, pliant arms, and carried the sweet beauty of their bloom into other folks' quarters, notably of the blackthorn and pithy elder, both of which, from jealousy no doubt, grew crookedly, with twist and ugly knot. In and out and everywhere the stealthy woodbine crept upward with innocent trailing tendril, content to be little seen below, knowing well that overhead, outstripping every other growth, its redeeming flower was fairest of all, diffusing the sweetest breath into the air.

Winyard's horse was young and unsteady, consequently he had but little time to admire the scenery; also he appeared to prefer for contemplative purposes, when his animal allowed of such, a slim and graceful figure slightly swaying to the movements of a sleek little mare in front. At length the lane was brought to a sudden termination, as is the fate of all such lanes, by a high-road running at right angles to it.

The Sandfords were simple people of a North country type, now, alas! growing rare. Already "Old Sandford," as he was universally called, was beginning to find that his daughter had imported all sorts of new-fangled ideas from her South-country boarding school, that the old home was too simple for her enlightened tastes, and that even his own little personal habits jarred upon her sensitive nerves.

His forefathers, he opined, had always been content to live in Sandoe, though Mabel complained that it was a common farmhouse. They had always found the prospect of hills and low-lying meadow sufficient for their eyes, and the knowledge that it was all Sandoe land was happiness enough for their quiet hearts.

The house was, indeed, little else than an enlarged copy of the solid farmsteads of the neighborhood; but the Sandfords were not farmers, and never had been, though why folks should be ashamed of an honorable occupation Old Sandford could not understand. Born, bred, and now growing old amid the solemnity of his beloved hills, where all goes slowly and surely except the clouds overhead—and God's hand guides them, so their speed need alarm no one—the old fellow was himself a slow man, but very sure. Above all, he was a gentleman by heart and by head as well, though he had never been farther South than Morpeth for his education.

When the Broomhaugh party entered the roomy, old-fashioned hall, which was used as a sitting-room at Sandoe, they found Old Sandford stamping his feet after a long ride.

"Ah, Win, my boy!" he exclaimed. "Thank God we've got you back to the North country again!"

Then followed the introductions, and the old gentleman shook hands heartily with Lena and her father, for he had no faith in those new-fangled bows with which strangers honor each other nowadays when they are supposed to be strangers no longer.

"Glad to meet you, sir!" he said to the Colonel in his quick, abrupt manner, with an expressive jerk of the head, which seemed to say: "I may be an old country bumpkin, but I know all about *you!*"

Then he proposed an adjournment to the summer-house, where they would no doubt find Mabel. "Reading novels, I expect!" he added, with a glance toward Winyard.

Mabel Sandford was indeed there, and, moreover, she laid aside a yellow-backed book as she rose to meet them. Winyard she greeted with an effusion which he, at least, thought rather overdone. She was dressed too well for the occasion, and her bright black hair was arranged somewhat more elaborately than was necessary. Nevertheless, she was decidedly pretty, with large dark eyes of the type usually called "fine," and a graceful figure full of lithe strength.

Leaving the two old gentlemen to amuse each other, Winyard began the question of theatricals at once.

"Charlie is stage-manager," he said, "but he asked me to get things on as far as possible before he came, because we have no time to waste—he goes to the Mediterranean next month, and I may be called away at any time."

101

Young Mistley

"It is a shame," exclaimed Mabel Sandford, with an exaggerated pout of her full red lips, "the way in which we poor females are deserted by everyone! I have not seen Charlie for months; and as for you, Win, I am surprised to see you now!"

"I expect," replied Winyard, with rather a short laugh, "that you will be heartily tired of us both before these theatricals come. You have read through the piece, of course."

"Oh—yes!" replied Miss Sandford. She had just picked a little spray of monthly roses, and was fixing it in her dress, glancing occasionally at Mistley as she did so.

"Well, we want you to undertake the longest part!"

"The heroine?"

"No, the young widow; there is a great deal to learn, mind," replied Winyard innocently, carefully avoiding Lena's eyes, and meeting Mabel's with infinite audacity.

"If you think I can do it, I am quite willing."

"Oh—I am certain of it! Miss Wright will play the heroine, Charlie the hero, and I the villain. Walter says he will act the old man's part, does he not?"

"Yes. By the by, he is somewhere in the garden. I will go and call him."

Mabel Sandford was a little disappointed, but she had too much spirit to show it; and Winyard's great interest in her part, displayed in the subsequent rehearsals, at length convinced her that although she was not the heroine of the piece, her part was by no means unimportant.

Her brother, who presently appeared, was a simple, good-natured fellow two years younger than herself. He openly confessed to being in a "mortal fright" about appearing on the stage, but expressed a humble readiness to do his best.

Young Mistley

Winyard Mistley was not in the habit of allowing the grass to grow beneath his feet. Without appearing to have or even desire his own way, and by means of gentle suggestions, he arranged all the preliminaries, and even fixed the day for the first rehearsal before leaving Sandoe that evening.

Heavy clouds had been stealing up over the hills for some hours, and, as the gate swung to behind the Colonel's horse, large sullen drops began to fall into the dusty road.

The Colonel led the way down the green lane, keeping up a steady trot despite the roughness of the path. At last the rain began in earnest, and he pulled up to suggest that Lena should put on the jacket she had strapped to her saddle.

"You two light-weights can soon catch me up," he said, riding off.

Lena stopped in the middle of the lane, and proceeded to endeavor, unaided, to loosen the straps round her jacket; but her gloves were wet, and the slippery leather refused to submit. Then Mistley forced his horse into the ditch, and so reached her side.

"I have no gloves on," he said quietly, as he leant over and took possession of the straps.

"Thank you," said she, looking rather anxiously after her retreating parent.

In a moment Winyard had unbuckled the straps and shaken out the short thick jacket. Then he took her bridle in his disengaged hand, and so left her free. But fortune was against her; the collar of the jacket got turned in, and Mistley had to take both reins in one hand while he leant back and assisted her. When he had done this, and Lena had secured the last button, she held out her hand for the reins; but he retained them for a moment longer.

" Am I forgiven ? " he asked.

" For what ? "   Lena looked rather markedly up at the sky, as if in gentle protest against being detained in the rain.

" For having my own way."

" Oh, I do not mind acting the part," she replied, with a short laugh.

It is in little incidents—in the trivialities of every-day life—that a man shows his knowledge of human nature. Winyard now suddenly abandoned the subject, and drew aside to let Lena pass.

" And now for a scamper home! " he exclaimed cheerily, as the horses sprang forward at a long canter.

CHAPTER XII

THE following evening Charles Mistley arrived. This event, unimportant though it may appear, had been awaited with some dread by Mrs. Wright; indeed, perhaps Mrs. Mistley herself may have had some misgivings on the matter, though she betrayed no signs of such.

The former lady, however, was by no means happy on the subject of her daughter. Of course it was natural, she confessed to herself, that the two young people should seek each other's society in a household composed of an older generation; and this great friendship (if such it was) might have been expected under the circumstances. But an equally close friendship had existed between Charlie and Lena before Winyard appeared on the scene; and the remembrance of this was not pleasant to the cheery little lady's soul. To her Lena was a puzzle, as, indeed, she was to a great many people. No subject had hitherto been quite sacred from the girl's raillery; life had, up to the present time, been a very pleasant affair—mostly laughter, and with no sorrows too serious to be laughed at later on. But now this unwearying mother thought she detected a graver look in Lena's eyes, and, mother-like, she set to work to find out what this shadow could portend. Mrs. Wright loved to look on love, as all good women do; but she had lived long enough in the world to know that where there is a victory there must be a vanquished, and the old foreboding came back to her that there was danger for Lena in this visit to Broomhaugh.

In fact, this little lady was puzzling over a question which has never been answered yet. This was the possibility of a true friendship existing between a maiden and a youth. It is very easy to give an opinion upon it in a general way, and many of us consider ourselves perfectly qualified to do so; but during life we will have to alter that opinion several times. This peculiarity, however, is common to every generality, because in speaking generally we invariably think individually. We boldly apply generalities to the entire human race, or to one-half of it, without deigning to inquire from whence the inspiration has been drawn; and on investigation it usually transpires that the opinion applies to one individual only. Indeed, it cannot well be otherwise, as there are no two human lives alike, and, in consequence, no two natures identical. This habit of speaking collectively is usually a youthful fault, which vanishes as experience wears out the bristles of our mental broom. When we are young, and the bristles are all astir with self-opinionated and mistaken zeal, we make great broad sweeps around us, collecting—like other new brooms—a little dust, and leaving unsightly streaks behind us, which only serve to show where the dust lies thickest; but when the bristles are worn down a little, we go to work more carefully, not in broad sweeps, but in little sidelong movements, clearing no great space, but leaving no streaks behind us.

Mrs. Wright had, like most people, her ideas upon this doubtful friendship, though she was too wise to hazard a decided opinion upon the matter. Like many of her sex, she knew men better than women, and, having attained a certain age, was capable of judging them impartially.

106

In fact, she saw the gingerbread without that gilt which is so apt to dazzle younger eyes. It is a lamentable fact that there is remarkably little gilt or gleam of any true metal about young men, until they have acquired it from contact with finer wares. The result of Mrs. Wright's observations—which may be worth recording—was that the man is to blame in almost every case of a spoilt friendship; that most girls are capable of forming a friendship with a youthful member of the sterner sex, but that the vanity of the latter invariably spoils it, and renders its existence an impossibility. He, in fact, in his superb self-appreciation, cannot realize that a girl may show a liking for his society without being in love with him, which, after all, he thinks is the most natural thing in the world.

Now Mrs. Wright had, in a few days, formed a much more correct estimate of Winyard Mistley's feelings than that astute young gentleman suspected. She knew his to be a heart wherein Ambition had found its place before Love. It is so in some cases, and when Love arrives he finds himself in the position of a dog who comes home to discover his kennel occupied by a determined and resolute cat. Some dogs—such characters as our friend Adonis—will make a rush at the kennel, and probably, at the expense of a few scratches, accompanied by much vituperation, will turn the cat out. Others will be more wary, and their tactics will perhaps partake more of the orthodox method of warfare: result—scratches galore, and the intruder still in possession. Others, again, will feign to be ignorant of the intrusion, professing a great interest in various objects of refuse that may be lying around, taking care at the same time to turn an unobservant back upon the kennel, and thus afford the cat an opportunity of honorable escape.

Young Mistley

Mrs. Wright shrewdly suspected that the intruder, Ambition, was in possession of Winyard Mistley's heart; but, womanlike, she promptly thought it possible that the sad dog, Love, might be prowling round in search of his own rights; and her instinct told her that the plan of assault most to be feared was the Adonis-like attack, sudden and daring.

During the last two years Lena's mother had thought a good deal upon the subject of young men in general, and Charles Mistley in particular. The more she saw of that grave young sailor, the stronger grew her liking for him. She soon learnt that his gravity by no means denoted a dulness of intellect, and discovered each day some new proof of his thoughtfulness for others and forgetfulness of self—qualities which find greater favor with elderly than with young ladies. Gradually she had dropped into the habit of encouraging the friendship which had sprung up between him and Lena, reflecting that if it grew into something stronger than friendship, Charles Mistley was worthy of any woman's love. There was, however, that grim fact of his being a sailor, which was forever forcing itself upon her notice, and would not be permanently quelled by the reflection that there are many appointments on shore within reach of sailors who, like Charles Mistley, have a moderate income and a certain influence at headquarters.

The younger brother, Winyard, had never entered into Mrs. Wright's thoughts in the matter, and lo! here he was, barely a fortnight at home, complicating things most terribly by calmly establishing a friendship remarkably like that which had caused so much uneasiness already. Whatever the result might be, this shrewd little woman of the world knew that no good could come of it; she held the opinion that the influence of a young woman

over a young man can be of no earthly good to him.
Altogether, Mrs. Wright had no desire to witness the experiment between her daughter and either of the Mistleys.
It is a dangerous experiment and a desperately unprofitable one, O youthful inquirer—an experiment best left alone, as the writer of these poor lines can testify, having burnt his fingers over it!

In the meantime, Winyard and Lena seemed to be cheerfully progressing down that flowery path which is so lovely at first sight, so disappointing on nearer inspection, and so exceedingly thorny as one penetrates into its depths.

They drove into Walso together to meet Charlie, and all three arrived in the highest good-humor with themselves and everyone else, as the first dinner-bell pealed through the house.

Despite her cheerfulness, however, Lena was a little thoughtful at intervals that evening, and during the mystic arrangement of her hair she was so absorbed that she not only forgot to hum a ditty to herself, but displayed a most unusual awkwardness in the insertion of sundry pins, more or less calculated to keep her head in order, and consequently the entire erection presented, even more than was customary, an appearance of approaching collapse.

A second attempt, however, was eminently satisfactory, and she tripped down-stairs, a demure and fairy form, long before the second bell rang. With maidenly dignity she entered the drawing-room, cool and serene, as if there were no such thing as dressing in fifteen minutes; but it was only to find Winyard standing at the open window, cooler and more serene, as if there were no such thing as reducing fifteen to ten. He did not speak, but held back the soft curtain for her to pass out into the garden.

"Not on the grass," he said with paternal anxiety, as

he followed her; "your shoes are too thin!" And she obediently walked on the gravel.

"Will you be so kind as to wear that dress in the third act?" asked Winyard presently.

"Why?"

"Because . . . oh, because it is the most difficult scene, and I think I could do it better if you wore that particular dress. Do you understand?"

"Hardly . . ." replied Lena truthfully. She was trying hard to find out whether he was serious or not. "But still, if there is stimulation in it to do great things, I suppose I must wear it; but I do not think it will be quite appropriate to the scene."

"Why not?"

"Well, that is just the most pathetic part of the whole play, which is in itself by no means cheerful; and white with a yellow sash is not exactly pathetic!"

"Tell me," said Winyard, with exaggerated gravity, "why white with a yellow sash is not pathetic."

"I do not know," she replied with a laugh; "but that is my view of the case."

"But do you not think that a strong contrast is always effective? I have never yet understood why people on the stage should persist in dressing in sombre garb on account of the sorrow that is coming, and of which they are supposed to know nothing. The most touching thing I ever saw on the stage was at the Comédie Française years ago, when I was at school at Fontainebleau. It made such an impression on me, that I have never forgotten it. The heroine was in a ball-dress, and the hero in ordinary evening clothes, with a decoration in his button-hole. It sounds prosaic, but it was wonderfully effective. The saddest things that have happened on

110

earth have been in the gayest towns, within the very sound of music and laughter.''

"Then you think I ought to be gay until the last minute!''

"I think so, certainly. It is a principle which one can safely go upon until the end of the chapter, and never regret it. Talleyrand originated that idea, I believe. I am quite certain that half of our troubles are only worthy to be met with laughter.''

"Do you speak from experience?'' asked Lena, thinking of her father's description of Winyard Mistley's dauntless spirits.

"No, because I have had little or nothing to experiment upon, having always been a lucky individual; but I cannot help admiring people who can laugh when they do not feel like it.''

"What a prosaic way of putting it!''

"Perhaps so—but you know what I mean, nevertheless. Now, if you were to wear that dress, I am sure it would prove most effective. There is something about a white dress—a soft, simple sort of dress like yours—with a yellow sash, which always makes me feel most sentimental; and I am certain that such a result could not fail to be edifying to every onlooker. If you were to add some flowers it would be still better—say jasmine. We will try the effect to-night.''

And he stopped to gather a few sweet-smelling sprays, which somehow took so long to arrange satisfactorily that the bell had to be rung again for their special benefit before they obeyed it.

"We will consult the stage-manager about it,'' said Mistley, as they turned toward the house.

"No!'' she said quickly. "Please do not do that!''

CHAPTER XIII

AT breakfast next morning, Colonel Wright explained at some length that as the stage-manager had now arrived, he failed to see any obstacle in the way of Winyard and himself indulging in another morning's fishing. This proposal Winyard agreed to with his usual readiness, and immediately after the morning meal they sallied forth together.

According to arrangement, Winyard went down-stream again, while the Colonel fished up. It was not really a good day for sport. The sky was brilliant, with dazzling white clouds scudding before a strong breeze. Altogether, matters did not go well. Several times Winyard stumbled as he made his way up the bed of the stream, very nearly breaking his rod on each occasion. Before he had been at work half an hour, he caught his fly twice in a tree, having to cross through deep water to release it. In fact, he was fishing atrociously. Now, when a man who is an adept with the rod fails to catch fish, and occasionally hooks a tree, it is fairly safe to surmise that he is not giving his mind to the work before him. Such, indeed, it is to be feared was the case with this cheerful young fisherman.

The strong will of a strong man is a tough antagonist for the best of us—that is to say, for the best of women, who are superior to us in matters wherein endurance counts heavily. Under a happy and careless **manner**, Winyard Mistley concealed a certain dogged determination, and all this was now centred on the profession which he had adopted. Ambition, determination, and patriotism fought together in the young man's heart—a strong combination under a resolute leader, for ambition has led men upward to the highest pinnacles of fame, despite every obstacle. Pitted against these allies was one small foe, his only arm a bow and arrow of the frailest workmanship. But he knew no fear, for he had fought the miscreants before, and vanquished them. In his plucky little heart was the knowledge that those three restless giants (one of whom he loves as a brother) are but mortal, whereas he is a god. He can lurk within the inmost citadel unseen, unsuspected; sometimes, even, he is content to lie hidden until the battle is over, and he laughingly appears with cynicism curling on his rosy lips.

To Winyard Mistley, Ambition and his allies whispered: "Leave home and love, cast aside comfort and ease, sacrifice all in order to pierce through the ruck of mediocrity—and pierce you must!" On the other hand, a small voice urged: "I am worth more than fame, more than glory and a country's gratitude, for I outlive them all!"

No wonder this angler caught trees instead of fish, when such inward voices were striving for the mastery. But the strife was destined to be settled by an event, and not by thoughts. It is ever so in our lives—we think great huge thoughts, and, like the waves of the sea, they roll on and are no more, while a tiny event may make a great man greater, and a poor man greatest. We often wonder, in profitless moments of self-study, how we would act in a crisis; imagining the while that the crises of our lives are ushered in with due regard to stage-effect, whereas they are in and out again before we realize it. It is only in looking back that we find the true turning-point, as a man having lost his way goes mentally back over the road to discover where his mistake occurred.

While he fished, Winyard Mistley was actually pondering over the advisability of abandoning his new profession. What conclusion he might have arrived at it were hard to say, had he been allowed to think the matter out; but suddenly a new light shone upon it. A light all lurid with the hate of man, red with the gleam of aggressive treachery, yet shining with the glory of a steadfast purpose.

Amid the solitary grandeur of his native hills, by the side of peaceful Broomwater, an event was destined to take place on this fair summer morning which left its mark on Winyard Mistley's life. It was here that the long pursuit, so steadfastly carried out by Marie Bakovitch, was to come to an end. As will be learnt hereafter, he was fully aware of the girl's purpose, and even knew her name and description, but had always treated the matter lightly, as the passing freak of a highly strung and ignorant girl. Now he was about to learn his mistake; he was about to face a sudden and unexpected danger, alone and unaided, as he had faced most things in his short life. And the result of it all was to be the appearance of a new ally against the little god who had laid his siege so skilfully. Dogged British pride joined ambition, determination, and patriotism, and drove their small enemy shrinking back.

Winyard Mistley had made his uneventful way up the stream for about a mile, and was now approaching a spot where the water broadened out, losing, after the manner

114

of earthly things, profundity in so doing. Here were stepping-stones, and on each side a natural unmade footpath.

Although he was fishing carelessly, Winyard's eyes were fixed upon the water; and he therefore failed to perceive the form of a girl at the edge of the stream, upon the opposite side, and a little higher up.

This young lady had apparently no intention of making her way across the stepping-stones, being quite content to stay where she was. Every now and then she glanced down-stream, as if expecting someone; and yet when Mistley appeared, unconsciously and placidly angling, she appeared surprised and somewhat disturbed.

At first she made a movement as if to draw back; and then, suddenly stepping forward, she resolutely planted herself at the water's edge, with pale agitated face and quivering lips, while her small ungloved hand went to the pocket of her dress.

Adonis was some distance behind his master, engaged in botanical discoveries, and therefore oblivious to all around him. With aggravating deliberation the fisherman came slowly on. The water below the stepping-stones was of no use to him, so he raised his rod to gather in the line and pass on. As he did so he lifted his eyes, and found himself face to face with the girl. Her attitude, the paleness of her lovely face, and the wild excitement gleaming in her eyes were instantly observed by Winyard, and in a flash of thought he connected her presence there with himself, and with the tall artist whose face he remembered having seen at Victoria Station on the morning of his arrival in England.

There was no ignoring the girl's evident excitement; he could not pretend to treat her as a villager, and pass

115

on with a local greeting. For a moment the ruddy color left his face; but it was not due to cowardice, for men grow pale in moments of excitement who do not know what fear is. Then he raised his cap, but never smiled or inclined his head.

The girl ignored his salutation, standing motionless and pale as a marble statue.

"I am Marie Bakovitch," she said simply, the musical tone of her deep voice rising above the brawl of water.

"I know it," he replied. Even in face of her pale, set features, and under the gaze of her cold blue eyes, he could not check the quiver of his lips. He was too chivalrous to let her see his smile, so he said: "You have caught me at last!"

Then, rod in hand, he stepped into the running water, while Adonis stood upon the bank with his left ear raised, watching these proceedings uneasily. The brook sped past Winyard's legs, rippling and laughing, while with its voice mingled the sad murmur of the pine-trees overhead, like the sound of the surf on a deserted shore.

Slowly he made his way across, feeling with his encumbered feet for each standing-place, for he dared not remove his eyes from the girl's pale and defiant face. Suddenly she seemed to realize what he was doing, and she raised one hand convulsively to her throbbing temples. Then hastily she withdrew the other hand from her pocket. Mistley saw the gleam of polished metal flashing in the sunlight, and a moment later he was facing the muzzle of a pistol, while behind it he still met those lifeless blue eyes fixed on his face, with no light of hatred in them.

The sight of the little black orifice, with its rim of blue steel, drove the smile away from the young Englishman's lips; but still he slowly approached her with the dogged coolness of his race—not blindly, but calculating his chances as if he were gifted with a dozen lives.

"If," she exclaimed, in her pretty Russianized English, "you come one step nearer to me, I kill you!"

No reply came from his lips. The stream laughed on. Overhead the pine-trees sighed, and far away in the blue ether a solitary curlew gave forth his weird cry of warning.

Facing the mouth of the grim little pistol, Winyard never hesitated. He was half-way across the stream, and with the same surefootedness he continued his way.

Then suddenly the girl dropped her arm.

"For God's sake, *stop!*" she hissed, stamping her foot on the soft turf.

Still he came on toward her, with steadfast gray eyes fixed on her face. Then she slowly raised her arm again, and turned the pistol toward him. While facing it, he was calculating his chances with a deliberation that was surprising even to himself; and there flitted through his mind the recollection of his own failure to shoot a disabled horse, because its eyes met his without flinching.

The bed of the stream was now rising at a gentle incline beneath his feet; a few more steps, and he would be in shallower water; yet another few, and that small white hand would be within his reach.

Suddenly a streak of white flame almost blinded him, and a ringing report well-nigh burst his brain.

The little puff of gray smoke rose slowly on the breeze, and Marie Bakovitch saw Mistley standing in the shallow water.

"Pah!" he exclaimed, as he passed his disengaged hand across his eyes.

The sulphureous smoke had half choked him, and some

grains of unburnt powder had flown into his face, causing a momentary sting; otherwise, he was unhurt. The pistol was of German manufacture, and threw high, having been made (as might have been expected) to sell, and not to shoot with.

He gave her no time to attempt a second shot. In an instant he was on the bank, having sent his rod quivering on to the turf beside him.

He grasped her wrist, but not too fiercely, for even then he remembered his manners, and the wrist was very small and shapely.

She made no attempt to resist, and relinquished her hold on the weapon as he firmly took it. Suddenly he felt the life go from her hand, and was just in time to catch her as she fell, unconscious and helpless, forward into his arms. It took him a moment to realize what had happened; then he laid her gently on the slope of the bank, and turned to get some water, which element he supposed to be necessary under the circumstances.

Across the stream Adonis, with all his sportive instincts aroused by the sound of a firearm, was hunting eagerly, with ears erect and officious tail, for the slaughtered game.

"Adonis," said Winyard, with comic vexation, "you're an idiot!"

A man is not seen to advantage when administering aid to an unconscious woman. He is apt to be clumsy and ridiculously awkward, feeling all the while that this is no fit occupation for him, that he is meddling with a delicate machine of which the sensitive workmanship and motive-springs are to him a profound mystery. He is oppressed with the notion that another woman would instantly put matters right by the simple means of unhooking something, or the performance of some similar trivial office of which he knows absolutely nothing, and would rather not attempt in view of returning consciousness. With a sufferer of his own sex it is a different matter; and from the time of the good Samaritan down to these ambulance days, a man ministering to a man has always been an edifying and wholesome picture.

However, it was Winyard Mistley's custom to make the best of most things. There was within him that true British conceit which prides itself upon being equal to every emergency, provided it be human, and the cause more or less a righteous one. Therefore he filled his cap with the cool water that flowed from the Northern hills, and set about to vanquish this unknown foe.

Now, it happened that sunstroke was a visitation with which he was more or less familiar, having had experience of it on several occasions; moreover, he was a great partaker in a certain insular love of cold water applied outwardly, and it appeared to him that he might do worse than treat this fair patient as he had treated many (less attractive) suffering from sunstroke.

Carefully holding his cap by the rim, he suddenly tipped it over, and cast upon the girl's lifeless face a cold shock of water, which immediately trickled down her graceful neck in a most uncomfortable manner. But what man, under the circumstances, could have been expected to think of that? This vigorous treatment met with its due reward, for Marie Bakovitch promptly opened her eyes, just in time to save herself the infliction of a second capful.

"Where am I?" she inquired in French, that being the tongue in which she prayed and thought, having spoken it before any other.

119

Winyard was never averse to satisfying harmless curiosity; but to answer this question was a matter of some length, so he ignored it, and said in the same language: "Now you are all right again, is it not so? Come, let us sit on that great stone. There you will get the breeze."

He slid an arm under the light form of his would-be murderess, and gently supported her toward the rock indicated. She allowed herself to be placed thereon in dazed silence, and then slowly raised one hand to the bosom of her dress.

"I am afraid you are rather damp," said Winyard apologetically, but with a cheerfulness of manner which seemed to indicate that all had occurred for the best. Then, being a gentleman, and perhaps a little soft-hearted, he turned away, busying himself with the top of his flask. This gave the girl time to rearrange the soft masses of hair which had become a little loosened, and to give one or two little cunning touches to her apparel, which a woman with only half her senses will still do.

"Here," he said, holding forth the cup of his flask, "take a little drink of that."

Obediently she took the metal cup and drank. If only Ivan Meyer could have seen how Winyard commanded and Marie obeyed, he might have learned therefrom an invaluable lesson, for the girl was of those who need to be domineered over, and are happiest in obedience. What Ivan Meyer the thoughtful failed to perceive in length and fulness of years, Winyard Mistley the superficial saw in exactly two minutes, and knew how to profit from it. The cordial appeared to revive her; a reawakening of life dawned in her eyes, and a faint pink, like the sunny side of a peach, rose to her cheeks.

"Did I faint?" she asked, without looking up; indeed, her eyes were fixed on the cup she still held, the contents of which were evidently not to her taste.

"Yes; but you are all right again now," was the cheerful and inspiriting reply.

Then she looked up, and appeared to recognize him for the first time, for she started back, exclaiming, "Oh —oh-h-h!" and covered her face with her hands, as if in horror of a recollection just rising in her brain.

CHAPTER XIV

WINYARD MISTLEY watched her in silence. He almost expected some hysterical display, or perhaps a vain onslaught upon himself. The color slowly left her face, and her level red lips were pressed together painfully.

"Now, do not go and upset yourself!" he said masterfully, as he picked up the cup she had cast from her. "Let us be business-like and quiet. Do you feel better now? Is there anything I can do for you?"

She looked up at him in vague amazement. Then, pressing back her hair with both hands, she said:

"I cannot understand you Englishmen . . . do you know who I am?"

"Oh yes, mademoiselle," he replied; "I know who you are."

He stooped and picked up the revolver which had so lately been pointed at him, and Marie Bakovitch watched in silence while he dexterously removed the five remaining cartridges and threw them into the stream, much to the astonishment of Adonis. Then he politely handed her the firearm.

"I have a favor to ask of you, mademoiselle," he said, "and then, if you feel restored, I will leave you."

"Of me?" The poor girl was piteously pale, but showed no sign of womanly tearfulness or emotion.

"Yes," he replied, stepping nearer. "Will you tell me whether you were sent by your Government or not?"

"I was not."

"And yet," said Mistley, watching her face closely, "your Government knew of your purpose. They placed every facility in your reach; they encouraged you as much as they *dared*. . . ."

She winced as he emphasized the last word. She sat twining and intertwining her ungloved fingers, but never spoke.

"They," he continued bitterly, "found themselves outwitted by simple straightforwardness, which, because it was not their mode of acting, was not expected by them. What they failed to do by telling lies, breaking treaties, and ignoring the commonest points of honor, they attempted to accomplish by foul means, calling in the aid of a woman . . . of a *lady*, mademoiselle, whose hands should never have been soiled by such dirty work. I shall never cease to regret that this has occurred, and I need hardly tell you that the matter will rest between ourselves, with the exception of Colonel Wright, who must be informed of it, not as a personal matter, but as a question of policy. To yourself personally I bear not the slightest malice; but oblige me by telling the man who signed your passport, who gave orders to the spy Marloff to watch me and report to you, who, in fact, did his best to make you a murderess—tell him that from henceforth I work no longer from a sense of duty to my country, but from feelings of the fiercest hatred toward himself and his despicable agents. Ah! you need not look frightened. In England we say what we mean, and are not afraid of treacherous ears being ever on the *qui vive* to report every compromising word uttered in confidence."

He was roused at last, and the gray eyes, hitherto so calm and restful, flashed as only gray eyes can.

The girl rose and faced him bravely; although of a singularly *fébrile* and nervous temperament, she felt at that moment no bodily fear.

"It is for my country that I strive, and not for any man," she said, in a low, concentrated tone which was wonderfully musical. "*I*, too, am a patriot; *I*, too, love my home, and count my life as nothing beside my country's good. You have power, and you are a man whose words are listened to; but for me it is a different matter. I am powerless, and can never hope to raise myself to a position of power. My life is of no value to Russia; but by losing it I could make it of value, if, by that sacrifice, I could remove from her path an enemy as implacable, as influential, as yourself."

It is painful to have to record the fact that Winyard Mistley shrugged his shoulders at these words. Such patriotism as shows itself in the forming of societies and making of fiery speeches was particularly distasteful to him. Indeed, it was by his extreme reticence that he made his mark in the diplomatic world. He had shrewdly suspected that Marie Bakovitch was the victim of unscrupulous men, who, possessing a certain gift of hysteric oratory, urged on others to deeds of violence, while religiously avoiding all danger to their own persons. This suspicion he now found confirmed by the girl's speech.

Perceiving that Winyard Mistley had no intention of being dragged into an argument, and was indeed preparing to leave her, Marie suddenly changed her manner.

"I, too, have a favor to ask of you," she almost pleaded. "I am in your power, wholly and inevitably;

but as an English gentleman I beg of you to keep . . .
this matter . . . a profound secret from Ivan Meyer.
I am strong again now . . . I will go! ''

With a grave inclination of the head, she passed him,
stepping firmly on the dry turf. He watched her as she
made her way along the edge of the stream by the little
path that led to Walso. Adonis having gravely undertaken a search on his own account for the five cartridges
thrown into the river, now returned unsuccessful, and
took his stand by his master's side, with sturdy legs set
well apart for greater convenience of the draining water.
He also watched the maiden depart, turning occasional
glances toward his master's face with a brisk and questioning movement, as if to ask what this was all about.

Winyard was in the habit of taking life cheerfully,
seeking out the sunny side of every cloud, but now he
was exceptionally grave. It was characteristic of his
somewhat reckless ancestors that he gave no thought to
the danger he had just passed through.

"Poor girl!" he muttered; "she is desperately in
earnest, and consequently she is miserable!"

Then he suddenly stooped to pick up his rod.

"Adonis," he said; "Adonis—I wonder who Ivan
Meyer can be. He does not know that she was waiting
here for me to-day. There is more in that than meets
the eye!"

Adonis placed his head slightly on one side, at the
same time elevating one ear, a habit he had when puzzled.
He also had his thoughts upon all this, but, alas! he
could not speak them.

When Winyard reached Broomhaugh with rather a
poor basket of fish upon his back, he was told that Colonel Wright had also returned, and was changing his fish-

ing-clothes. When he came down-stairs a few minutes later, he found his chief waiting for him at the door of a little smoking-room which was specially set apart for the gentlemen.

The old fellow looked grave, and, ignoring Winyard's inquiry as to what sport he had had, he motioned him to enter the room, and followed closely. Then the Colonel closed the door, and held out a telegram.

Winyard took the pink paper, and read aloud:

" Would suggest Mistley engaging a valet whom I can recommend. Marie Bakovitch is in England."

The message bore only the initials " M. L.," and had been despatched from the Westminster Branch Post-office. Winyard read it over once for his own edification, and turned toward his chief with a smile. The Colonel was standing with his broad shoulders against the mantelpiece, his eyes fixed on the carpet. His hands were thrust deeply into his jacket-pockets, and he moved restlessly from one foot to the other.

" As usual," said Mistley, still smiling, as he took a seat on the edge of the table, and carefully tore the telegram into small pieces. " As usual with news from headquarters—this comes just too late."

" How ? " asked the Colonel, looking up rapidly.

" I had the pleasure of meeting Miss Marie Bakovitch this morning."

" You—here ? "

" Yes. She had a cock-shot at me with a very nice little revolver at a distance of about five yards, and missed me ! "

" Whew—w—w ! " remarked the Colonel. Words

usually failed him at a critical juncture. Mistley
laughed as he dropped the remains of the telegram into
the waste-paper basket—his usual laugh, which had little
hilarity in it, serving, nevertheless, very well as a stop-
gap.

"She was in the train by which we came. I remember
seeing her at King's Cross. No doubt she is staying at
Walso. Privately, I think she is a little vague in the
upper regions; she did not appear to know exactly
what she was about, and—and it was—desperately poor
shooting!"

The Colonel tugged pensively at his gray mustache,
while his kindly eyes rested with an expression of wonder
on his companion's face.

"Now that I come to think of it," he said slowly,
"when I drove your mother and Mrs. Wright into Walso
the other day I saw a foreign-looking girl accompanied
by a tall, fair fellow, who looked like a Scandinavian.
The ladies were in a shop, and I was waiting outside."

"The foreign-looking girl was Marie Bakovitch," said
Winyard, partly to himself. He was slowly stroking
Adonis with a soft pressure of his slim brown hand on
the shaggy head. "If," he continued, after a long
pause—"if it had only been a man, the whole affair
would have been intensely funny; but, somehow, since
I have seen the girl, the humor of the thing has vanished."

Lena and Charlie, passing the open window at that
moment, heard Winyard's remark. There was no mis-
taking the neat enunciation, no misconception of the
meaning; and as they passed on, each wondered a little
over those words caught on the wing.

Presently the Colonel walked to the window, still pondering over the event just related to him. Then, without looking round, he asked:

"Will you have this valet?"

"No, thank you! I do not believe in that system, for one reason; and I require no one to protect me from a girl, for another!"

Then the Colonel turned sharply round, and faced his companion.

"Who was the man I saw with her?"

"I was just wondering," replied Winyard adroitly.

After a short pause the Colonel spoke again.

"I think, Win, you are a little too rash—too indifferent to life; either the indifference is counterfeit, or there is something radically wrong."

"Let us say," replied Winyard imperturbably, smiling, "that it is counterfeit—at all events, there is nothing radically wrong. But that has not much to do with the question. If this girl is going to be a nuisance, she must be made to go; and, above all, the ladies must not get wind of the affair. There is no reason why they should, I think."

"Suppose I go and see the girl—she must be made to leave at once!"

"I think," replied Winyard, "it would be as well to give her one or two days' grace—say till Tuesday. There is not the slightest fear of her making herself obnoxious in the meantime; and if she is not away by then, we can put on the screw. Somehow, I think she will not be heard of again; her patriotism has been satisfied by the mere smell of powder, like a French journalist's honor. She was desperately frightened, I think, and very much relieved when she found she had made a bad shot."

"Well, then," said the Colonel, with some determination, "you do not go out of my sight till Tuesday!"

Mistley laughed—a boyish laugh, all glittering with lightness of heart—and made a movement toward the door, for he heard a sweet, clear voice trilling a very well-known air about the house. But Colonel Wright did not respond to the movement. He stood at the window, still tugging at his gray mustache—still contemplating the carpet.

"I often wonder," he said at length, with a quick upward glance toward his young companion—"I often wonder why this girl ignores me, and directs all her mad hatred against you. If the matter is, as she and her precious companions state, merely a political question, it appears to me that my name, and not yours, should be on their list of persons considered dangerous and likely to be harmful to Russia."

Winyard Mistley made no reply. He stooped to caress Adonis, who was sleeping on a low chair, and the expression of his face was a masterpiece of innocence and utter emptiness.

"I think," continued the Colonel, who felt he was gaining ground, and therefore grew bolder, while his kindly eyes acquired a new keenness—"I think . . . I will go and see . . . Marie Bakovitch."

"No!" exclaimed Winyard incautiously; "you must not do that!"

Then there followed rather an awkward silence between these two men who knew each other so well. The younger busied himself with Adonis, while the Colonel looked on with a strange misty look about the eyes.

"You must think me a great duffer, my boy!" he said at length, a little grimly.

Winyard shook his head, but did not look up.

"I am afraid," continued the old soldier, "that I must be one, or I should have suspected it before. Now —when it might have been . . . too late, I see it all. That first letter from the Society of Patriots . . ."

"Lunatics," suggested Winyard, with rather a lame little laugh.

"No, let us call them Patriots, for some of them, at least, are sincere. Their first letter threatened us both. You answered it, and, contrary to your custom, you forgot to keep a copy of what you wrote. Since then there has been no question of me, but only of you. Oh, what a fool I was not to have thought of it before!"

As usual, Winyard laughed, but the Colonel held to his point.

"Win, my boy," said the old fellow slowly, "during the last two years we have been very good friends, and that under exceptionally trying circumstances. We have gone through a good deal together, and we have shared everything; I think it would have been right and fair . . . in fact, you must see for yourself that I have a claim to share this additional danger with you as we shared the others."

Winyard was very much occupied with the buckle of Adonis's collar, and did not look up at once. Then he looked toward the door, and said:

"Listen!"

Adonis, who knew the meaning of the word, instantly cocked his left ear and obeyed. Slowly he wagged his tail with little awkward jerks from side to side, and looked round into his master's face as if to say: "*I* know who that is!"

Without, in the low-roofed hall, Charles Mistley was

relating some incident to Lena and her mother. It was evidently amusing, because occasionally the somewhat monotonous rhythm of his deep voice (the softest in a drawing-room, and loudest in a gale) was broken by a laugh; clear and merry from Lena, or soft and true from Mrs. Wright. At last the tale came to an end, and the two voices were mingled in one happy burst of merriment.

"No, Colonel!" said Winyard, shaking his head very wisely. "I think you had no right whatever!"

And, with a low laugh, he passed out into the hall to join the laughers there.

CHAPTER XV

THE little parish church of Broom was remarkably full on the Sunday morning following these events. This fact was observed by the young vicar without surprise, and moreover without prejudice.

The Reverend Charles Renforth was a Christian who managed fairly well to hide the muscularity of his ideas; but in the recesses of his charitable heart there lay a mighty worship for all strong things. Under such heading he classed Charles Mistley, having contracted a great friendship with the young sailor during the short intervals of holiday spent by the latter at Broomhaugh. Of Winyard he had not seen so much, but of his actual deeds knew more. Colonel Wright was a public man, and the young parson read the newspapers assiduously in his quiet little study, watching events at home and abroad, and learning of the deeds of Englishmen who serve their country by wandering away from it. "It was never our Government that made us a great nation. England was made by adventurers, not by its Government; and I believe it will only hold its place by adventurers." These true words, written by the greatest adventurer of the nineteenth century, apply to such men as Colonel Wright and Winyard Mistley, of whom there are many in our very midst, unappreciated, unadmired, and cast into the shade by a low type of hero-worship, which takes for its idols wordy politicians, mere ranters, wind-bags, and self-seeking humbugs, unworthy of the name of patriots. Such men, however, failed to impress the athletic young parson of Broom. His heart warmed toward a stronger type, and the hardy old Colonel was his ideal Englishman.

The Reverend Charles Renforth was therefore by no means surprised when his little church filled with unwonted faces and unknown bonnets from Walso, and even beyond that ancient burgh. Nor did he take unto himself any undue credit by attributing this enlarged attendance to a laudable desire to hear him discourse upon the Scriptures.

He shrewdly suspected that these strangers had come, not to worship by preference in his church, but to see the well-known Colonel Wright and his distinguished young coadjutor; yet he thought no worse of them for that, and was honestly glad to see them all, remembering that a seed sown by the wind may well find a fruitful resting-place.

During the progress of the second lesson, wherein there were many short pauses, the vicar discovered a face among the congregation which, by reason of its unfamiliarity, called for further glances. It was that of a young man—a pale, intellectual face with a square jaw and closed lips, softened by a pair of wondrous blue eyes, wherein lay the shadow of anxiety or hopeless sorrow. The gentle despair of those eyes disturbed the reader, and awakened within his honest breast that sympathetic yearning which the coldest of us cannot but feel in the presence of one whom we know, or imagine, to be bearing the weight of a genuine sorrow.

Ivan Meyer had not come to church from mere curi-

osity, but with a set purpose. Marie Bakovitch had
been more incomprehensible than ever during the last
few days, and her patient lover was slowly awakening to
the fact that her mind was no longer reliable. Nevertheless he hoped on; but to continue hoping and watching in silence and alone was a heavy task for one of his
impulsive nature. He suddenly determined therefore to
seek assistance, and this from Winyard Mistley himself.
Something in his artistic soul, some strange love of a
crude contrast, prompted him to do this; and so convinced was he of the wisdom of his appeal, that he had
come to Broom Church with a little note in his pocket to
be passed into Winyard's hand.

By chance the Colonel and his secretary were sitting
next to each other, forming, as they invariably did, a
striking contrast. The old soldier sat motionless, with
his powerful gray head reclining against the panel of the
black oak pew—a calm and thoughtful face, with eyes a
little inclined to be dreamy at times, and vacant in their
gaze; while Winyard, with his quick glance and erect
head, was the very incarnation of energy and resource.
Here was no dreaming, no absence of mind, but a cheerful readiness to face every emergency, and a merry suggestion for every difficulty.

As the preacher preached, and looked over the heads
of his listeners, his eyes frequently rested on the two
men; and every time they did so, he felt humbled. He
could not help comparing and weighing in the balance
of his mind the relative merits of words and deeds. His
words, and the deeds of these two men. His own work,
he was convinced, was the noblest that is placed in the
hands of man; but at times it appeared to him essentially a work of words, and a young man at some period

or other of his existence is sure to conceive a sudden hatred for the vanity of words. The necessity for action comes to us all at some moments, and this usually happens between the ages of twenty-five and thirty-five—after the growing and before the vegetating period; when the human plant has attained its full height, but has yet to form its own wood from a green and pliant stalk, which, if slightly bent, will grow in crookedness, hardening as its growth gains force.

As the congregation trooped down the narrow aisle, Winyard caught sight, for the third time in his life, of Ivan Meyer; and in his eyes he saw the gleam of recognition which is so difficult to conceal, and with it he thought he detected a peculiar pleading expression which he failed, at the time, to understand.

Without turning round to lock, he felt that the tall foreigner was immediately behind him as he passed out of the low door, and it was characteristic of his readiness of mind that he showed no surprise when a note was thrust rather clumsily into his hand. He must have slipped it into his pocket with wonderful celerity, because he was shaking hands the next instant with Miss Mabel Sandford, who appeared to be completely satisfied with the effect of her new summer costume.

Her interest in the theatricals was rather too ostentatious; and Mrs. Wright, with a woman's quick insight, saw, as she came out of the porch, that she was displaying her intimacy with the young diplomat for the sole benefit of her lady friends.

Mrs. Mistley had for some days been trying to secure a *tête-à-tête* with her son, and with little difficulty she now succeeded in arranging that they left the churchyard together. For some moments the mother and son walked side by side in silence, then Winyard glanced over his shoulder, and said:

"The Colonel has been caught by Old Sandford, which means that he will not get away for at least a quarter of an hour."

Mrs. Mistley smiled vaguely, but made no reply for some moments.

"He told me yesterday," she said at length, "that if any further mission were offered to him, he should refuse. He says the work is too hard for a man of his age."

"Yes . . . I know. He has often said the same to me. . . . Perhaps it is better that he *should* give it up, though of course that is a mere excuse. He is as strong as ever, and as capable, but he has had a long life of wandering, and it has been weary work for Mrs. Wright . . . and Lena. He feels *that*, I know—he feels that Mrs. Wright's life has not been an easy one, though she is so brave and cheery. She seems to have no relations—no sisters, I mean, or brothers—or even old friends."

"Only Laurance Lowe!" said Mrs. Mistley, in a low voice full of gentle sympathy.

"I do not understand Laurance Lowe," said Winyard thoughtfully.

"No . . . I think . . . very few people do!"

They were now walking by the Broomwater, and the ripple of the stream as it danced and tumbled along filled in the intervals of the conversation, and led to long, thoughtful pauses.

"Tell me, Win," said Mrs. Mistley at length, with a hesitating glance toward him. "What do you think of doing in the future?"

"I?" he began vaguely. "Oh, I told them at

headquarters that I was ready to go anywhere at any moment!"

"You have no thought of settling down yet?" gently and suggestively.

"Settling down?"

"Yes; marrying and going into Parliament, and behaving generally as a well-off and somewhat ambitious young Englishman ought to do, according to precedent!"

"I have no respect for precedent, mother!"

"Nor I. But why not give up wandering, Win, and go into Parliament!" she asked softly. "A man who has mastered a speciality, as you have this Russian question, is certain to get on there."

"But I have not mastered it yet."

"Well—you and the Colonel are the acknowledged authorities upon the matter. I do not see what more you can require. Whether you have mastered it or not, you know more than any other man."

"Yes, but it is like exploring a new country—there is no end to it. One must keep up to the times and be ever in the front, or it is useless competing. Once the ground has been travelled over by another man, the interest is lost. While I am here, the Russians are not by any means idle; and if I started for Central Asia to-morrow, I should find that things had moved onward since I was there before—onward for them, backward for us!"

"Then you have not altered your plans. You intend to continue being a wanderer on the face of the earth, a man whom the Cabinet keep in sight, as being reckless enough and clever enough to send on any wild-goose chase they may have in hand!"

"Do they keep me in sight on that account, mother?"

"I was told so by a Minister."

"I am glad to hear it. A man may get very good sport after wild-geese, and who knows what may come of his knowledge of the country at some future day! I tell you, mother, this is an age of specialities—universality is at an end. My speciality is this Central Asian question. At any time, at any moment, we may find ourselves upon the brink of the biggest fight the modern world has seen; then my time will come. Then the first words of the War Office will be: 'Send for Colonel Wright and Winyard Mistley'—the one to plan, the other to execute. When that time comes, mother . . . *nous verrons!*"

"In the meantime, it seems to me that your entire life is being sacrificed to be in readiness for an event which may never occur."

"Ah! Of course it may not come in my time, but that is a chance I must be content to run."

"There is a view of the question which you appear to have overlooked, Win," said Mrs. Mistley, with quiet firmness.

"Yes?"

"Suppose you wished to marry!" As the little lady uttered these words she suddenly raised her head, and looked keenly into her son's face.

Beneath his mustache, Winyard slowly drew in his lips as if to moisten them, though the air was cool enough.

"As the tree stands, so must it fall!" he said with a sudden laugh.

"Which being translated means?"

"That no man who feels the restless spirit of the wanderer within him has a right to ask a girl to marry him."

He looked down at her, and smiled calmly.

"But the girl may be stronger than the spirit."

"Temporarily?"

138

"No, permanently."

"I doubt it," said Winyard. "Look at a case we have before us now. Colonel Wright has never settled down."

"Perhaps, Win, his wife has never asked him to. Perhaps she has thought of his career in life before her own happiness. Women have been known to do that before now."

The practical young man looked doubtful.

"And do you consider that her life has been a success?" he asked.

"Most certainly I do. And you men may be thankful that women have the power of loving for love's sake; that absence makes but little difference with them. Especially you of the great army of wandering Englishmen, who turn up in all parts of the world with your brown faces and ready hands. You are all the same; the only soft part of your heart is reserved for the love of Nature; and unfortunately women love wanderers, and soldiers and sailors, more than other men."

"Mother," said Winyard, with a cheery laugh, "you are getting sentimental, and that will never do. If you infect me, I shall die off in a week. And as for talking in that insinuating manner about settling down, how about a certain elderly lady who is always flying about the world—Scotland, London, Paris, Rome, and even St. Petersburg—nursing the stricken, and consoling such as are love-sick or martyrs to indigestion?"

"When you marry I will settle down in a cottage near at hand, take to needlework, and worry your wife. There is Lena coming alone; run away and meet her while I go in and take off my bonnet."

They were now upon the stone terrace, and Mrs. Mistley pointed down the valley as she walked toward the house.

"I expect," said Winyard partly to himself, "that Charlie has been caught by the Sandfords."

At the head of the narrow steps which he had just ascended, he drew the note handed to him in church from his pocket. It was in French, one line in a fine clear handwriting:

"*Meet a friend to-night at the bottom of the small steps.—I. M.*"

"I. M.!" mused Winyard—"Ivan Meyer; and he calls himself a friend. I am gradually getting into a fog with all these muddling conspirators."

Then he thrust the note back into his pocket, and ran lightly down the steps to meet Lena.

"You are polite!" was her greeting.

"I am," he replied, bowing low. "I am nothing if not polite."

"Then you are nothing," she answered saucily.

"Thank you. I was afraid you did not think much of me."

"You have allowed me," she continued severely, "to walk home from church alone, and to carry *this* unassisted."

She held out for his inspection a tiny Prayer-book, of which the weight might safely be set down as three ounces.

"Good gracious!" exclaimed Winyard, "you do not mean to say that you carried that all the way!" And he gravely took the burden from her hands. "I thought Charlie was with you," he continued apologetically.

Young Mistley

"No, Mr. Mistley, I was alone."

"It shall not occur again, Miss Wright."

"It is not polite to mimic people, Mr. Mistley," said Lena, looking straight in front of her. They were at the foot of the stone stairs cut in the wall, which were just broad enough for two persons to pass. Then her humor suddenly changed.

"How very foolish we are!" she exclaimed, laughing. Just as she spoke she slipped backward, and her laugh turned into a little cry of fright.

Winyard, who was a step behind her, appeared almost to have foreseen the mishap, for his arm was round her before it was possible to know whether she would have fallen or not. It was doubtless owing to the narrowness of the steps that he found it necessary to throw his arm right round her, instead of contenting himself by supporting her with his hand.

"Perhaps we are," he observed gravely, as she recovered herself quickly and passed on.

"Perhaps we are what?" she asked, keeping her face studiously turned from him, and plucking little tufts of lichen from the wall as she passed.

"Foolish!"

"I am, at any rate," said Lena, with a little laugh. "I never do remember that silly step. The way it tilts forward when one stands on it is most alarming. Now, I am sure you had forgotten it."

"Excuse me, I remembered it."

"And you did not warn me. Perhaps you wished me to tumble down to the bottom, and come to an untimely end in the depths of the Broomwater."

Winyard did not answer at once; he appeared to be pondering over the words before he spoke them.

"Perhaps," he said in a voice so low that Lena could scarcely hear it—"perhaps I wished to have the pleasure of saving you from all that."

Then the ingenuous youth changed the conversation skilfully, knowing that maidens are delicate in their susceptibilities, and love little a joke that is pressed too far. That loose step, with its alarming weakness, was never again overlooked by Lena; and by some strange sinuosity of her maiden mind, abetted by her imaginative heart (an unfathomable shallow, all crisscross currents), she came to loving it beyond its forty-seven mossy fellows.

Even gray, dead stones can be endowed with individuality by the associations of a past that never comes again. The power and memory of them lie round us as we pass on through life, like landmarks left behind the westward-travelling wanderer, who, facing the glorious uncertainty of sunset gold, turns back and looks on that which he will never see with quite the self-same eyes again. We think that our ancestral halls are dear to us by the power of their own individuality, but it is not really so. It is the magic touch of human sympathy, human love, and human interdependence that awakens the quick thrill of memory. All earthly things—and more particularly all human things—live by past association in the human heart. To this there is but one exception—the sea, which, like a wayward mistress, demands a life's devotion, to be repaid by fickleness and cruelty. She scorns all outward aid of human origin; but with simple blend of cloud, sunshine, and blue water, offers a variety of aspect unequalled by wood and mountain.

CHAPTER XVI

THE moon had bravely taken up her nightly task of sweeping clear the heavens. But there were some huge clouds that promised to strain her cleansing powers to the utmost. The good folks walking home from church had clasped tight their woollen wraps as they spoke of coming rain; but that was three good hours earlier in the night, before the moon had risen and set to work with all the ardor of a new broom. Here and there in the clouded vault little puffs of silvery white betrayed weak spots in the canopy of vapor; and through these the white scavenger was boring assiduously, leaving no breach unattempted. In some places she had even broken through, and the stars twinkled faintly down toward the laboring earth.

The cool night wind came smoothly over the bare hills, moaning through the stately fir-trees, while the smaller and more demonstrative undergrowth of beech and thorn rustled with the crispness of approaching autumn already in their leaves.

Far up on the hillside some fond ewe, whose maternal heart was not reconciled to the inevitable, bleated dismally; and after waiting vainly for an answering cry, bleated again, and wandered on over the brow of the hill. The inevitable in her case was the progress of little woolly legs from awkwardness to sprightly gambollings, and thence by natural sequence to the dread companionship of mint sauce.

Winyard Mistley sat on the stone sill of his bedroom window, ten feet from the ground, with his legs dangling in the darkness, and listened absently to the distant lamentation. It may be that he was picturing to himself the lonely mother's clumsy anxiety as she stumbled on, totally disregarding the inequalities in her own path, and gave forth that unheeded wail to the grim hills and laughing stars.

The ears of a man who has seen the darker side of human nature become very keen, with that blessed adaptability which characterizes all our senses; and Winyard was waiting for the sound of a footfall or the crackle of a branch on the little path far down below the wall, knowing that in the stillness of night he could not fail to hear it.

The monotonous cry of the sheep was not the only sound of woe in the air, for in the darkened room behind the solitary watcher the silence was every now and then broken by a little muffled whine. Adonis was allowed to sleep in his master's room, and he was now lamenting gently and continuously that it had been considered expedient to attach him to the bed-post on this occasion. Apart from the indignity of being held prisoner by such an extremely domestic device, he felt deeply that he had not been trusted to obey orders. But Winyard knew the dog's simple character too well. He knew well enough that while the command was still fresh in his mind, Adonis could be implicitly trusted to obey; but the most ardent watcher is open to a sudden attack of sleepiness, and the shortest nap inevitably drives an unsympathetic order from the canine memory. This result Winyard wished to avoid, as Adonis would undoubtedly have undertaken a vigorous search for his master, despite such a trifling obstacle as a ten-foot drop to the ground.

The scene was so lovely, the thousand night-odors so sweet, that the time slipped rapidly away, while the watcher almost forgot to note its passage. He had been sitting there nearly half an hour, when at length he heard the rustle as if of someone moving through the underwood upon the slope down toward the stream. With a last whisper of admonition to Adonis, he placed his two hands on the window-sill and threw himself far out into the darkness. He lighted softly on the mossy turf, and crossed the lawn.

His eyes were now accustomed to the darkness, and he could recognize the form of each stately tree, drawn in sharp black filigree against the gray sky. In the shadow of the wall at the foot of the long flight of steps he soon discovered a tall figure leaning against a tree, with the leisurely patience of one who knows that his waiting is not vain.

For a moment it struck Winyard that if this man had evil intentions, nothing would be easier than to shoot him as he descended the steps with the moonlight shining full upon his face; but the thought was only fleeting, and untinged with any likelihood of turning to a fear.

As the young Englishman approached, Ivan Meyer stepped forward, and, with an artist's ever-present love of harmless effect, raised his hat as he said:

"Monsieur Mistley?"

Winyard was one of those unfortunate people whose sense of humor is irrepressible—unfortunate, because it invariably strikes at the wrong moment, and because the possession of it makes one see deeper pathos in every-day life than those whose smile is slower. The incongruity of the whole affair suddenly forced itself into Winyard's thoughts, and he was thankful that his face was in the shade as he raised his hat slowly and coldly, with a truer knowledge of dramatic effect than Ivan Meyer possessed.

"I am *Winyard* Mistley," he explained. "It is, perhaps, my elder brother with whom monsieur wishes to converse."

It may have been that Meyer thought he detected a slight shade of irony in the formality of this reply, for he instantly dropped the ceremonious mode of address in the third person.

"No, monsieur, it is yourself whom I seek," he said, with a nervous hesitation which did not fail to raise him considerably in his companion's estimation. "You will pardon my indiscretion, but I was hard pressed before I sought assistance—you can believe that?"

With characteristic foresight the young Englishman began to wonder how much money he had about his person, as he bowed in acquiescence.

Instantly Ivan Meyer saw that his words had been misconstrued, and hastened to explain.

"I am here," he said, in a tone showing more self-assertion, "to ask a strange favor!"

"I will endeavor to assist you—Monsieur . . . ?"

"Meyer—Ivan Meyer. I am a Russian by nationality; a Swede by rights, for I am a native of the Baltic Provinces."

Again Winyard bowed, and waited with the same unsympathetic silence for further information.

"You know the name of Marie Bakovitch, monsieur?"

"I do."

146

Young Mistley

"She is at present in Walso, near to here."

"Do you come to me on the part of mademoiselle?" asked the Englishman somewhat coldly.

"No; I come on my own account."

"Indeed!" Winyard moved restlessly from one foot to the other, and by casting glances up at the clouds, down toward his own boots, and indiscriminately around, indicated gently that he was not desirous of prolonging an interview with this mysterious youth.

Suddenly Ivan Meyer took courage, and stepping closer to his companion, he said passionately:

"I come to you because you have ruined my life. I am the lover of Marie Bakovitch. Her love for me, or the prospect of winning it, was the one bright spot in my existence, which has been as dark as that of every young Russian. For her I worked night and day, in the hopes of one day becoming a great artist; for her sake I would willingly have thrown my life away. But for her sweet influence I would have become a Terrorist, fighting a glorious battle by means so foul that God can only frown upon the righteous side and uphold the tyrant. For her sake I forgave my father's exile, my mother's death, my own miserable childhood; and, just at the moment when happiness seemed within my reach—when I felt sure of winning Marie's love, you rose upon the bright horizon of my joy—and now . . . now you are driving her mad. I should have hated you; at one time I thought I did, but now I know that it is not you but your power that I hate. I have known of Marie's project for a year, and have ever since striven to make her give it up. It is not for your sake that I have done this, but for hers—nevertheless, I have some claim upon you. Surely I am justified in calling upon you now, in the name of the Blessed Virgin, to obey me—to come, now, with me to Marie Bakovitch!"

"But," said Winyard, with true British calmness, which appeared almost cruel in its striking contrast to Meyer's excitement—"but what good can I do?"

"I do not know—we are in the hands of Providence; but she is forever asking for you," replied the Russian defiantly.

"For *me?*"

"Yes; in her moments of calmness the name of Mistley is ever on her lips, and when she becomes excited she attempts to come out to seek you. I have locked her in our little sitting-room, promising to come and find you. Sometimes I think she is mad, monsieur, and at other moments I think I am so myself. Will you come? I have provided for everything. Marie is calmer to-night, but she never sleeps now. Mrs. Armstrong, our landlady, has her room in an outbuilding—all Walso is asleep; it is safe!"

Still Winyard hesitated; Ivan Meyer evidently did not know of the meeting by the stream, he reflected; and the sight of the man she had attempted to murder might have a terrible effect upon the girl.

"Is it . . . possible . . . that you think this a trap?" asked Meyer slowly.

That decided the young Englishman.

"I will go with you," he said simply. "The thought you suggest never entered my head."

"Thank you, monsieur. The way is not long if we go by the fields. The path is too narrow for us to walk together—shall I lead the way?"

"I think I know this path better than you; I will go first."

"I thought——" began Meyer, and then suddenly checked himself.

Winyard turned, and in the moonlight the two young men looked into each other's eyes for a moment in silence. The Englishman was smiling, but his companion was grave.

"You thought?" said the former interrogatively.

"I thought that you might consider yourself at an undesirable disadvantage."

With a shrug of the shoulders and a short laugh, Winyard turned again and led the way. At the first they were silent, but later, when they were able to walk side by side, they talked—or, to be more correct, Meyer talked while his companion listened. Thus they made their way across the dewy fields together—the artist and the diplomat, one whose feelings are his greatest aid and virtue, while to the other such commodities must necessarily be a drag and hindrance. The impetuous foreigner, transparent as the day in his unreserved sorrow, and the cool Englishman, with his ready smile, as impenetrable as the ripple on the surface of a mountain lake, which hides the depth and dissembles unsuspected recesses beneath the glance of superficial merriment.

The young Russian made no pretence of talking on general topics. Marie Bakovitch was the one interest of his life, and of her he spoke with that *naïve* enthusiasm which is less apt to make us smile when it is expressed in French. To Winyard, however, these raptures had a peculiar interest, and he was far from laughing at them. Gradually he learnt the true character of the girl who had devoted a year of her life to the quest of his, and the more he learnt the more he wondered. It is difficult for a strong man, whose control over his mind and heart is almost as great as that exercised over the more mechanical portions of his body, to understand the character of a girl, passionate yet weak, firm and yet *fébrile*, like Marie. Still more difficult is it for him to sympathize with such a character. In his eyes the passion has no grandeur—it is mere weakness; the firmness is nought else than unreasoning obstinacy. As Meyer talked on, Winyard was half ashamed to find that he could only despise Marie and pity her lover. It is not a pleasant sensation for a young man to feel that he despises a girl, especially if she be young and beautiful, as this strange maiden undoubtedly was. The thought jars against his sense of chivalry, and seems almost a sacrilege; it upsets, once and for all, one of youth's most precious illusions.

With a man's impartiality (for no woman ever yet placed both sides of a question on an even footing—thank goodness!), Winyard combined the happy possession of an intuition delicate and sensitive as that of a woman. It is by aid of this mental sensitiveness that women gain in a short conversation, or even a momentary glance, an impression which was never conveyed by words or passed from eyes to eyes. It comes—and there, long after the remembrance of the accompanying incidents has passed away, it is found like the precious deposit at the bottom of a gold-digger's pan.

Upon Winyard's mind this midnight conversation— the only one he ever had with Ivan Meyer—left a distinct impression, without, however, any reasoning to bear it up. No doubt the more delicate machinery of a woman's mind would have turned out neater handiwork; but such as it was, the impression was there: and ever afterward he knew and *felt* that Marie had never loved Ivan Meyer, and that therein lay the explanation of her strange conduct.

CHAPTER XVII

THE streets of Walso were deserted when the two men entered the little town. The moon, now rapidly clearing the heavens of a few fleecy clouds that still remained, shone placidly down upon the gray-stone houses with their red-tile roofs. No window was lighted up, and the clean white blinds gave back the soft moonlight, and seemed to speak of healthy, quiet slumber, the reward of a hard day's toil.

Meyer opened noiselessly the door of Mrs. Armstrong's cottage.

"I covered the windows," he said in a whisper, "from inside, so that one cannot see the light of the lamp."

Winyard followed his guide into the dark passage, closing the door behind him. A moment later his companion pushed open that of the tiny parlor, and a stream of light poured out on to the plain wall and oilcloth-covered floor.

"Come, monsieur," he said, after glancing into the lighted room; and as Winyard obeyed he mechanically and critically noted the hideous pattern of the oilcloth upon the floor.

Marie was seated near the table, with both arms resting upon its dull red cover. The soft lamp-light gleamed upon her flaxen hair, and defined her white profile against the dark wall beyond. She turned her eyes wearily toward the door as the two men entered, but

151

there was no light of recognition in her face. It was at that moment that Winyard was struck for the first time by the wonder of her great beauty. He had never before seen her without her hat, and in the soft light her lovely supple hair had a gleam of gold upon it, borrowed from the lamp's rays. Her light blue eyes looked darker by the same reason, and from the red tablecloth there arose a pink glow which cast over her pallid face a rosy hue of life. But it was a soulless life, and the young Englishman winced as he met those vacant, pleading eyes.

Meyer motioned him to stand aside in a corner near the "ikon," where the tiny oil-lamp flickered little ruby shafts of light across the holy picture. Then he approached her and said:

"Marie, I have brought him."

The girl took not the slightest notice; indeed, she did not appear to hear his voice, but sat gazing dreamily at her own hands lying idly on the table before her. And now the patient lover went to her side, and laid his hand upon her lifeless wrist.

"Marie!" he whispered, speaking Russian for the first time in Mistley's presence. "My little Marie! I am Ivan—do you not know me?"

She slowly raised her eyes from the contemplation of her own hands, and fixed them searchingly on his face.

"Ivan!" she said at length, in a sweet deep voice. "You have come already! Are they waiting to take me away?"

"Who, my Marie?"

"The soldiers, for I have killed him—I have killed him!" Her voice died away to a whisper.

"No, you have not killed him, Marie. He is here!" said Meyer, speaking slowly, as one speaks to a child.

Young Mistley

"Who is here?"

"Winyard Mistley—he has come at your own request!"

"No, Ivan; no! I shot him at the stream. I killed him. I shall never see him again, for he is dead. I told him to stop, but he came nearer; he never took his eyes off mine—he never hesitated; and as he came—as he looked at me—I thought it was the *other*. He looked so brave and calm, but . . . but the *other* is bigger . . . bigger and braver!"

When Winyard was excited, or at moments when his nerves were on tension, awaiting the time for action, he had a peculiar habit of drawing in his lips, first the lower and then the upper, as if they were parched and needed moisture. This action made his square jaw look squarer, and by sympathy his gray eyes grew dogged and dark beneath the motionless lashes.

All this time he had been standing in the darker corner of the little room, with keen observant eyes upon the lovers. One brown hand was religiously executing Mr. Czerny's No. I. five-finger exercise on the top of an old three-cornered oak cupboard; and his lips were slowly moistening each other. Perfectly calm and collected, watchful, alert, and keen, he waited his time. At last he stepped forward, and with a little sign to Meyer to let him speak, he said:

"No, Mademoiselle Bakovitch; you are entirely mistaken. You did not shoot me."

The girl looked up at him with eyes vague at first and wondering; but gradually the rays of a reasoning soul shone through them, and with a motion of her hand toward the soft hair over her temple, she spoke:

"You—here," she said; "*you!* Why have you

153

come? Where is the other? He does not come. I want him; not you."

She rose from her seat, and wandered vaguely up and down, glancing at the two men from time to time furtively, with troubled, distrustful eyes. It seemed as if reason had completely forsaken her brain, for she murmured incoherently in a strange medley of languages. After a few moments she suddenly recovered her senses, and appeared to recognize the two men again. It was a terrible sight, and even Winyard Mistley looked pale and bewildered, while his companion watched Marie with the dull calmness of despair.

With a gesture, which was almost a command, he bade her resume her seat, and then in a masterful tone he spoke:

"Mademoiselle," he said, "I must ask you to leave England at once. You will return home, and immediately send in your resignation to the Society of Patriots on account of your approaching marriage with Monsieur Meyer, which will disqualify you as a member. Have I your promise that you will leave here—if not to-morrow —as soon as possible? I ask this of you, though it is in my power to command. And now I beg of you, for the sake of Ivan Meyer, for the sake of all you love on earth, to give up forever your connection with any political society. Politics are not for women; it is a man's work —leave it to men. Every woman who has meddled with them has brought misery to herself and sorrow to those who loved her."

The girl slowly raised her eyes to his, and watched his earnest face as he spoke. There must have been something strange in her gaze, for the young fellow winced beneath it. It had never been his lot to look on genuine, hopeless misery before; but he instinctively recognized what he saw in those sad blue eyes.

"I will go," said Marie softly.

Then Winyard mechanically moved toward the door. With a silent inclination of the head he left them. Meyer alone returned the salutation, but did not stir from his position near to Marie Bakovitch.

With deliberate care and noiselessness the young Englishman passed out into the passage, and raised the latch of the outer door. The little street lay silently in the white moonlight, which touched the old houses and moss-grown tiles with a fairy-like glint. As he paused on the threshold he heard a quick footstep behind him, and Ivan Meyer stood at his side.

"You see," he whispered, "she is going mad!"

In all and through all Winyard Mistley was eminently practical.

"Are you quite alone?" he asked. "Have you no friends in England? Has she no maid, even, with her?"

"Yes; she has a maid who is now sleeping in her room. She is young, but intelligent."

"You must rouse her. Let her persuade mademoiselle to go to bed, and she must remain by her side to-night. In the morning, if mademoiselle is better, you must get her away from here at once. If . . . if she is worse, send to me, and my mother will come to her . . . a woman will know best what is to be done. I cannot understand . . . *anything;* but I am convinced that mademoiselle is not going mad; it is only temporary. I think it must be what is called hysteria. Have you *no* friends in England?"

"We have but one—a Monsieur Jacobi, of London."

"Monsieur Jacobi, of London . . . who is he?" asked Winyard.

"I know him very slightly; but he has been kind to Marie. He is a musician, and . . . and is connected with some society to which Marie belongs."

Winyard shook his head. "He is no good, then," he said. "You must go to your Consul, that is all. If I do not hear from you by eleven to-morrow morning, I will know that you have left Walso; but if you require assistance of any description, write to me or telegraph at once. Put my name in full—Winyard—W-i-n-y-a-r-d—in the address, so that no mistake can arise. Do not thank me, for I have done nothing yet. Good-night."

And so they parted. With everything to make them bitter enemies, they had yet been friends. Their acquaintance had been of but a few hours' duration, for they never met again. To one it was a mere incident in a busy life, a few hours taken from the many; an unavoidable divergence from the clearly-defined path of his career, to aid a straggler on the mountain-side. To the other, it was an event of some importance in an existence overshadowed by persistent ill-fortune. It was a ray of light upon the darkness, which only passed away and left the shadow deeper by comparison.

Ivan Meyer re-entered the cottage, and closed the door. Marie was waiting for him in the little parlor. She was sitting by the table, and her attitude was characterized by a peculiar stillness which had no feeling of repose about it. He stood watching her for some moments with weary, yearning eyes and haggard face.

"Marie," he said at length, in a voice that was no longer pleading as of old, "let us understand each other."

" Yes, Ivan," she replied softly. " What do you not understand ? "

He came nearer, and, leaning one hand upon the back of her chair, he bent over her.

" Will you do what the Englishman asks ? "

" Yes," she replied in a dull voice.

" All ? " he asked with trembling lips.

" Yes, Ivan—all. We will go to America as you desire. Oh, I am so tired—my head is throbbing! I will go to bed now. Good-night, Ivan! "

She rose and extended her hand to him. In a wondering manner he raised the delicate fingers to his lips —very tenderly, very lovingly—and held the door open while she passed out.

Then he dropped into a chair, and sat staring stupidly at the paraffin lamp till the distant chime of two o'clock aroused him, and sent him mechanically to his room.

Winyard Mistley walked slowly through the peaceful fields. He had lighted a beloved brier-wood pipe, and in the calm air the transparent puffs of smoke rose with a pensive regularity. He noted the soft mist lying over the lowlands by the river; he followed the bold outline of the distant hills against the glowing heaven, wondering at the lace-like fineness of the trees, each tiny branch of which stood in dark relief—and yet he was not thinking of these darksome glories. The hurried scuttle of an occasional mouse in precipitous retreat disturbed him not, for he knew the night, and loved it with the love of an Oriental.

A few hours before he had felt only an unchivalrous contempt for Marie Bakovitch—the contempt of a strong and steadfast mind for one weak and wavering—and now there was nought but pity in his heart. A change brought about by one long glance of her mournful eyes, and he despised himself a little for this same Christian weakness—pity.

"I know now," he said to himself beneath the still night sky—"I know now why women invariably come to grief over politics. It is because they cannot separate the two lives—the political life and that of a woman. There is something in this beyond me altogether—something that I cannot get at. Another fellow is mixed up in it, that is certain; but who he is, and what he is, and where he comes in, goodness knows! The 'other,' she calls him, and somehow it sounds like Charlie, which is of course ridiculous . . . unless . . . by George! . . . unless she has mistaken him for me, and he has been playing the same trick on me as I have been playing on the Colonel. But all that is practically impossible. There was something about the expression of her face that I cannot understand . . . perhaps some day I will."

His thoughts then drifted on in other channels, and he increased his pace.

CHAPTER XVIII

MONDAY evening had been fixed for the first rehearsal of the great dramatic entertainment; and, as the time came near, Lena discovered that she was growing just a little nervous. Her part caused her few misgivings, for she knew it perfectly, having passed a most stringent examination at Charlie's hands; to the acting of it she gave but little thought, leaving it, as actors should, to come of its own sweet will upon rehearsal. There were, however, some trifling remarks on the well-worn pages of her play-book that gave the maiden great misgivings. These were printed in italics, and read as follows, or to like effect: "Takes her hand;" "Places one arm round her;" and so on, being instructions to a young man as to the manner in which he should make love. Assuredly an utter waste of printing-ink, especially when Lena Wright was to be the victim of such scandalous liberties.

Charles Mistley, as stage-manager, had naturally spoken much of the play, giving, in his good-natured lazy manner, tentative opinions, and asking advice from Lena and his brother upon sundry situations to be depicted. Of all had he fully treated, excepting this one most trying scene between herself and Winyard; and this he appeared content to leave to their discretion. Once, indeed, he observed, with a little shrug of the shoulders, that the italics were often useless, and that different people had a perfect right to read the parts in different ways. This vague remark Lena took as referring chiefly to those italics which somehow seemed to her to be most prominent in the whole book; and she even gained some comfort therefrom, though Winyard, who heard the speech, only nodded his head, and let the subject drop. At times she regretted woefully that she had undertaken this most difficult *rôle* of a maiden who loved a villain, knowing him to be such, to the detriment of an upright man whom she could only respect. She almost wished that the whole affair had never been planned, and looked back in wonderment to the time when she herself had been the prime mover in it. What had come to her since then—what had made Charlie so different—what was this great change in everything and everybody? Ah, Lena! Ask what it is that makes a cloudy sea look bright and happy—what gives the sound of sweetest music to the mournful rustle of autumn leaves—what makes sad people gay, and gay folks sad?

Instinctively she knew, however, that the part was within the scope of her little-tried histrionic powers. She felt that she could endow it with life and semblance; and, above all, she understood the character of the girl she was intended to represent.

Such stage intercourse as she had with Charlie gave her no trouble. He was, indeed, supposed to be her lover, but of an old standing in love, and therefore less embarrassing; while the difficulties that lay in Winyard's path, of a cross and undercurrent stream of passion, flowing into and discoloring with its villainy the purer and colder river of mild affection, required a tact and dramatic delicacy which Lena knew him to possess. Though, indeed, she knew nothing about it, only divining by aid of maidenly intuition, which turns from evil as surely as the compass-needle turns from the south.

But these were only Lena's thoughts, and sacred to her own heart. When she and the brothers talked of the coming representation, so keen was their delight in it, so sparkling the shafts of their wit, and so inconsequent their remarks, that the two mothers (who complained that the onus of the whole affair rested with them) gave it as their opinion that the piece would turn out to be an absurd farce, the true and skilful pathos of it being beyond the comprehension of such light-headed performers.

The first rehearsal bid fair to realize the misgivings of the elder ladies, so intensely ludicrous was it after the preliminary nervousness had quite worn off. This was the result of a deliberate plan on the part of the stage-manager, whose experience taught him that rehearsals beginning with laughter usually finished up with successful acting. Winyard and Lena were not in the first scene, and Charles Mistley's part was too unimportant to have effect on it, the consequence being that it passed off very solemnly; and Mrs. Wright, who was prompting, had but little work to do. The second scene began in the same manner.

"Win—this will never do," whispered Charlie. "It is more like a Board-school examination than anything else. We must wake them up somehow."

Winyard promptly obeyed his brother's instructions, and on receiving his cue, introduced two new elements into the performance—merriment and earnest acting, which can be combined with great facility. He set Walter Sandford at his ease by a passing joke, and a demand for his advice as to the placing of some furniture.

Miss Mabel Sandford he pleased and amused by beginning to make love to her in mistake for Lena, calling forth from her ready tongue a maternal reproof. In short, this quick-witted youth carried out to perfection his manager's wish in pulling the company together, and setting everyone at ease.

Mrs. Wright, instead of prompting, helplessly wiped the tears of laughter from her eyes; while Walter Sandford, the shy and awkward, rolled on a sofa in an ecstasy of amusement, which found vent in loud and unrestrained guffaws.

The end of the third act was approaching, and Lena felt with some misgivings that her difficulties were at hand, in the parting between her and the villain she was supposed to love, despite his villainy; a way which women have.

She thought that Winyard must have forgotten the coming scene, so cheerful and thoughtless he appeared to be; but in this she was mistaken. It is so easy to pass from one emotion to the other, the difference between a possible comedy and a possible drama is so infinitesimal, that we get sadly fogged in real life, hardly knowing whether we should laugh or weep; and so mixed up in this respect are our cheerful neighbors across the Channel that they have only one name for the two, calling everything a comedy, which perhaps is wisest after all.

In the midst of all the laughter, the idea suddenly came to Winyard that it would be a worthy triumph to quell the merriment, supplementing it with the opposite emotion, which is so near at hand.

In a whisper he said to Lena:

"Now we will show them what we can do!" leaving her to understand it as she could.

But soon she did understand, and aided him beyond
his expectations. The difficult scene appeared to pass
away as if it were a portion of their real and earnest lives
—for life is as real and earnest to the merriest of us as it
is to those who pull long faces and suffer from dyspepsia.
Lena forgot all about those embarrassing italics, though
Winyard obeyed them, and more. By the sheer force of
his dramatic power he carried her away, and brought
forward the talent of expressing pathos which he had
detected when she had sung unwittingly to him. For
the moment she was no longer happy Lena Wright (for
assuredly nothing could whisper of sorrow in her young
life), but the heart-broken girl, parting from her lover
forever; and he, Winyard Mistley, acted the part as if
he knew too well the pain and anguish he depicted so
cleverly.

First the laughter died away, then vanished the last
smile, as these two searched deeper and deeper into every
human heart for the emotions which cannot fail to be
hidden somewhere there. It was almost an inspiration,
and quite a passing stroke of genius. No word of forethought had passed between them, and yet no mistake
could be detected—the art, if art there were, was so well
hidden, so craftily covered, that none could determine
where it lay.

The spectators were hushed into silent wonder. With
the majority of them, however, it was merely a piece of
clever acting—an exhibition of dramatic talent such as
lies in the power of most of us, though the demand for
it may never come. But to two of them it was something more. The prompter drew in a long deep breath,
and glanced nervously toward the stage-manager. Of
course it was acting—mere acting—but Mrs. Wright did

not like it. Such acting, such rehearsals were dangerous; and why had that gray drawn look come over
Charles Mistley's calm face?

When it was over there was a momentary silence, as
if each person present were waiting for someone else to
speak. Winyard dusted some imaginary specks of carpet from his knees, as if family prayers had just been
offered up, and proceeded to move the furniture and rearrange the improvised stage. This he did quietly and
mechanically, which served very well to ease the breaking
of that silence, and to allow Lena time to come back to
work-a-day speech and thought.

"There," said Mrs. Wright at length, "you have
made your prompter feel quite 'choky,' which must be
a triumph of acting."

"Well done!" said the Colonel softly; and Charlie
suddenly clapped his strong hands together, and spoke a
little rapidly.

"Splendid!" he said—"splendid! Everybody is all
that a manager could desire. We will bring down the
house with applause, I am certain. I am very much
obliged to everyone for the intelligence and diligence
with which they have studied their respective parts!"

They were all accustomed to Charlie's peculiar grave
jocularity, and laughed readily enough.

It was too late, Mrs. Mistley thought, to go through it
again, and also she was sure they must be tired. She
glanced at Lena as she spoke; but she, at all events, did
not appear fatigued, for she was talking and laughing
gayly with Charlie Mistley.

Soon afterward the carriages began to arrive, and the
visitors left in twos and threes.

When, at length, the two brothers were left alone to

smoke a last pipe before going to bed, they sat for some
time without speaking. They had never been much
together, these two, and perhaps it was owing to this
that they were somewhat different from other brothers in
their mutual love. Mutual respect had an important
place in the love they bore toward each other, and, as a
rule, brotherly affection is without it. Charlie knew
that his younger brother was cleverer, quicker, and in
every way more brilliant than himself, and he was content that it should be so. Indeed, he was proud of it—
proud to be the brother of Winyard Mistley. And Winyard, the observant, was fully aware that this big, grave
brother of his was a better man than himself. He could
not exactly define this feeling; he could not determine in
what characteristic, in the possession of what virtues, or
the freedom from what faults, this superiority lay; but
he felt its presence, and respect was mingled with his
love. Perhaps the consequence was a diminution of that
sense of easy familiarity which is considered nowadays a
necessary adjunct to love. The Mistleys were not familiar. Without being formal, there was in their daily intercourse a peculiar, half-expressed deference for each
other's feelings which is more often found in the north
of England than in the easy south. Their paths in life
had divided very soon, and, as each had pressed on with
firmer stride upon his chosen road, the space between
had grown apace. Sons of a roaming race, contemporaries of an independent generation, they were eminently
capable of managing their own affairs, living down their
own sorrows, and passing through their own joys, each
in his individual way. The thought that they were
drifting apart had never occurred to either of them, and
Mrs. Mistley—a soldier's daughter, a soldier's wife—had

early recognized how hopeless it was to attempt to draw together two men whose walks in life lay so far apart. One lost in the Punjaub, the other in the China Seas, how could they correspond, how could they hold together? And yet withal the love was there—that shy, awkward love of man for man which is the most beautiful conception of the human heart. Mrs. Mistley's life had been one wherein the shadow predominated over the sunshine; but one of the brightest periods of it was that short time at Broomhaugh—those few weeks wherein the brothers had come together again—and she found that her anxiety had been but vain, that the wonderful tie of kinship had never snapped through all the strain of years.

On this particular evening, Winyard felt a strange increase of affection toward his brother. Never before had they possessed so many interests in common; never had the thought come so prominently before his mind that too little had been said between them, too much left to the imagination.

Charlie sat by the open window of the little study in a low basket-work chair, and smoked with that good-natured placidity and sense of strong repose which suited so well his fair face and splendid stature. Winyard, seated near the screened fireplace, smoked more rapidly, as if to keep pace with his quicker thoughts, consuming more tobacco, enjoying it perhaps less. The calm peacefulness of his brother's demeanor quelled the words that were within his heart, bade him be as self-contained and self-suppressing, drove back the restless eagerness of his soul, and spoke of a quiet attendance on the course of events which was beyond his comprehension, and had no place in his character.

Young Mistley

If Winyard could only have seen beneath that calm and indifferent exterior, he might have found encouragement, he might have put into words the unusual thrill of brotherly love that warmed his heart. But Englishmen are not made so, and the moment passed, never to return; the opportunity came no more, and Silence numbered another victim to her ruthless bow and spear. It is only on the stage that men have time and opportunity to make that little farewell speech which is to put a graceful finish to our comedy, clearing up the doubtful passages, explaining away misunderstandings, and mingling a prayer for charitable remembrance with the rumble of the curtain roller. It almost seemed as if Winyard Mistley knew that this was a last chance of breaking down that invisible barrier which stood between his brother's heart and his own, a barrier which was nought else but shyness and a habit of reserve on either side.

It almost seemed as if his imagination could span the four hundred miles of silent, night-ridden land that lay between him and two gray-haired, grave-faced men who were at that moment speaking of him within a little curtained room beneath Westminster's great tower. It seemed as if he could read the message addressed to him, and containing the mandate of an almost certain doom that lay beneath the anxious statesman's hand.

CHAPTER XIX

THE following morning, at the breakfast-table, a telegram was handed to Winyard, with the intimation that the messenger was awaiting the reply. The young man broke open the envelope, and read the flimsy pink paper. It took him scarcely a couple of seconds to glance over it, and he proceeded immediately to fill in the address on the reply-form enclosed. All at the table noticed that there was no hesitation, no indecision in his movements, and they remembered that incident later. Then he added the single word "Yes," and handed the reply over his shoulder to the servant.

"May I trouble you for the jam?" he said, with an impudent smile toward Mrs. Wright; and it was only after he had helped himself largely to that condiment that he tossed the telegram to his brother at the head of the table. Life had, it seemed, for him no earnest side at all.

The bite of toast which Mrs. Mistley had just placed between her strong short teeth tasted as no toast had ever tasted to her before. It was a peculiar mixture of absolutely no flavor and a nauseating bitterness. She *knew* that this telegram was important, and meant the end of these happy days; all her five senses were lost in one great throb of sad foreboding.

In the meantime Charlie had read the telegram; and his face had remained inscrutable beneath the quick gaze of two pairs of undeceivable eyes. Lena was at his side, and therefore could not see his face. She was smiling bravely at some cheerful remark of Winyard's. Strange to say, Charles Mistley did not raise his calm eyes to his brother's face after having read the message; he looked past the pink paper, sideways, down at Lena's hand, which rested on the table close to him. The small white wrist was trembling as if from extreme cold; and as the sailor saw this, a momentary contraction passed across his eyes.

The Colonel had laid down his knife and fork. One brown hand lay on the tablecloth in striking contrast to its whiteness, with fingers slightly apart, as if in readiness to grasp something. His solemn eyes, beneath their heavy brows, were fixed upon his secretary's face with an old man's deep and silent expectation.

Only when the door had closed behind the servant who bore the unhesitating answer did Winyard speak of the telegram.

"You might let the Colonel see it, Charlie," he said coolly.

"Business?" inquired Mrs. Mistley, with well-suppressed anxiety, as the folded telegram was passed from hand to hand.

"Yes," answered her younger son, with his ever-ready smile; "my valuable services are once more required by a grateful country."

"What!" exclaimed Mrs. Wright, with sudden indignation, which might have been partly assumed; "after a fortnight's holiday? I should refuse if I were you!" The good little lady was desperately anxious to keep the conversation going, for she had seen her husband change color, and look up gravely at Winyard. She also knew that Lena had seen this too.

"He that has put his hand to the plough should not look back, as Shakespeare or someone has observed," said Winyard readily.

"I think," said Lena, with a clear, brave laugh, "that it is in the Bible."

This was precisely what Winyard wanted, and he laughed promptly by way of encouraging the others.

"May I have half a cup, mother—only half," he said presently, handing his cup, but without raising his eyes from the table.

"Certainly. I beg your pardon!" Mrs. Mistley proceeded to raise the lid of the coffee-pot and look inside, as if she were about to make the strange mistake of adding water. She even extended her hand toward the hot-water jug, but somehow Winyard's finger and thumb reached it first, and held it firmly to the table, though the part he held must have been unpleasantly warm. The unwonted resistance sufficed to recall Mrs. Mistley's wandering thoughts, and she glanced quickly at her son to see if his action had been the result of intention and rapid observation, but he was looking the other way. It did not strike her at the moment that it would be difficult for anyone to hold the bottom of a hot-water jug and be so supremely unconscious of it, but the incident was remembered afterward.

"I suppose," said Colonel Wright, handing back the telegram, "that you said yes?"

"I did," replied the young fellow cheerfully.

"And," observed his mother pleasantly, "are you going to tell us where you are going, what you are going to do, and when you are going to do it?"

"Certainly," he replied, looking at his chief, whereat the old soldier smiled, the meaning of which was that the elder man's simple diplomacy consisted chiefly of a discreet silence; while, in contention, Winyard advocated a seemingly rash straightforwardness. "Certainly. I am despatched to Central Asia on a mission of some sort; but having no details yet, I am specially warned against disclosing them."

No one spoke, and no one made a pretence of continuing the morning meal for some minutes. Outside, the rattle of a horse's hoofs on the hard road broke the silence of the quiet valley. Mrs. Mistley looked toward the window, and listened to the dying sound. Central Asia again! That dim, unknown land was destined to haunt her life. She knew only too well its dangers and manifold horrors. The sound of the horse's hoofs upon the road seemed to resolve itself into a weary repetition of the words "Central Asia"—"Central Asia"—"Central Asia!" until it gradually died away in the low hum of the Broomwater. All at that table were more or less connected with the East—all felt the presence of that lowering cloud which grows and subsides again from time to time, like the clouds of heaven; and all knew that one day it will swell and gather darkness until the storm bursts at last. The meaning of that brave word "Yes" was patent to them all.

But Mrs. Mistley was a brave woman; also she was born (as could be seen from her soft, inscrutable gray eyes) on the sunny side of the barren Cheviots, where folks do not hold much by an undue display of feeling. So she smiled upon her son, and asked: "When?"

"I must be in town," he replied, studiously looking out of the window, "on Friday afternoon."

Lena it was who broke the silence that followed this announcement.

"Then," she said very quietly, "we must have the theatricals a day earlier."

This remark, uttered in a most matter-of-fact voice, had the effect desired by its utterer. It relieved the tension, and gave Winyard something to chatter about. Charlie also, in his slow way, took advantage of it to create a diversion with the toast-rack, which terminated in a resumption of breakfast. It was rather strange that, with two clever women of the world at the table, these young people should thus have to take matters into their own hands.

"I have a better idea than that," Winyard hastened to say. "We cannot well have the theatricals a day earlier now that everyone has been invited. Mother, tell me, is there not a train from Newcastle at five in the morning?"

"Yes," replied Mrs. Mistley promptly. She was one of those rare women who can at a juncture give a decided opinion as to the time of day.

"Well, then, if the Colonel will be so good as to lend me his horse, we can manage it beautifully! We have not an animal in the stable that I can thoroughly trust—mine is too young."

"Do you mean to say," observed Lena, "that you would ride into Newcastle after the theatricals and the dance, at some unearthly hour in the morning—twenty-something miles?"

"Certainly; it would be rather a joke!"

"Winyard's idea of a joke," said the Colonel with some deliberation, while he kept his eyes fixed upon his plate, "has always been peculiar."

The old soldier looked very grave, and made no attempt to keep up the conversation. This did not at all suit Winyard, who said cheerily:

"Will you lend me your horse, Colonel? I will be most careful with him, and will send him back by train from Newcastle."

"Oh yes! You are welcome to the horse, my boy," said the old fellow; and Lena noted the rarely-used expression of endearment.

"You had better take my mare," she said airily. "She is faster than Socrates."

Winyard was about to refuse, but, looking up, he met Lena's eyes, and then for a moment he hesitated, finally saying:

"Thank you!"

Thus the question was left open, but gently biased on one side, like a woman's impartial judgment.

Breakfast over, Charlie accompanied the ladies out on to the terrace, while the Colonel followed Winyard to the little study. When the door was closed, the old soldier looked suddenly round at his companion with a characteristic brusqueness of manner.

"Why have you undertaken this wild expedition to Bokhara?" he asked.

"Because," replied Winyard, with a certain playful pride, "I am about the only man who has a chance of getting there unknown."

"And do you believe that any good will come of it?"

"No."

It was in such incidents as this that the young fellow occasionally betrayed his military training, and the old soldier loved to see it. Blind obedience to orders, yielded by intelligent, *thinking* men, has been the making of England.

"How will you go about it?"

"Through Russia, I think. I want to have another

look at Moscow, and would perhaps have a chance of picking up some maps there."

"But," said the Colonel, "you will never get into the country now. They know you too well."

"My idea was," said Winyard thoughtfully, "to get a new passport written out by that fellow they have at the Office, who writes such an atrocious fist that no one can read it. I would go from Hull to Cronstadt by sea. The officials there are so numerous and so self-satisfied, that in all probability I should get passed through under a name of their own construction; through no fault of mine, you understand, but owing to the badly-written passport, and my own unfortunate inability to speak any language but English. If that way fails, there are others equally simple. Then to Moscow by a slow day-train; there I would get other passports from some of our terribly mysterious Polish friends of the 'English Club,' go out of Moscow to the South a different person to him who entered from the North, leaving my passport in the hands of the authorities to file away among the State archives. By the time the police began to wonder why the passport was not called for, I should be beyond their reach. The plan is more underhand than I quite care about, but with such despotic people there is no avoiding a little trickery. It is simple, and likely to succeed on that account, I think."

The Colonel was accustomed to Winyard's quickness of thought, and evinced no surprise at the rapidity with which this plan had been conceived, worked out, and laid before him "cut-and-dried" within ten minutes of the event which had called for its birth. For half an hour the two men talked over the matter, calmly and in detail, seeking to be honorable and straightforward, as behoves Englishmen even when in intercourse with men who know not the meaning of such words, and determined to carry out the mission intrusted to one of them at all risks, and in face of every difficulty, as behoves brave men and patriots.

It was not without a sigh of envy (that sad and hopeless envy of old for young) that the Colonel listened to Mistley's plans and hopes; but he felt all the while that even in his best days he would never have been equal to this daring young traveller in brilliancy of conception, rapidity of execution, and steadiness of purpose. There is no greater antidote for cankering envy than this same suspicion of inferiority. There was also in the old soldier's heart a pleasant glow of self-congratulation that the man chosen for this hard task should be his subordinate, a rough-riding young diplomat (a race quite distinct from the scented, wordy intriguers of audience-chamber or conference-hall), whose *début* had been made under his own leadership, and whose knowledge came from his own teaching and experience.

Both men fully knew the dangers likely to be incurred, though neither spoke of them. Both had stepped over the threshold of that mysterious land of the far East, and for them the half-forgotten names of its cities had no halo of Arabian-Night-like glory. They took small account of these, except to denude them of the untold splendor and lavish wealth bestowed upon them by travellers' fables, and to reduce them ruthlessly to squalid townships. The hopeless, trackless wastes of desert sand and rounded stone were of much greater import to the solitary traveller. To him these spoke of months spent in weary travelling by burning sun and chilly night; they spoke of a maddening monotony—hunger, parching thirst, a gruesome solitude, and an unrecorded death.

CHAPTER XX

PRESENTLY Winyard left the Colonel. The old traveller was poring over a map, the greater part of which was occupied by notes of interrogation implying doubts on the part of the geographer. Of course it was by the merest chance that Winyard should pass out by the window instead of the door, and that he should cross the smooth lawn and go straight to the far corner of the old wall. It was that particular corner from whence the sea was at times visible far away to the east.

Adonis followed at his master's heels. Occasionally he raised his rough muzzle and sniffed at the air. There had been rain in the night, and from the valley there ascended a subtle odor of refreshed verdure. All around was fresh and cool and wholesome. Winyard Mistley crushed up the telegram within his jacket-pocket, so that the crinkle of the paper mingled with the whisper of the leaves above him. Then he looked round over the green hills, and softly whistled a popular air in the most matter-of-fact manner.

Doubtless it was owing to the merest coincidence that he found Lena at the corner of the wall when he approached. She was looking the other way; indeed, she was leaning sideways over the wall to gather some sprays of woodbine which had climbed up within reach. The air was scented with a thousand autumnal odors; but the breath of the woodbine penetrated, somehow, through all, just as love is popularly supposed to penetrate through stone walls and the dead thickness of accumulated years.

Then these two foolish young people deliberately did the worst thing possible under the circumstances. They did nothing, and said nothing. He stood beside her, and looked away down the valley to the spot called Mistley's Gap, where the line of the meeting hills cuts the sky. She sat there, and waited for him to break the silence, expecting some laughing suggestion. But for the first time within the last few days Winyard was serious in her presence.

Lena, finding nowhere else to look, also gazed down the valley, where the shadows were blue and hazy, and the sheep as tiny insects upon the treeless turf.

Adonis now conceived the brilliant idea that something must be wrong, and promptly proceeded to put his paw into it, as might have been expected from a blundering old gentleman dog. He looked at Lena, long and thoughtfully, with many a blink of his pink-rimmed eyes; and then, without opening his teeth, he observed:

"Um—m—m!" A plaintive protest, which seemed to say, "If there is anything to be explained, explain now, and be done with it!"

Ah, happy Adonis! In his canine philosophy such were wisdom indeed. He did not know that there are many things we would fain explain but dare not. Many a sentence left unfinished, to be filled up with little mental dots—thus, ". . . . ." as the hearer's taste may dictate. But, after all, most of these are better left unsaid forever. In one case out of the proverbial ten, speech might alleviate present sorrow; in the other nine, it would but increase the pathos of life. If preaching were of any profit, what sermons might we, who have passed through the mill, reel off for the benefit of those who follow us! It is so easy to say, "Never keep a letter—never preserve brown and withered floral products about which there hangs the vestige of a scent, strong enough yet to waken up a slumbering memory!"

Lena stooped forward, and, taking Adonis by the fore-paws, she hauled him bodily up on to the wall, during which process he did his best to look dignified.

It is strange how cruel men can be. Winyard looked down at Adonis as he stood on the wall with Lena's white arm round him, and, as if speaking to the dog, said:

"You have never congratulated me."

He did not raise his eyes from the contemplation of the faithful Adonis during the little pause before Lena spoke.

"I congratulate you," she said indifferently.

Winyard smiled suddenly. The reply and manner of delivering it were so exactly as he would have done it himself, that it seemed as if she were mimicking him.

"I am sorry I have to go at such a short notice," he said conventionally; but he laid his hand on Adonis's rough back close to her wrist, which somehow changed the burden of his remark.

"Yes, it is a pity," she replied cheerfully, as if he were leaving to keep some pleasant engagement.

"However," he said, stooping to examine the name inscribed on the dog's collar, which could not have been very new to him—"However, we will get the theatricals in."

"Ye—es . . . we will get the theatricals in."

He was not looking at the dog now, but at her.

178

Young Mistley

"Did you really mean that offer of Fairy to ride into Newcastle to be taken seriously?" he asked.

"Of course I did—quite seriously."

"Then you think . . . I am to be trusted?"

She hesitated for one brief moment, then raised her eyes to his bravely, and said:

"Yes—I think you are to be trusted."

Winyard was slowly stroking the dog's shaggy back, and in the confusion of the fur his fingers touched Lena's hand which was resting on Adonis's shoulder; whereupon she moved higher up on the woolly neck, thus leaving a larger piece of canine person free for caresses. But Winyard was clumsy—again his hand touched hers, so that Lena was at length obliged to withdraw altogether.

Woodbine is a wayward growth, hard to lead when growing, and loving little to amalgamate with other flowers when gathered. The few sprays that Lena had procured were peculiarly difficult to arrange with any degree of satisfaction, despite the efforts of ten nimble fingers; perhaps, however, these were not quite steady, especially when beneath Winyard's quiet gaze.

"I am afraid," he observed meditatively, "that I will find no woodbine in Central Asia."

"Not being well versed in the vegetable products of Central Asia, I reserve my opinion," replied Lena demurely.

"I am afraid," repeated the ingenuous youth with a sing-song intonation, "that I will find . . . no . . . woodbine . . . in . . . Central Asia."

His hand, resting on Adonis, was half open, as if expecting something. Then very slowly two sprays of woodbine were separated from their brethren, and extended, perhaps two inches, toward the expectant hand. With her head poised slightly to one side, Lena gravely admired them. Still the open hand did not move. One inch more, and Winyard's fingers moved to meet Lena's; still another inch, and the two sprays bid farewell forever to their brethren in misfortune.

Lena rose from her humble seat upon the clean gray stone and moved toward the house.

"I know," she said, "that Charlie is patiently working away at the scenery. Let us be virtuous, and help him."

And so she led the way into the house, Adonis and his master meekly following.

Since the midnight interview with Marie Bakovitch and her lover, Winyard had heard nothing from or of those unsatisfactory foreigners. He had duly advised Colonel Wright of the entire proceedings, and they had sought in vain some likely explanation of Ivan Meyer's peculiar conduct, for diplomatists grow sadly sceptical regarding the disinterestedness of human motives. Also is it difficult for the practical Western mind to comprehend the strange Quixotism of the Slav nature.

Winyard was somewhat uneasy about the whole affair. His own personal risk in the matter did not appear to him very great; but he was fully aware that he ran great risk of misapprehension, or, worse still, misrepresentation, if the circumstances of his connection with Marie Bakovitch should transpire. A story such as that could so easily be twisted and turned into something quite different. He would have felt still more apprehensive had he known that his beautiful enemy had actually been a guest in Mrs. Wright's house under the name of the Baroness de Nantille, and that she was therefore person-

ally known to his mother, Mrs. Wright, Lena, and his
brother Charlie. But Winyard was spared these additional complications. Ivan Meyer had faithfully fulfilled
his promise of leaving Walso with Marie as soon as possible, which, however, was not before the Wednesday morning, as the girl's condition was not such as would allow
of a long journey. Had Meyer known that the slight
amelioration in the state of her physical and mental
health was only a temporary lull, he would have felt even
greater relief than he did at turning his back upon the
peaceful little town. The girl bore the long journey
well, but it was written that a higher Hand than Ivan
Meyer's was now to guide her troubled steps. A blessed
oblivion came over her tottering reason, and while the
mind wandered, the body throve and prospered.

It was only on the Thursday morning, in the midst of
preparations for the theatricals and ball, that Winyard
learnt of their departure from Walso. A groom had
been sent into the little town to make some purchases,
and when, on his return, he delivered his parcels to his
young master, he mentioned that the "furrineering
folks" had left. It was a great relief. For although
Winyard was not the man to bow down before an untoward wind—meeting, rather, every breeze of heaven as
it came with watchful eyes and steady lips—his was a
courage of that type which can afford to disguise no
danger by detracting from it.

They were all working in different parts of the old
banqueting-hall, which had for the time been converted
into a tiny theatre; working, each in his characteristic
way: Winyard with a dashing rapidity; Charlie with
easy-going indifference, accomplishing much without appearing to exert himself—directing everything without

appearing to have a will of his own upon any one question. There was no fuss, no undue haste about his movements. As usual, he was ahead of his time, and could afford to waste a few moments here and there with some grave pleasantry. Colonel Wright was quite content to occupy a subordinate position. He was ready to lift the bigger flower-pots for Lena, hand the tacks to Charlie, or climb up a ladder with a hammer for Winyard. It was during the last-named service, when they were both perched high up on a ladder, that Winyard imparted to his chief the news he had just received.

"I have just heard," he said in a low voice, as he took the hammer, "that our foreign friends have left Walso."

Then, without waiting a reply, he turned and began driving a long nail into the hard beam. Most of us love to drive a nail, though few care for the more tedious task of first boring the hole. And so many deals are split in this world, and many hearts are broken.

Colonel Wright from below watched the steady swing of the hammer, and noted the almost boyish delight which Winyard took in his noisy occupation. It seems that with some people a proper sense of responsibility—a realization of life's gravity—never comes; and, what is stranger still, they appear to get on very well without it.

When the nail was driven, and the curtain duly arranged, the two men descended and stood back in the hall to enjoy the effect of their handiwork. They were out of earshot, and Charlie was hammering somewhere behind the drop-scene on the stage, so Winyard took the opportunity of saying:

"Colonel—it is just possible that something may come out in time about Marie Bakovitch—something untrue, I mean, that might do her harm. If my name should in any way get on gossips' tongues when I am away, do not trouble to contradict anything to the general world. For her the contradiction would be worse than the slander, for it would mean a charge of attempted murder. For myself . . . I thought I did not care . . . but now I find I do. I should not like your . . . Mrs. Wright and your daughter to believe anything they might hear. You understand?"

"Yes," replied the Colonel slowly. "I understand. Shall we put up the other curtain now?"

CHAPTER XXI

THE critical moment had come. The stage was ready, the footlights burning cheerily, and Colonel Wright was at his post with the curtain-cords held tightly. Through the curtain came the buzz of many voices, slightly hushed by expectation.

Charles Mistley, cool and good-natured, was clearing the members of his unruly little company off the stage. After a last glance round, he made a sign to Colonel Wright, and the curtain ran smoothly up. The first two acts went off merrily enough. The audience was charitably inclined, and their charity was not called for, which phenomenon invariably has a most pleasing effect. The young manager was more and more surprised at the excellence of his little company, especially as regarded the judgment they displayed in gradually toning down the merriment as the play progressed and the last pathetic scene approached.

It was a cunning play, written by a master-hand, and cunningly acted. Moreover, it had been well rehearsed. Charles Mistley rose to the occasion quietly and steadily, as was his wont. He appeared to know everyone's part as well as his own; but only displayed this knowledge when absolutely necessary, for he possessed a virtue without which no man is a leader—absolute faith in those beneath him.

Young Mistley

The curtain descended at the end of the second act amid great applause; but when this had died away, a sudden silence supervened. There was a vague feeling among the auditors that a crisis was coming—that they had been made to laugh, simply in order that they might the more easily be made to weep. Sad and softly sighing music—which works on the human feelings like water on a penny bun, softening and enlarging—now followed.

Charles Mistley had decreed that the longest interval should be between the third and fourth acts, on the consideration that suspense sharpens the mental appetite. Few alterations were required on the stage, and Winyard was setting straight things that were already straight, a way we sometimes have when expectation is pressing on us, when Mabel Sandford hurried out of the ladies' dressing-room.

"Winyard," she said in a whisper, "I am awfully afraid Miss Wright is going to break down. When I went into our dressing-room just now, she was as white as a sheet. She said there was nothing the matter, and went out into the conservatory, I believe; but I saw her lips trembling, and she walked unsteadily. I don't want to alarm you unnecessarily, because I am sure you must be getting tired yourself, but a glass of wine or something would probably put her right."

Winyard never liked Mabel Sandford as he did at that moment. For the first time in his presence she had forgotten herself, and in consequence appeared, as she in reality was, a very good-natured girl.

"Thanks, Mabel," he said simply. "I only hope it is not nervousness. I will take her some wine, and will also send some into the ladies' dressing-room. I ought to have thought of that before. Mind you take some yourself, because your work is not over yet, and remember you will have to dance till daylight after this!"

"Oh, I am all right, thanks!" laughed the girl, turning away. "I have plenty of time to change my dress, have I not?"

"Yes, plenty!"

For some moments Winyard Mistley stood motionless, alone, upon the little stage. Then he stooped down, and with peculiar care smoothed a wrinkle out of the carpet. Who can tell what were that young fellow's thoughts? Perhaps he could not have analyzed them himself. This evening, a merry little company—laughter, chaff, and gayety. To-morrow, a breaking up; a dismantling of all this hollow scenery; a gray, dusty hall, with here and there a flower, brown and withered, thrown into a corner; a dull atmosphere, heavy with the scent of perfume and paraffin cynically mingled. Perhaps he realized then that a woman's lot—that aching sorrow of one left behind —is infinitely harder than men quite recognize.

Slowly he walked across the stage, and passed out into the garden. In the dimly lighted conservatory he found Lena sitting alone. She was leaning forward with her bare hands clasped upon her knee. In crossing the garden, the little curls above her temples had been blown aside, and now the pale light of the lamp suspended among the ferns above her fell lovingly on the brown hair, and drew forth little golden gleams. She heard the footstep in the darkened doorway, but did not look up or move.

Winyard stood for a moment in the doorway. The light fell on her face in such a way that he could see the gleam of tears in her eyes. There was a little movement in his throat and in the muscles of his firm chin, as if he were swallowing something with an effort, and then he advanced toward her with the usual misleading smile. It would appear that he attributed those tears to over-excitement in connection with the last act of the play. Indeed, there was nothing else for him to do, no other cause for him to seek, under the circumstances. No doubt he felt that the evening was far from its close as yet, and preferred to ignore the farewells with which it was to terminate. Men cannot do things well without giving their whole mind to the work they have in hand at the moment, and Winyard was, without doubt, thinking only of the theatricals.

"Tired?" he said interrogatively.

Lena nodded in acquiescence, and slightly turned her head so that her face was in the shade.

"Miss Wright," he said with mock severity, for he was desperately afraid of appearing serious, "this will never do!"

She did not reply, and made no attempt to acknowledge the brilliant sally.

"Lena," he said suddenly, using her Christian name, which he did but rarely—"Lena, this is not like you!"

She was dressed for the third act—in white, as he had desired it, of a soft, silky material that clung round her sweet young form in cunning folds. There was in her whole being a subtle sense of refinement. Her dress was perfect; what little jewelry she wore was faultless; even the manner in which her hair was arranged spoke of the deft handiwork of practised fingers. As he stood at her side, the scent of the white jasmine at her throat reached him, and brought back the memory of his request. In an instant he saw that all was exactly as he had desired it. Was it blindly, or with wondrous foresight that he persisted still in his jocularity?

"I am a little limp myself," he said cheerfully.

Then Lena recovered herself, and mentally stood at bay, as every true woman would have done in her place.

"It *is* very tiring—is it not?" she said indifferently.

There was one weak spot in the armor of her pride. Her voice was calm and perfectly steady, but its tones were singularly at variance with the unshed tears that trembled on her lashes. She had trusted to the advent of an opportunity to conceal these before he could see them, not knowing that it was too late.

It is strange how little incidents remain fixed upon the human memory, like the few tiny leaves still green upon a stricken tree when the others have fallen from it. This small inconsistency of tearful eyes and a cheerful voice never quite left Winyard's memory. Gradually he came to look upon it as peculiar and individual to Lena; typical of her sweet, gentle courage.

And so they acted their little parts alone in the dim light of a single lamp, without the aid of stage-effect or music. An unrehearsed effect, an unpremeditated scene; vain empty words spoken with averted eyes.

"I cannot quite understand you," said the girl in the same conventional tone of forced interest. "I am very much afraid you must be heartless, and devoid of filial feelings."

"Inasmuch as how?" he asked, slowly pulling an innocent fern into small pieces.

"Because you completely ignore the fact that you practically start to-night, after all this is over, upon a journey which in all probability will be . . ."

"My last!" he suggested frivolously, as he threw all

the particles of fern into the air, and watched them flutter to the ground as if it were a most interesting experiment.

She was silent, and appeared to be entirely absorbed in removing from her dress a small end of thread left there by a careless seamstress.

"At all events, there are risks attached to it."

"I think," he said, "that you are overrating things a little."

That wretched little white thread would keep swimming about in the most unaccountable manner. Lena longed to give even the most hurried touch to her eyes; and even as she longed, Winyard turned his back to her, and went beneath the lamp to consult his watch. Though he contemplated the bland face of that reliable piece of mechanism for some moments, he never saw the time; but that did not matter very much.

"It would be rather hard to overrate Bokhara," she said quietly.

Then he turned and slowly came back to her side. There was an uncomfortable, drawn look about his lips, and his eyes were dull as he watched her mechanically smoothing the folds of her dress.

"How do you know that it is Bokhara?" he asked in a low, steady voice.

"I made . . . papa . . . tell me."

"I am sorry you did that . . . extremely sorry. Tell me . . . does my mother know?"

"No! No one beyond myself. But you *must* tell her. It is better that she should know—even that it is Bokhara—than be kept in ignorance and suspense. I think . . . that you do not quite understand . . . women!"

"I thought there was something on the old gentleman's mind," said Winyard, suddenly changing his manner. "Nevertheless, I still maintain that you are looking at the worst side of things. There may be one or two risks, but . . . I am a very lucky fellow, you know, and generally turn up smiling at the end of a difficulty."

"I think," said Lena, remorselessly refusing to smile, "that your talents are a decided loss to the British stage!"

He looked fixedly at her, as if attempting to penetrate the obscurity; but she kept her face averted, and he could read nothing from the dainty coils of hair turned toward him. Then the tone of his voice changed again; he dropped his usual semi-bantering style, and spoke as she had never heard him speak, except on the occasion of the first rehearsal, in a voice which conveyed a happy mixture of pathos and philosophical indifference.

"I have a difficult part to play," he said, "and you are making it doubly so."

She did not understand him. Her only feeling was one of anger at her own slowness of comprehension; she felt that there was a deeper meaning in the words than she had caught, and the moments were slipping—slipping by.

"Come!" he said briskly, offering her his arm; "we will go and get some wine, or *you*, for one, will never get through the next act. Charlie has been dosing the whole company, I believe; it is a way far-seeing stage-managers have."

It was something new for Lena to be spoken to like this—she who never confessed to fatigue, who could dance till sunrise; but she meekly obeyed him.

Young Mistley

They got through the third act successfully, and the curtain descended in silence. This only lasted, however, a moment, and was quickly followed by deafening applause. It had been almost too real. The music, the lowered lights, and perhaps the dull excitement of the approaching farewell, had affected the actors, and into their parts they threw an intensity and earnestness which in the business-like rehearsals had been beyond their powers.

It was one o'clock before the last of the guests at length drove away, and Winyard ran upstairs to change his clothes for the long journey before him.

CHAPTER XXII

WHEN the traveller came down-stairs again, he found the whole party assembled in the drawing-room.

His rough tweed suit formed a strange, uncomfortable contrast with the evening dresses around him. Despite his fatiguing evening, he appeared quite fresh and energetic.

Charles Mistley was the only other person present who did not look worn and tired; nothing seemed to affect him.

"Half an hour before I need leave," said Winyard cheerily; "I mildly propose that you all go to bed."

"I propose," amended his mother, "that everyone goes to bed except me. If my son does these wild things, I should be the only sufferer thereby."

"And I propose," said the Colonel, with his grim smile, "that we all go and have some more supper."

"I could not eat a thing," remarked Mrs. Wright decisively.

"Nor I!" "Nor I!" came from other parts of the room.

"Mother has had no supper, I know," said Winyard; "and the Colonel was carving, so *he* got nothing to speak of. I propose that we bring something in here. Come along, Charlie!"

The brothers presently returned loaded with plates and other necessaries.

"I think," suggested Winyard, looking sideways at

Lena, "that it would be most appropriate to finish up the whole entertainment with a song."

The girl silently went to the piano, and, after a short search, found a small manuscript-book. Winyard came up at that moment, and, taking it from her hands, opened it at the unpublished song which she was singing when he first saw her. It was on the first page of the book, written out in a girlish hand, the notes large and very inky.

Lena began the harp-like accompaniment, and sang. Slightly behind her, on a low chair, her father sat and ate cold chicken with an old man's deliberate enjoyment. Winyard, in his light-colored suit, was perched on the high end of the sofa, with his thick boots dangling. Charlie stood near at hand, pouring champagne noiselessly into a glass.

The girl appeared to sing the first verse with a studied disregard for the meaning of the words, doing her best to render them expressionless. The second, however, she rendered with more of the true intensity; but at the end of it she stopped abruptly, and closed the book.

"It is rather *too* appropriate," she said, wheeling round and pointedly addressing Mrs. Mistley.

Then she rose from the piano, and, crossing the room, dropped wearily into a low chair.

"I wish you would go to bed, Lena," said her mother; "you are thoroughly tired out."

"I? Oh no! I am not a bit tired. If I look pale, it is the result of paint and powder. Professional people are always pale when the paint is washed off—are they not, Charlie?"

"Oh yes," replied the sailor gravely. "Look at me, for example!"

Everyone did so, and laughed at the sight of his brown

13   193

and weather-beaten face, which was exactly what he wanted. Perhaps he had more faith in his own powers of bearing a general scrutiny just then than in Lena's.

They talked on in a vague, uninterested way, as people do at a wedding or a funeral, while waiting for a curtain to rise, or to kill time while a ship is sinking beneath their feet. We are getting very clever nowadays. Soon the flora and fauna of the world will be exhausted—soon we will know everything worth knowing about every animal on earth; but of certain phases of the human mind we know no more now than Noah knew of the inward thoughts of Shem, Ham, and Japheth. At last the gravel outside grated under the light feet of Lena's mare and the heavier tread of a sleepy groom.

Adonis, who had been tranquilly sleeping in the hall, now sidled his way through the slightly open door. He looked toward the window, listening intently the while; then, remembering that life is not all repose and furry mats, he looked briskly at Winyard with uplifted ear.

"Is this anything to do with us, my master?" he asked with his honest, sorrowful eyes.

It happened that there was silence in the room just then. Mrs. Mistley was breathing a little quickly; she glanced almost furtively at her younger son's face. Everyone else was looking vaguely at Adonis, except Charles Mistley, and he was watching Lena quietly and indifferently.

"Yes, Adonis," said Winyard, breaking the silence, "you and I must go. There is no continued rest for sinful dogs!"

It had been arranged that Adonis should henceforth live in Seymour Street, as Mrs. Mistley was going to Paris, and Broomhaugh would be empty.

Young Mistley

The stupid dog then deliberately turned to Lena, and gave a little jerk of his stumpy tail, accompanied by a bland smile which seemed to say:

"Of course you are included in this arrangement?"

"Come here, you dear old thing," said Lena in reply, "and I will carry you to the door."

Adonis, who was a philosopher, concluded that it was no business of his to heed a few crushed laces. If people liked to embrace him and carry him about, throwing cool arms around him and pressing his rough side against silks and soft muslins, assuredly that was their affair. Only he tried truly to behave like a gentleman, and to look as if he liked it. With due preservation of a courtly smile, he wondered in his inmost dog what that was a-pitter-pattering so hurriedly against his muscular ribs.

On the doorstep his surprise was somewhat increased (though in nowise betrayed), when a pair of fresh young lips lightly touched his shaggy forehead. However, he gravely cocked his ear for the whisper that followed:

"Adonis, darling, I think my heart is breaking!"

He heard, and wagged his tail.

In the meantime Winyard had donned his gloves. He slipped two fingers beneath the girths, and gave a preliminary tug at the stirrup-leathers; then he turned to say good-by.

"I expect," he said, "to see you all in town in a week or so. We will not call this good-by, because I have not got all my pretty farewell speeches quite ready. They require further rehearsals. Do not stand at the door," he added, with his imperturbable cheerfulness. "You will catch horrible colds, and abuse me behind my back!"

Then he mounted. The last person with whom he

shook hands was his brother Charlie, who had been standing at the horse's head. It was strange how the young
sailor invariably found something to do, and was never
to be discovered idle.

"Come, Adonis!" Winyard called out, and then he
vanished in the darkness.

Despite his injunction they stood at the door. Through
the still night air the sound of Fairy's doings came distinctly to their ears. At first the springy walk that
betokens a desire for more exhilarating work, then a
flighty unsteady trot, soon followed by an even thud of
armed hoofs with a ringing promise of many miles before
a lag or halt.

Once they heard him say "Come along, old man!" to
Adonis, and then the steady "clapperat—clapperat—
clapperat" rose and fell again. That was all the watchers heard—that and the low murmuring voice of the
Broomwater.

Slowly, slowly, like the memory of our dead, the sound
diminished as Fairy sped along, till finally it was lost in
the brawl of the stream away down in the dark valley
beneath.

Then Mrs. Mistley, Mrs. Wright, and the Colonel
turned and entered the house. Lena and Charlie were
left alone. They stood side by side, and listened for a
sound that was dead. So still were they that Charlie
could hear the hurried tick of his own watch. Lena
stood motionless, and showed no sign of moving. Her
companion waited for some minutes with the peaceful
patience of a sailor, and then he said in little more than
a whisper:

"Come, Lena!"

She turned and looked at him vaguely, as if she had

not been aware of his presence. He was standing in
front of the open door; a beam of light flooding out into
the darkness rested on his upright form, and gleamed on
the dead white of his linen. He was motionless and
quiet as usual—the personification of equability and
strength. From his unusual height he looked down at
her gravely.

"Come," he repeated. "We have had a hard day—
let us go in. Beware of that little step."

And, under pretext of guiding her, he took her hand
within his arm, and entered the house.

They found the old people in the drawing-room.
Something detained Lena in the hall, so Charlie passed
into the room first. He had a peculiar way of ignoring
what people are pleased to call the necessity of speech,
and now he leisurely crossed the room without a word.
Upon the mantelpiece a candle was flaring up and smoking, something having become attached to the wick. To
this Charlie directed his footsteps, and began quietly to
extinguish one candle after another. Mrs. Wright noted
the action, and wondered whether he was diminishing
the light of the room with a purpose, or whether his
occupation was aimless.

When Lena entered the room, she found that everyone
except Charlie was looking toward her.

"Well?" she said, smiling, as she crossed the room.

"Well!" replied Charlie at once, without turning
round.

"I think," said Lena, without addressing anyone in
particular, "that it was a great success, don't you?
Everybody *said* they enjoyed themselves immensely, and
I really believe they meant it."

"I am sure they did," affirmed her mother readily,

with a little contraction of the eyes. "The floor was lovely, I know, because I tried it. Charlie led me astray as usual, and made me dance, against my principles and despite my gray hairs."

"I heard," said Lena mischievously, "several people talking about an elderly lady from London being the best dancer in the room. But . . . there is papa pulling his mustache to keep himself awake. You old people keep such shockingly late hours. Puff . . . there goes a candle—puff . . . there is another. Good-night, Mrs. Mistley—good-night, mother—good-night, poor sleepy old gentleman. . . . Good-night . . . Charlie."

CHAPTER XXIII

No man can speed through the night air without experiencing a more or less clearly defined sense of exhilaration. One is almost raised above mere human feelings, which, as we all know, are fleeting as the sunset redness. It makes one envy those grand old forefathers who careered along the broad highroads through night and day. It is not merely the speed itself and the mighty rush of severed air round bravely prominent ears, for one can get those by embarking on one of the fast trains that rush away nightly from London, like a family of spiders racing from the centre of their web outward to where the tissue is of firmer make, and life less great with pressure. No! there is something more—something gathered from the merry stars or the pale, sad moon—something inhaled with the cool night-odors of the earth. To enjoy it all, it is perhaps necessary to have the gentle companionship of a horse, himself slightly nervous by reason of the huge shadows and ghostlike heaps of broken stone—to feel him testing, as it were, your reliability in case of emergency by gentle mouthing of the bit.

It could not be stated, with that rigid regard to the truth which the present writer has invariably endeavored to observe, that Winyard Mistley went on his way rejoicing; but he was not insensible to the glorious scene around. A half-moon was setting over the western heights, her light as yet too feeble to impair the modest beauty of her attendant stars. The great sombre hills lay silent and deserted beneath the brilliant canopy of night, cutting the dark heavens with their darker outline.

The sweet, subtle odor of the slowly waving pines mixed with the cool air, and refreshed all drooping nature with its tonic strength. Winyard inhaled deep draughts of it, and rejoiced. The wonderful freshness of our Northern nights is a gift fully appreciated by those who have lived beneath a warmer zone.

Fairy peeped back with white-gleaming eyes, and gently tongued the bit in vain endeavor to find out who this might be upon her back. The hand upon the bridle was as light as Lena's; but the weight upon the saddle a very different matter. Also, she felt a greater watchfulness upon the movements of her dainty head, as of one who knew her not, and yet was inclined to kindly thoughtfulness. There was no longer the ripple of the habit tickling, yet comforting, her shining flank; but still it could not be the groom (though the odor of tobacco-smoke was in the air), for the legs were longer and less cruel in their grip.

The home-like creak of warming leather had a certain sense of companionship, however; and as this grew regular with her more even trot, Fairy began to settle down to her work with a pleasant respect for him who was her guide and trusty guardian through these shadowy horrors of the night.

Then her ears, becoming motionless, at length discovered the measured tread of four unshod feet upon the road beside her. Devoting one ear to the investigation of this, while the other was deputed to look out for other

surprising matters in front, she soon arrived at the conclusion that the flying feet were the property of that
pleasant but rather distant dog of unprepossessing and
dishevelled appearance who had lately arisen upon the
scene.

Adonis felt instinctively that this was no pleasure-trip,
but serious work at last. This was no time for stopping
to inhale at closer quarters those delightful ratty odors
that every now and then assailed his sportive nostrils—
no time to pounce through nettle and low tangle upon
some affrighted little scuttler who had not the common-
sense to lie quiet till all danger was past and over. So
he set his ears well back, avoiding, like a clever mariner,
all inequalities such as catch against the wind; and,
allowing to hang from the leeward side of his mouth his
red and dewy tongue, he sped along. He turned his
eyes neither to the right nor left, but fixed them on
his master's foot passed through the stirrup-iron above
his shaggy head.

Winyard carried no whip—perhaps from some Quixotic
dislike for dealing such admonishment to the willing
little steed that knew Lena's touch and voice so well.
And in justice to Fairy it must be recorded that she took
no undue advantage. At the summit of the steep, old-
fashioned bridge spanning the Broomwater, she stopped
by command, and drew into her widespread nostrils the
fresh, water-tainted air, while Winyard, peering under
the swaying branches, took a last long look at the brawl-
ing trout-stream, and wondered if ever he should look on
it again—if ever the same trio, Adonis, Fairy, and he,
should stand again together and listen to the sweet
laughing water—those thousand musical ripples dear to
the heart of a fisherman through all his life.

Young Mistley

Then Fairy bravely faced the steady ascent of the narrow road, zigzag up the bare hillside. Already the yellowing moon was kissing the lofty horizon; already the eastern sky was changing color.

The black intensity soon lost its sense of utter opaqueness; gradually a light green shade rose, in fan-like rays, up from the distant ocean. As the traveller reached the summit of the pass this slowly acquired a pink hue of coming richness, creeping softly up like the blush of pleasure mounting to a maiden's brow.

Now the rich lowlands, awakening, drew over themselves a veil of pearly gauze, leaving the black tree-tops standing out in shamefaced bulk amid a sea of cloud.

Fresh morn was hard at work, sweeping away all shades and mysteries of night; even as the light of the great Dawn will rest upon the shadows of unanswered questions, and show up in a blaze of glory the mighty scheme of which we form a detail, sweeping off all web and tanglement where dust lies thick and choking.

And now a clear straight line appeared low down in the eastern sky, dividing the growing light into two separate shades of pearly-green.

Winyard Mistley looked on this, and knew it was the sea. Distant objects on the vast plain beneath him now began to loom up from unexpected quarters, like skirmishers when the bugles call. Beneath this great unlovely level Nature had, with characteristic waywardness, hidden broad seams and strata of her richest treasures.

Above the damp mist towered here and there, among the sparsely-growing trees, strange, gaunt erections, black chimneys, and huge whirling wheels held high aloft.

As the light increased, a breeze from the cold North Sea came bowling over the level, rolling away before it like a huge soft blanket the morning veil, and laying bare the thinly-populated land.

Then, from the height, Mistley saw the distant seaport villages, and followed with wondering eyes the intersecting railway-lines, each running from its coal-pit to seaboard, or to join the broader iron-way running north and south. Around each pit was grouped its little coaly village, tiny cottages and hovels clustering near the great smouldering heap and spider-like erections, like starlings round a raven.

On its surface the land was meagrely tilled, for all the cultivation lay below. Away beneath those deserted squares of salty pasture were passages and crossways, lines of rails and darksome caverns, intersecting, crossing, recrossing, climbing and descending.

Creeping, crawling, and grovelling, black-faced, hardy men were forever under there, following with tiny tunnel the bent of every seam. When the coal-dust is washed off these grimy toilers are strangely pale, for there is assuredly more night in their lives than in most human pilgrimages.

By the time that Mistley had reached the plain, the glow of coming sunrise was over the sea. All Nature was awakening to the fact that another day was at hand. In the trees and low hedges the birds were twittering tentatively and low, like an orchestra tuning up. Doubtless they were clearing their little pipes (for the east wind from the North Sea makes all throats gruff) in order that their Maker should be praised with clear and ringing notes.

Presently the sun raised one merry beaming eye over the line of the horizon, calling all the world to laugh and rejoice in that he had come again. Across the placid sea shot he one golden shaft of light which lay lovingly on the broad yellow sands, where the hardy Vikings had of old hauled up their marauding war-ships.

And now the young traveller spoke cheerily to Fairy, and bade her be glad that her work was more than half accomplished.

Already the trees looked happier by reason of a more lusty growth generated by kindly companionship.

Gosforth was awake as Fairy threw up the black dust of the road. Every cottage chimney was smoking with a promise of housewifely preparations for the weary night-shift men, even now coming up from the bowels of the earth with dazzled eyes, and a wondrous great appetite for breakfast.

To the southward the whole atmosphere was darkened with the heavy poison of strange-smelling smokes, rising sullenly from the banks of the busy Tyne. Tall chimneys broke the line of distant hill, and below, in a dull blue haze, lay the much-tried city of Newcastle.

Within this impure haze of smoke and night-damp was a whole army of chimneys, tall and short, dimly discernible like soldiers on a battle-field when the smoke lies low.

Respectable Jesmond was asleep when Fairy clattered through; Northumberland Street, now gradually launching into retail commerce, likewise. In Grey Street, a solitary policeman gazed sleepily at the solitary horseman, and thought of some poor doctor who was doubtless about to be called from his warm bed.

Then horse and rider parted company with mutual esteem warming either heart; for Fairy loved a gentle hand and a kindly voice, and was justly proud of the white lather near her girths.

Twenty minutes did Mistley devote to her welfare—for

the ostler was sleepy, and rubbed with little vigor—and ten to his own, beginning a new day, as he had begun many, with no other mark between it and the previous day's work than a good splash in icy water.

The train was poorly filled, folks over the border being marvellously careful of their own comfort, and there was little difficulty in securing an empty carriage.

Adonis gravely seated himself opposite his master, and waited like a well-behaved dog till he was spoken to.

This happened very soon after the rumble of the huge High-Level Bridge was left behind.

"Adonis!" said Winyard, with great gravity, "has it ever occurred to you to find out that you were not so clever as you thought yourself? I have just made that discovery, old fellow, and it is not pleasant. I thought that I had my feelings and inclinations under perfect control. I imagined that the world was an oyster, which would spring open at the first touch of my sword. But I was a fool, Adonis—a blind fool. Yes; that is right—grin and wag your tail; pretend you know all about it, when you don't. I do not understand it myself; but there is something wrong, Adonis, my boy . . . something wrong, and somehow . . . I think things will never be quite the same again."

Before the train glided slowly into Durham Station, master and dog were sleeping the sleep of the weary.

CHAPTER XXIV

THE rays of the setting sun, piercing the frosty air, gleamed luridly on every dome and minaret of grand old " Mother " Moscow. The bell suspended in the white tower of Ivan Veliki was thrilling the entire city, far beyond the Kremlin gates, with its deep, continuous voice. There was no sound of metallic concussion, but one great unbroken hum vibrated over all, like the buzz of some huge winged insect. It was a feast-day, and the Metropolitan was about to bless the people from the jewelled altar-steps of the cathedral. Prince and pauper, soldier and insolent official, passed beneath the red arch of the Holy Gate together, hurrying toward the already over-filled cathedral. Passing into the shadow of the sacred portal, each bared his head and humbly carried his hat in both hands until he was through the arch, for this token of respect must be paid by infidel and Christian alike. High up in the crumbling brickwork hung the holy picture, from whence the Saviour's mild and loving eyes gazed down upon the ignorant multitude.

The shopkeepers in the Slavonski Bazaar were busy closing their little narrow booths, knowing that their commerce was finished for the day.

From one of the arcaded passages there emerged an old man, bent and limping. He was clad in a long garment confined at the waist by an old leather strap. His high boots, reaching almost to the knee, were innocent alike of grease or blacking. On his head was a black astrakhan cap, all glossy with newness, and in his hand he carried five or six more. This type is common enough in Moscow—the man was an itinerant vendor of astrakhan caps, and, like the rest of his kind, was quite ready to take that from his head to offer to any would-be purchaser.

As he came out of the Slavonski Bazaar, he turned his head as if a dog should have been at his heels; then beneath his shaggy curls of grizzling brown he smiled a little grimly.

Painfully he made his way across the broad market-place, not in the direction of the Holy Gate, but toward the marvellous Basil.

Opposite this, the most lovely building ever erected to the glory of God by a man who knew not His love, the old hat-seller stood and gazed. For greater convenience he laid his cone of fur-caps upon one arm, and raised his two hands to the crook of his staff.

The eyes that rested on the glorious curve of varying cupola and minaret were strangely youthful and penetrating. Admiration for this triumph of Eastern architecture was expressed therein, but wonder there was not. It was as if the old man knew every line and turn, and was now gazing on them as one who bids farewell.

The sharp, concise tread of an officious police-agent sounded on the stones behind the old fellow, but he never turned or heeded it.

He seemed lost in a reverie, wherein perhaps figured the grim personality of Ivan the Terrible, who had caused this same Basil to be built; and then, when it was finished, seeing, despite his coarse and barbarous nature, that it was almost superhuman, had blinded forever its nameless architect. But what should an old hat-seller know of these things?

"Thou wilt sell no caps here," said the obtuse police-spy at his elbow.

"No?" answered the old man quietly, without looking round.

"No; go on, one way or the other."

"Then in Moscow one may not even look at a church?" said the old man, turning to go.

"No. I turned away an Englishman from here yesterday; and if an Englishman (for they see everything) may not look, surely thou mayest not."

"Same fellow, my man. Same fellow, you thickhead!" muttered the old man in perfect English, as he hobbled toward the Holy Gate.

In passing through he reverently bared his head, looking sideways up with senile awe toward the sacred picture.

He shambled past the gates of the Imperial Palace, and stood for some moments beside the great bell, resting on its pedestal at the foot of Ivan's Tower, silent forever with a crack from base to summit.

The great bell overhead had ceased ringing, but the air was still vibrating with a dull thrill of dying harmony.

The people were still thronging past with stupid, awe-struck faces, crossing themselves occasionally as they passed a shrine built into the wall with a fervor which was piteously blind and ignorant. For religion here is conducted on the same principles as the enforcement of the law.

The old man looked at them with a strange, quizzical philosophy, and from their dense and ignorant faces, rendered miserable by many generations of utter poverty and oppression, he raised his eyes to the gorgeous Imperial Palace behind them.

Then he shook his head, which showed a palsied readiness for such exercise, and wandered back past the brilliantly-painted railings and black-and-white-striped sentry-boxes, under the holy gateway into the vast market-place.

He ignored the officious limb of civic law, who, however, kept a stern eye fixed upon him; and, skirting the Slavonski Bazaar, the old hat-seller passed out of the Kremlin.

He quickened his shambling pace, but stopped suddenly in one of the narrower streets of New Moscow. A blue letter-box was fixed to the wall, and upon this he laid his stock of fur-caps, separating them and shaking out the little black curls of hair with a practised hand. He arranged and sorted his diminutive stock-in-trade for some time, till the street was clear of passers-by. Then he slipped one hand into the breast of his long coat and produced a letter. After glancing at the address he dropped it into the box, and murmured in English:

"There goes the last link. I am off at last, and a week ago to-day I was putting up scenery at Broomhaugh!"

When the Post-office collector came shortly afterward with his bag to clear the box, the old hat-seller was still examining his wares, one of which he pressed upon the letter-carrier with a little clumsy pleasantry about the cap coming in useful when he received his pension. The old fellow spoke the guttural, coarse Russian of the South.

Beneath his shaggy brows he watched his letter fall from the box into the canvas bag, and then turned away toward the highroad leading to Nijni Novgorod.

Young Mistley

Thus Winyard Mistley turned his back on civilization, and started on his lone and wearisome journey of three thousand miles. The hurried leave-taking at the porch had been indeed a farewell, despite his cheery assurance to the contrary. Twenty-four hours after leaving Broomhaugh, he was on board a little merchant steamer gliding slowly down the Humber. An interview at Whitehall, a second at the War Office, and he had received his instructions. No outfit, no letters of introduction, no baggage. " Was there anything to delay his starting immediately ? " he had been asked. " No—nothing! " The answer was not very prompt—there was the shadow of hesitation in it; and for a moment, the white-haired anxious soldier who had asked the question relaxed the coldness of his official demeanor.

" It is sometimes better," the old worn-out traveller said, " to find that there is no time to say good-by—do you not find it so ? "

" Yes—perhaps it is better so," Winyard had replied with a sudden smile, and all was said and done.

And now that was all over—a mere memory of the past. The hurried preparations, the difficult letter to Mrs. Mistley, written at a club amid the laughter and merry-making of men who would have been silent enough had they known. The uncomfortable farewell at King's Cross Station, and the last grave pressure of the hand from the two old travellers, who, partial strangers as they were, had made a point of seeing him off.

Now he was fairly at work, and his old confident delight in the attendant difficulties was returning to him. In the midst of enemies he calmly defied them all, meeting treachery with an apparently rash straightforwardness, pitting against their suspicious watchfulness a keen and educated discernment which was infinitely superior. Alone, unrecognized by his country, and unprotected by her avowed interest, he set forth into those weird untrodden deserts of the far East, where untrustworthy fanatics are restlessly scheming with and against the unscrupulous envoys of Russia; where treason and falsehood are in the very air, and where truth forms no part or portion of manly honor.

Leaving behind him home, moderate wealth, and perhaps love, he was facing discomfort, deprivation, and the probability of a lonely miserable death. It is a hopeless task to seek for human motives. Who can say why thousands of Englishmen deliberately choose a wandering life, when ease and comfort are within their reach? It cannot be said that ambition alone drove Winyard Mistley to take this journey, for he was fully aware that no public reward can be assigned for private service, in a country governed by the Press. He knew well the dangers that lay ahead, first in the semi-barbarous and wholly tyrannical country through which he was passing; and beyond, dangers of desert and rapid rivers, of burning sun and ice-cold nights, of ruthless nomads and treacherous schemers.

It was a match between educated cunning and ignorant, but the latter had the advantage of numbers.

What drove this refined Englishman to face the innumerable terrors and hardships of a journey in the untrodden East? Patriotism. For patriotism is not dead, let cynics write what they like.

Winyard Mistley did not hesitate to risk his life on a journey to that unsettled land where, one day, will be fought the greatest fight the earth has ever quivered under; where the Lion and the Tiger (dogged bravery

211

and cunning courage) will stand side by side to repel the encroachments of the shambling Bear. And then will be seen to rise from the ashes of Ease and Indifference a very phœnix of Patriotism.

This is essentially an age of words; we are a verbose generation, loving to sit at a table with closed window and crackling fire, and there to write on any subject that comes to the fore—of distant lands which we hardly know by name; of peoples whom we have never seen, whose tastes and habits are strange to us—but action is not yet dead among us, as England will find when her hour of need has come.

There is a very present satisfaction in serving one's country with rifle on shoulder, beneath the shadow of a fluttering standard, to the sound of martial music. The cheers of the excited populace, the roll of the drum, and that terribly fascinating "trub—trub" of a thousand trained feet, send a man forth to fight for his fatherland with a glowing heart. He feels that death is not so terrible after all with those red-coats around him, with the inspiration of patriotic music throbbing through his brain.

Winyard Mistley had none of these. Surely his was a higher standard of courage than that of the trained soldier. He followed no chief; he was not forced on by men who depended on his leadership. No "pomp and circumstance of war" was his, no cheering populace, no trusty comrade. Neither was his duty comprised in a blind obedience to superior orders, which if it may be somewhat galling to one man out of five, is an intense relief to the other four.

Despite what he said to Marie Bakovitch, it was no hatred toward Russia that impelled him to devote his life

to the study of her crooked politics. He was too much
of a cosmopolitan to be influenced by such ignorant and
insular prejudices as affect the ruck of untravelled and
unread Englishmen. It is strange, in this enlightened
nineteenth century, how many of our countrymen honestly believe that there is no land in the world equal to
England, no soldiers equal to ours, no intellects so lofty
as ours, no literature except ours. And these, also, men
of education and some slight reading, though the latter
has necessarily been confined to the writings of other
Englishmen.

This curse of "insularism" militates against England
throughout the whole world, and will one day fall back
upon our own heads in such a manner as to cause a very
rude awakening. Then, perhaps, it will be seen that the
teaching of effete and bygone tongues, which we persist
in considering more beautiful than those that have super-
seded them, is a mere folly. Then the fathers of sons
will perhaps conceive the brilliant idea that because they
know enough Latin to understand in some degree the
maudlin prosings of fifteen hundred years ago, it is no
reason why their sons should not be allowed to enter into
the cultivated thoughts of modern writers, who (to their
own detriment, no doubt) write in language only fit for
Frenchmen, Germans, or Italians to read.

Travel is doing much for us, there is no doubt; and
already there are glimmerings of light entering the brains
of the more liberal portion of the rising generation.
Already these are beginning to realize that this planet
does not consist of England, with a few partially necessary countries existing around her, by her kind permis-
sion and endurance.

Winyard Mistley was neither blinded by national pride

into a mistaken and vainglorious confidence, nor subject to the pusillanimous misgivings of a mere alarmist. He looked at the entire question with the impartial eye of an outsider, having learnt from his many wanderings abroad to forget that he himself was an Englishman when judging of English affairs. No man could give fuller justice to Russia than he, and no man knew better the restless nature of the half-civilized men whom a sudden freak of fortune had raised to a position of power in the far Southeast. For this reason he was feared and respected by them more, perhaps, than any member of the British Government. His strict honesty, combined with a certain blunt way of suddenly exposing to public ridicule unscrupulous schemes, which they thought to be unknown, was particularly repugnant to their overweening pride.

CHAPTER XXV

ONLY a fortnight had elapsed since Winyard Mistley's departure from Broomhaugh, and Colonel Wright was already beginning to experience some anxiety at the absence of news from him. The old soldier, too impulsive for a diplomat, grumbled aloud at the prolonged silence of his pupil. He knew that there must be good reason for it; but felt at the same time that he, of all people, might reasonably expect to be kept fully posted as to Winyard's movements.

Lena, whose spirits were singularly high (in an unusual *jerky* manner), watched her father in his anxiety, wondering whether there were any real cause for it; and Mrs. Wright, for reasons best known to her own maternal heart, watched Lena.

On the fifteenth morning the tardy letter arrived at last, having been forwarded by Mrs. Mistley from Paris. The Colonel read it slowly, for it was written in pencil on the torn-out page of a sketch-book. Then he turned the paper over again, and read it aloud:

"DEAR COLONEL,

"I leave Moscow this afternoon, walking to the first station on the Nijni line. I am fairly off now— right in the heart of the country, and no one the wiser. Give me twelve months before you think of getting anxious, *eighteen* before you show your anxiety, and *twenty-one* before you send Wilson and Bates. Let them come unknown to the newspapers. If either of them be unable to come (I do not anticipate unwillingness), someone else must. Do not on any account send one man alone. If I should not get back, and Wilson fails to hear of me, shed a friendly tear, but shed it in private; our white-coated friends must not hear of it. By the by, on second thoughts, please tell your ladies and the mater *all* about Marie Bakovitch. It will be safer. Do not lose sight of the mater, and take care of the respectable Adonis.

"Yours,

"W. M."

The Colonel's voice quivered a little as he finished reading.

Lena, slowly sipping her coffee, looked over her cup toward her father, with an interested but somewhat critical expression on her face.

"It is to be hoped," she said, "that 'the respectable Adonis' will appreciate the interest shown in his welfare."

"Ye-es," said the Colonel vaguely, as he slowly folded the letter. "There!" he continued more energetically, as he placed it in his pocket—"you know as much as I do!"

Mrs. Wright slowly raised her eyes from her plate, and looked across the table toward her husband.

"Except . . ." she said suggestively, ". . . in the matter of Marie . . . something or other."

"Marie Bakovitch . . . yes, I must tell you about her. It would interest you, I think."

Lena was still sipping her coffee indifferently.

Young Mistley

"Marie Bakovitch," continued the Colonel deliberately, "is a young lady, beautiful and . . . accomplished. Two years ago she undertook to remove me from the face of the earth. She is what is called in some countries a patriot, and that is the form taken by her patriotism. Of course she belongs to several crackbrained societies, and one of these was kind enough to inform me by letter that I was condemned, at the same time warning Mistley. He had the effrontery to reply to their formal communication, but I did not see the letter. Since then I have heard nothing more about it. Some time later Mistley received a threatening letter, and since then this girl has followed him like a shadow . . ."

Lena slowly set her cup down upon the table. With one white finger she began polishing the top of the silver coffee-pot with peculiar attention, like a child who is being gently scolded.

"By some means," continued the Colonel, "he turned the wrath of these mistaken patriots from my head, and called it down upon his own. Marie Bakovitch followed him to Walso, and actually attempted to shoot him, down at the Broomwater one day when he was fishing. She missed him, and then fainted into his arms—in the most confiding manner, Winyard said. The fellow managed to make even *that* into a funny story. He generously kept the whole affair quiet, and succeeded in getting the girl away from Walso. She even promised to leave England, but whether she will keep her promise or not, I cannot say. He was afraid that they might have been seen together, and that gossip would get about, so he asked me to tell you the truth about it."

The two ladies were silent. Lena bent her head over the coffee-pot as if she were short-sighted, and wished to see the result of her prolonged polishing. It was only when he looked across the table and met his wife's eyes that Colonel Wright fully realized what Winyard Mistley had done in taking this danger upon himself.

"And you knew this all along," said Mrs. Wright presently, with gentle severity. She was recalling, with the unerring memory of a woman for such details, the thousand passing incidents in which Winyard Mistley and his chief might have betrayed their anxiety concerning Marie Bakovitch and her presence in Walso.

Women usually consider that they have the monopoly of the minute diplomacy of every-day life. They love to comment on the clumsiness and want of tact with which they are pleased to endow their husbands, brothers, and sons; and when a revelation comes to them, as it had now come to Mrs. Wright, the result is a trifle humiliating. Most women learn sooner or later in their lives that the men whom they pride themselves upon blindly leading allow themselves to be led just so far as suits them, and not one inch beyond.

Lena must have been thinking of this also, for presently, without looking up, she said:

"I cannot understand it at all. If I had a secret like that upon my mind, I should be miserable. I should not be able to think of or take an interest in anything else, whereas you and . . . Winyard . . . were as innocent as lambs. You took an interest in the theatricals, in the trivial details of every-day existence . . . it makes one feel like a child to whom the nurse talks upon topics likely to amuse, and never thinks of what she is saying."

Before Colonel Wright had time to reply, the door was thrown open by the square-shouldered butler, and Laurance Lowe entered the room, closely followed by Charles Mistley.

"We met on the doorstep," said the younger man; while his companion silently shook hands with Colonel and Mrs. Wright, and kissed Lena.

"Early visit," added Laurance Lowe, by way of apology.

"I am glad you have come," said the Colonel genially. "I have heard from Winyard at last."

Then he rose and handed the letter to Charlie. The young sailor took the paper and walked to the window.

"Excuse me," he said, with a grave smile toward Mrs. Wright, before he unfolded it. Leaning against the woodwork of the window, he read the letter through slowly and deliberately. Then he came forward and gave it back to the Colonel, with a word of thanks.

Before handing it to Laurance Lowe, the old soldier unfolded the paper and examined it critically; then, looking up suddenly at Charlie, he said:

"It is such men as this who leave their mark upon a generation."

Charlie smiled in his lazy, grave way.

"Yes," he replied; "the energetic ones."

Laurance Lowe was holding out his hand for the letter, patiently and without any show of curiosity. As previously hinted, he was essentially an unemotional being, never displaying curiosity or surprise.

"Colonel," said Charlie, "I have brought you the new sheet-map I promised to procure you. It is a large affair, so I gave it to Jarvis to take into your study."

"Thanks—many thanks!"

"And," continued the young sailor, "and . . . I have come to say good-by."

Young Mistley

Laurance Lowe slowly raised his eyes. They rested on Charles Mistley long enough to notice that the young fellow carefully avoided meeting Lena's quick glance, and instantly turned away again.

"Good-by?" echoed Lena. "Surely *you* are not going away now?"

"Yes," replied Charlie quietly. "I have been appointed to the *Curlew*, on the Mediterranean station."

Mrs. Wright had risen, and was standing at the window with her back toward them. She turned her head.

"I shall be very sorry to lose you, Charlie," she said softly.

Lena said nothing. She was engaged in administering small pieces of toast to Adonis. She could not be expected to express surprise, as Charles Mistley had foreseen this appointment, and had spoken of it frequently.

Presently the gentlemen adjourned to the study to smoke cigarettes and inspect the new map. When it was spread out on the table, the Colonel took a pen and made a little cross over the word "Moscow," writing underneath it the date of Winyard Mistley's letter. With dotted lines he followed the track of the railway to Nijni Novgorod; then, turning south, traced the broad flow of the Volga. Carefully he portioned off each day with a line drawn horizontally.

As the mariner traces his course upon the chart, so Colonel Wright continued, in the months that followed, to make this imaginary track across Russia. Down the Volga to Astrakhan, by road from Astrakhan to Petrovsk, and from thence across the Caspian Sea to Krasnovodsk. Each day's journey was portioned off scientifically, each day the little dotted line advanced farther into the unknown East.

Young Mistley

The old traveller never spoke much to his wife or daughter concerning this map, doubtless considering it a detail of his profession necessarily of small interest to ladies. He was not aware that day by day a fair young face was bent over the gray paper, and a dainty finger followed with absorbing interest the growth of the black line.

CHAPTER XXVI

THE weeks passed slowly on. Autumn blustered out, and winter stole in with a keen black frost that enveloped London in fog and darkness. The muddy streets were dangerous, the air pestilential; and yet people lived on merrily enough, performing their daily tasks, extracting their daily enjoyment from existence.

At Broomhaugh it was a very different matter. A great and wondrous silence reigned there—even the voice of the Broomwater was checked. The huge brown boulders grew hoary with long ice-beards, and as the water fell day by day, little platforms of ice stood out from stone and bank. Then came a great fall of snow, and the dark pine-trees were at rest. They could not sigh and moan at the passage of every biting breeze beneath this real and tangible burden of chilly white, for pine-trees are like men who make a great moan when things are passable, but bear with manfully closed lips the weight of a real sorrow. In the pine-woods, however, as in the world, a sharp crack sometimes rings out, followed by a sickening rustle of falling strength, and the older trees hug their close-knit bark, gently whispering to each other that such and such a sapling has given in at last. But Broomhaugh was deserted; the old gray house was silent, and the snow lay in virgin purity over all the land.

222

Young Mistley

Through that long winter Lena was her father's constant companion. Indeed, the family of three wondered then how they had been able to manage life so well apart when the Colonel was away. The old soldier was very busy with both official and private writings, and in Lena he found a bright and intelligent assistant. Article after article flowed from his pen, and in review and magazine the weight of his experience soon found appreciation.

Also, there was much reading to be done. As an old sailor loves to hear about the great waters in quaint sea-sounding words, so the traveller loves to follow the wanderings of others " when travelling-days are done."

During those darksome months Lena grew very wise in Eastern lore. The Colonel's map was now common property, and his daughter openly displayed her interest in the ever-lengthening dotted line. Sometimes, even, she was consulted as to the journey to be adjudged. Thus, in the quiet study, father and daughter travelled Eastward together, by piteous little stages of one-eighth of an inch or so per diem, till at length the end of the black line touched the B of Bokhara; and the Colonel talked of gilded domes and minarets, of crumbling walls and narrow gateways built of the little flat bricks manufactured of old—" without straw."

Now this was all very fine and exceedingly pleasant—this prosperous journey devoid of hardship and danger—to be taken up after a good night's rest in a warm bed, followed by an honest English breakfast; but there came no news of the real traveller, who had become, as it were, a tiny insect crawling over the vast map.

Lena, from her reading, knew that there are occasional opportunities, even in the farthest desert, of sending back a few words by some return caravan or party of travellers; but no sign came from Winyard Mistley. Since the letter from Moscow, his silence had been as that of one who is in the grave. At times this imaginary journey seemed to Lena to be nothing else than a pitiful farce; but she could not make up her mind to mention this thought to her father, who showed no anxiety.

The Colonel was well aware that some news should by this time have reached England; but his simple trust in Mistley's powers was very great.

"If *any* man can do it, Mistley can!" he had said vaguely, one day when the soft dampness of the atmosphere seemed to speak of coming spring. This was no reply to some remark of Lena's, but merely in answer to his own thoughts. The Colonel was leaning against the mantelpiece gazing dreamily at his own boots, while Lena stood with her back toward him, bending over the map. She waited for more, but her father remained silent.

The summer brought an event in Lena's life of some importance. This came in the shape and form of a young gentleman named Walter Haughton, who had been her playmate in former years. But the playmate and the young man were two very different beings. There was nothing to be quoted against Walter Haughton—his manners were perfect, if somewhat too self-possessed—his appearance decidedly in his favor; but he invariably inspired a sudden distrust in the minds of experienced men and women of the world. The former called him a "bad egg;" the latter said he was a rolling-stone. Young ladies who aspired to "fastness" considered him great fun, and no two young men had the same opinion regarding him. When he presented himself at Seymour Street and talked of old times, throwing in a few sincere words of tribute to the memory of his mother, who had been a friend of Mrs. Wright's, he was received with much kindness. Certain rumors of wild doings were kindly forgotten by Mrs. Wright, and the new page was universally looked upon as spotless. Indeed, Walter Haughton now set up his stall in Vanity Fair as an irreproachable young man, and did very well. This took place early in the summer, and the new venture proved so successful that Haughton honestly determined to adopt for the future the paths of virtue. Mrs. Wright did her very best to aid him in this. She introduced him to her friends, took him out to houses where young men were required, and to his credit it may be recorded that she never had cause to regret having done so.

When, however, Haughton's visits to Seymour Street became monotonous in their regularity, and when he appeared at every ball, reception, or soirée, Mrs. Wright began to experience misgivings. The "prodigal," as she was pleased to call him, did not assuredly come to see her; it must therefore be Lena. However, for some reason the good lady was less anxious now regarding her daughter than she used to be. Also the relationship between Haughton and Lena seemed to make no progress —the keenest-eyed old dowager could not have detected anything more than mere friendship, and that of the description generated more by the force of circumstances than from natural selection.

However, this young gentleman called one July afternoon, and as soon as he entered the room Mrs. Wright saw that there was something different in his manner. His usual and somewhat remarkable self-possession was not there, and his blue eyes were less shifty than of old; but, on the other hand, they were entirely devoid of a

reckless merriment which was not without its fascination. Mrs. Wright was no mean scholar at human
nature's great academy; she could read faces as well as
most people; but Walter Haughton's manner puzzled her
that morning, and continued to puzzle her until Lena
entered the room, and then the meaning of it was clear.

Lena was dressed in readiness to go out. She had
made an appointment with some girl-friends to meet at
a picture-gallery, which they were desirous of "doing"
before the fashionable hour. Walter Haughton promptly
proposed accompanying her as far as the gallery, which
she acceded to without demur.

Mrs. Wright saw them to the door, which she closed
after them.

"Poor prodigal!" she murmured to herself, as she
slowly mounted the stairs. "Poor . . . prodigal! he is
as sure of his failure as I am."

Lena came home rather earlier than Mrs. Wright had
expected. The gallery had certainly not been exhaus-
tively inspected. The good lady glanced up from her
work for a moment as her daughter entered the room,
but made no remark regarding her quick return.

Lena walked to the window, and stood with her back
toward her mother, looking out on to the dusty, sunlit
street. She had not removed her trim little hat, and the
fingers on the window were gloved.

Then Mrs. Wright laid aside her work, and softly went
to her daughter's side.

"Mother," said the girl wearily, without looking round
—"mother, why is it that some people's lives seem destined to be failures from beginning to end?"

Mrs. Wright slipped her arm round her daughter, and
they stood side by side, looking vaguely into the street.

"My darling," she said presently, "I think *we* are meant to shape our lives as unselfishly as we can; but . . . still . . . we should not look too much on either side—there are so many to assist that the sacrifice of ourselves may be of little ultimate good."

"Walter—asked me to be his wife."

"Yes, darling."

"Do you think it would have been of any good?"

"No, Lena; I think it is best as it is. Poor Walter! luck does seem to be against him . . . but he is young yet. People are not unfortunate *all* their lives . . . unless they have themselves to blame."

The girl made no reply to this. Her confidence in her own strength of mind had been somewhat shaken that afternoon. Like many a ne'er-do-well, Walter Haughton had a most harmonious voice; and never had its tones been so pathetic, so musical, as they had sounded in her ears an hour ago. She actually shivered as she remembered how near to hesitation she had been.

"There is . . . Mr. Lowe," she said suddenly, but without evincing surprise; and with a little inclination of her head she indicated the direction in which she was looking.

Beneath them, Laurance Lowe was crossing the street. His active gait looked, even more than usual, out of keeping with his bent white head. A passing suggestion of pain flickered across Mrs. Wright's face—perhaps she was mentally withdrawing the statement she had just made.

A few minutes later, Lowe entered the room. He kissed Lena with a strange old-fashioned respect, and turned to shake hands with her mother, who had advanced to meet him less hurriedly. As his hand met

227

Mrs. Wright's, he raised his shaggy brows, and looked at her for a moment. There was distinctly a question in his quiet eyes, and in hers there was, as distinctly, an answer to it.

" Any news ? " he had asked, and the reply to it was: " No news."

Each time these two met he asked that same question, and hitherto that same anxious answer had been given.

CHAPTER XXVII

EARLY in September, Mrs. Wright received a letter from Gibraltar, of which the address was in an unknown handwriting. Charles Mistley's letters had of late borne the Gibraltar post-mark, but this could not be from him. Before she had read the first page, she exclaimed:

"Charlie is coming home!"

"Hooray!" said the Colonel.

"Oh . . . I am *so* glad!" said Lena, with more fervor than the occasion would appear to demand. But Mrs. Wright looked grave.

"He has broken his arm," she said, and then she suddenly laughed.

The letter, which was from an officer of Charles Mistley's ship, was a very humorous production, purporting to be written at Charlie's dictation, but interlarded here and there with observations from the writer's own fertile brain. Although the news was bad, it was so cheerfully imparted that the bright side of it was alone presented.

"At any rate," said Lena, when the letter had been read aloud, "he is coming."

"Yes . . . he is coming," replied her mother thoughtfully, almost anxiously.

Charles Mistley had been the only member of the little circle who had refused, persistently and continually, to acknowledge any feeling of anxiety at his brother's silence. His letters, written in the Mediterranean, seemed to have caught the sunshine and joyousness of that favored sea. No thought of anxiety, no suspicion of doubt, was allowed to find place in the closely-written pages. More than a year had elapsed since Winyard's departure, and the silence was yet unbroken. War had at times appeared imminent, and then from mere lack of interest had lapsed into peace again. Great storms had passed over the world—revolutions, murders, and blood-shed—but Charles Mistley's faith had never wavered. The black line on Colonel Wright's map had turned back; it had even regained civilization, and yet no word was forthcoming. Despite this, Charlie laughed at anx-iety. Worst of all, Winyard's name had gradually been dropped from conversation at the house in Seymour Street. The topic was tacitly avoided, as we avoid the mention of those dear names which gain no answer now.

It was to this that Charles Mistley was coming home.

A few days after the arrival of the letter he presented himself in Seymour Street. Although he had given no notice of his coming, he was fortunate enough to find everyone at home. There was, however, another visitor in the room when he arrived. This was a brother officer of Colonel Wright's, who had stopped his cab in passing through Seymour Street to call and leave two brace of partridges.

This old sportsman was holding forth upon the details of his sport when Charles Mistley entered the room in his usual unobtrusive manner, walking with a slow, strong step devoid of any litheness. The greetings and introduction over, Charlie, with true British instinct, displayed an immediate interest in the partridges which were lying on the hearthrug.

"You have been shooting, sir?" he observed.

"Yes; but I secured a poor bag."

Lena smiled openly.

"That is a good bird," continued Charlie, in the same make-yourself-at-home tone of voice, daintily holding up the largest partridge by one leg.

"Yes," replied the General, smiling vaguely.

"I am afraid I am a poor sportsman," continued the big sailor, meditatively placing his head on one side in order to examine the bird more minutely. "I could not stand a keeper by my side; and in the absence of some-one to keep me up to the mark, I should probably sit down on the lee side of a hedge and think the sunny hours away."

His slow enunciation conveyed an impression of pleas-ant laziness, such as one rarely meets with in these hur-ried days. He looked past the bird at Lena, and met her eyes fixed full upon his face with a smile of ill-disguised amusement. He quietly smiled back, and proceeded to keep the ball of conversation rolling, descanting with lazy gravity upon the utmost trifles.

At last the old sportsman took his leave, and the Colo-nel accompanied him to the door. When the latter returned, the fact had apparently slipped his memory that he had shaken hands with Charlie before, for he went through the ceremony again, taking Charlie's left hand in his right somewhat awkwardly.

"How is the arm?" he asked, glancing at the sling, which the young sailor somehow managed to wear so that it failed to attract attention.

"The arm is getting on splendidly, thank you," he replied in rather a constrained tone. The Colonel had left the door open, and now the young sailor crossed the room to close it. He stooped in order to see that the bolt had acted properly, and then he turned and faced Colonel Wright.

"I have news," he said quietly, "of Winyard."

"Ah!" exclaimed the old soldier, rising from the seat he had just resumed. "Tell me all about it—news at last, thank God!"

"It is a long story," began the other, in his slow manner.

"Then be quick with it," interrupted Mrs. Wright, with an impatient laugh. A little "catching" sigh of relief came from Lena's corner of the room.

"Let us hear all about it," said the Colonel, pointing to a chair.

But Charlie appeared to prefer standing. He took his station at the corner of the mantelpiece, and while he was speaking he fidgeted with the ornaments there, taking them up and setting them down again one after the other. He told his story with characteristic simplicity and shortness.

"The day before yesterday," he said, "I was at the club at Plymouth, reading a paper or something, when a fellow came up and said, 'Commander Mistley,' in a casual sort of way, and held out his hand. I shook it, and let him have it back; and then he said, 'I am Henry Akryl.' I was none the wiser, so I said 'Yes' in a vague way. . . ."

"I know exactly how you said it," interrupted Lena, with a little laugh.

"Well, it ultimately transpired that he dined with us one day in the Persian Gulf. He is an Eastern authority—writes books, or reads inscriptions, or something. Then he told me his story. In January he was at Kizil

Arvat. One day he was in the bazaar, and, of course, was being pestered by the scum of the place, who wanted him to buy rubbish of every description. He is the sort of man who never buys curiosities, and he finally got rid of them all except one fellow, who followed him most persistently even out of the bazaar. He turned down a narrow street where the grain-merchants have their stalls; but this fellow still followed him, and kept thrusting his wares forward. His particular line of business was old jewelry, Moscow crosses, cheap bangles from Kieff, and that sort of thing. He whined out a prayer for charity in the most aggravating manner, and once or twice Akryl struck his hand aside. Suddenly, however, he ceased whining, and said in perfect English, 'Don't look round—don't stop; but listen to what I tell you.' Akryl seems to be a sharp fellow, for he walked on without showing any surprise. Then the jewelry-merchant went on: 'When you get back, go or write to Colonel William Forster Wright, 109, Seymour Street, London. Remember the address. You had better write it down when you get back to the caravansérai. *Don't* look round. Tell him you met an Englishman in Central Asia—to-day—that is all.' Akryl said, 'Are you Mistley?' and the fellow replied, 'Shut up.' Akryl bought a cross. . . .''

Charlie stopped speaking. His thumb was hooked into his waistcoat-pocket, as if making sure that something was there. His eyes were fixed on the hearthrug—a tiger-skin, the stripes of which he was following with the toe of his boot. Suddenly he raised his lazy blue eyes, direct and with a certain deliberation, from the floor to Lena's face. He caught her eyes fixed wistfully on his hand. Then he moved slightly, and addressed Colonel Wright.

"It sounds like Win, does it not?"

"Yes," replied the old traveller, slowly pulling at his mustache. "Yes—that was Win."

"Akryl saw nothing but his hand," continued the sailor. "A small brown hand he said it was—almost the hand of a Tartar, but somewhat stouter, with compact fingers and light-colored nails. I asked him for further details, but that was all he could tell me. He had landed in England two days before I saw him, and was on the point of starting off to join the Fez Expedition, and was just going to sit down and write to you when he caught sight of me and remembered that I was . . . Win's brother."

"It is not much," said Colonel Wright slowly, "but it explains a good deal. He ought to have been across the Kizil Arvat desert before January. No doubt he has had difficulties to contend with which we did not quite foresee."

The old soldier was no adept at dissimulation. His manner implied disappointment, and in each heart there was a vague conviction that this news was not satisfactory. It was no explanation of the subsequent silence.

"And now," said Mrs. Wright, cleverly breaking the uncomfortable silence, "let us hear about yourself. How did you break your arm?—what are you going to do with yourself?—how long leave have you, etc., etc.?"

"O . . . h! I suppose I shall moon about, get up in the morning, go to bed at night, and take my meals regularly."

"Which," said Lena severely, "is his definition of a human existence. Charlie, you are as bad as ever—as hopelessly lazy, as incorrigibly unsatisfactory."

Charlie bowed with grave mockery.

Young Mistley

"No," said Colonel Wright, who was a wonderfully reliable judge of men. "No; he is not that. He is simply a humbug; he is pleased to assume laziness because it pays. He dawdles his life away because he is a philosopher. There are few books he has not read— few subjects upon which he could not tell us something; but he prefers to sit idly by and listen to a futile discussion when a few words from him would settle it at once. He is a shopkeeper who stores his best wares beneath the counter, and leaves the window empty."

Charles Mistley met this accusation with a mellow laugh, in which the ladies joined.

"I begin to regret," he said, "that I ever left the *Curlew*, for I was treated on board with the respect due to the gold lace upon my sleeve; but still, if anyone else wishes to add a few remarks, now is the time. I have no friends, I have not even the protection of a mother's love, as that respected lady does not arrive from France till to-morrow! I have just taken chambers for her and myself in Bedford Place!"

"Bedford Place—again!" exclaimed Mrs. Wright.

"Yes, Bedford Place again," he replied. "I think the mater likes the busy rattle of the cabs."

"What leave have you?" asked Colonel Wright.

"Four months, Colonel. Four months, with the probability of an extension to six, according to the doctor's report."

"You have not told us how it happened," said Lena.

"Carelessness," replied the young fellow, with a shrug of his shoulders.

"On your part?"

"No, on the part of someone else. A man was lowering a boat, and the rope slipped—a thing that might

235

happen at any moment. The boat was full of men, who would have been shot into the water if two of us had not stopped it."

"Who was the other?" asked the Colonel.

"The man who wrote home for me."

"I thought there was something in that fellow, despite his foolery!" said the old soldier thoughtfully.

When Charles Mistley left the house shortly afterward, there was in his mind a vague half-formed sense of misgiving. It was almost a prescience of coming evil. Lena was different; there was something in her manner which had no sympathy with the Lena of olden days. His memory went back to the time when she, little else than a child, had been pleased to make him her friend, her confidant, almost her brother; when he had laughingly taught her to dance, and had skilfully guided her through the little ball-room dangers that surround a lovely girl in her early youth. All this he thought of, and followed through it the natural growth and development of her mind—making every allowance for outward influence, giving full credit to maternal care. Although his mode of life had not afforded much opportunity for the study of such matters, the young sailor knew that there is no change so great in the nature of human beings as that which may, and often does, come to a girl between the ages of seventeen and twenty-four. It is during that period that all the infinite possibilities of good, all the chances of evil, are on the balance. In those years a woman realizes the object of her life, for it is then that love comes to her—love with its dazzling light of happiness, too perfect for mortal realization or enjoyment.

If love had come to Lena, and Charles Mistley thought

it had, what he saw was not a direct result of its influence. There was something beyond his powers to divine, and which he did not at the moment attempt to define. From whence the thought had come he could not tell, what passing word or glance suggested it he could not determine, but he only knew that Lena was concealing something from her mother. A change had come over the understanding that existed between these two. So slight was it and so intangible, that if Charles Mistley had not been much keener and much more observant than he pretended to be, he would never have detected it.

Then he began to wonder if any other person had noticed it, and his thoughts naturally turned to Laurance Lowe. If the change was there, Laurance Lowe would know something of it; and from him information was only to be extracted by a great exercise of patience. So the young sailor wandered on through the noisy, crowded streets, puzzling his brain over the most futile question man has ever set his mind upon—the question of a woman's heart.

CHAPTER XXVIII

WITH the advent of October came a succession of fogs. The atmosphere of London was such as only Londoners can breathe, yellow, noisome, and choking. The Wrights had talked of leaving town, and had even discussed the question of going abroad, but they were still in Seymour Street. The Colonel was busy, and seemed singularly averse to leaving town; he was now getting seriously anxious about Winyard Mistley. Political events had occurred making it a matter of congratulation to the English Cabinet that they had a man of Mistley's discernment and well-known ability in Central Asia; but, at the Colonel's urgent request, his presence there had been kept a secret. The information, however, which he would undoubtedly be able to supply was daily becoming of greater necessity. Relating as it did to the feeling of certain tribes, more especially of the Saruks, respecting Russian aggression, it was such as only an expert in Eastern matters could supply. The Foreign Office authorities were compelled to bear much abuse, and to submit to unlimited badgering at the hands of officious and scantily informed Members, who took the opportunity of getting their august names set up in type by taunting the Ministers upon having no other sources of information than those of such notable unreliability as Russian official journals.

Young Mistley

All this was of undoubted benefit to the solitary wanderer, and while it demonstrated to a nervous Cabinet the utter futility of half-measures and unrecognized envoys, it militated greatly in favor of Winyard Mistley, whose devotion to the cause he had espoused was so obviously disinterested. But to Colonel Wright—to the man who, despite his gray hairs, felt that his place was not with the talkers who are left behind, but with the workers who go afield—it was particularly galling and terribly anxious work.

Instead of getting better, things grew worse. Vague reports, originating sometimes in Berlin, sometimes in St. Petersburg, appeared from time to time in the newspapers. These rumors spoke of trouble on the Afghan and Persian frontiers, of tribal disturbances and religious differences, of boundaries overstepped and agreements broken. Added to all this, Colonel Wright received a blow from a nearer source, which aggravated matters greatly, and rendered Winyard Mistley's silence almost unbearable.

One morning, late in October, he was sitting at his study-table. Before him lay the large sheet-map which Charles Mistley had brought more than a year ago. A fresh route had been worked out across it with dotted lines of red, commencing at Kizil Arvat on the day mentioned by the traveller Henry Akryl. The Colonel had just completed the dotted line as far as Bokhara, and was looking, in an absently methodical manner, at a calendar. The date written above the word Bokhara was terribly far back into the spring, more than six months ago.

The study-door opened softly, and although the old soldier heard it he did not move or turn. Two warm hands were laid upon his shoulders with that marvellous touch of a woman's loving fingers. They were peculiarly steady hands, as white as Lena's, but firmer and somewhat heavier.

"Willy!"

"Yes . . . old woman."

"Willy . . ." repeated Mrs. Wright, looking out of the window into the hopeless dreariness of the October morning, "have you noticed any . . . difference—any change in Lena?"

The Colonel raised his eyes from the map and contemplated the chimneys of the opposite house for some moments in silence.

"A change . . . old woman," he said slowly. "Perhaps there is a change—she is no longer a child now."

"No, it is not that; there is something else. She never allows it to appear, but . . . she is miserable. She is wearing herself to death. We must go away from London."

It must be confessed that Colonel Wright had not given very much thought to the subject of his daughter's happiness, nor was he very clever at divining a motive.

"Is it," he asked, "anything to do with Charlie?"

Mrs. Wright appeared to be buried in thought. She uttered no reply, but leaning forward over her husband's shoulder, she placed her finger on the map, where the red and black lines met beneath the word Bokhara.

A pitiful silence followed, such as leaves its mark upon the human heart.

"Good God!" whispered the Colonel.

Mrs. Wright went toward the window. The band that held back the folds of the heavy curtain was twisted and somewhat out of place. Slipping it off the hook, she deftly put it right, and then she turned her face slowly toward her husband.

"Then you think . . . he has failed," she said in a monotonous voice.

The Colonel sat at the table with his chin resting on his folded hands. He was staring at the map.

"We should have heard from him six months ago," was his reply.

Mrs. Wright crossed the room, and sat down on a low chair near the fire. For nearly half an hour they remained thus, the white-haired old warrior and his comely gray-headed wife. After twenty-four years of married life they were lovers still; and as they sat there—he looking out into the yellow mist, she watching the changeful flames as they leapt up and fell again—they were recalling the weary years of waiting that they had passed through, ignorant of the love that lay hidden in either heart. They were looking back to the first happy days of their married life, days rendered almost sacred by the touch of sorrow and the ever-living joy of watching over Lena, according all their parental love to the little girl who only knew her elder brother by the name that demanded a lowered voice.

"With Lena," said Mrs. Wright presently, in a gentle voice, "it will be the matter of a lifetime . . . as, indeed, it is with most girls."

"Are you sure . . . there is no mistake about it?"

"Sure," was the soft reply. "We have been able to watch over her—to keep sorrow and sickness away from her, but this . . . this love is beyond us, Willy. It is very hard that love should bring sorrow with it at once."

"Has Laurance Lowe said anything?" asked the Colonel.

16   241

" He has said nothing—he never speaks of that sort of thing, but he thinks the same as . . . I do."

" And—Charlie ? "

" I cannot understand . . . Charlie," replied Mrs. Wright. " His thoughts, his feelings, and his motives are alike a mystery to me."

The Colonel opened one of the drawers of his writing-table, and, taking Winyard's letter from it, he spread the crumpled paper out upon the face of the map and studied the writing, now growing dim and faded. The formation of each letter was familiar to him; he knew the writing as he knew his own.

A thicker wave of fog came slowly over the town, and the darkness lowered its veil over everything like a short winter's twilight. The printed names on the map were no longer visible, and yet the Colonel sat and gazed at it, with Winyard's letter at his side.

Presently the door opened, and, with a flood of warm light, Lena entered.

" I verily believe you were both sound asleep! " she exclaimed with a cheerfulness which for some reason made her mother wince. " Is it not dreadful—lamps at eleven o'clock in the morning! "

CHAPTER XXIX

A MONTH had elapsed since Charles Mistley's return, and as yet he found himself no nearer an elucidation of Lena's altered manner than he had been on first discovering it. He had merely confirmed his original conviction that such a change existed. During those four weeks he had been much in the society of Laurance Lowe, as every frequenter of the Colonel's house was forced to be, but from him no information had transpired. True, they had talked together very little, both being silent men.

Laurance Lowe was not what the world is pleased to call a hospitable man. This arose less, perhaps, from that sense of economy which is the result of a solitary existence than from mental laziness. If he could have relied upon his guests to entertain each other, and make free use of what was placed before them, he would readily enough have returned such hospitality as he received; but unfortunately his friends were not selected from among people capable of that difficult task. He would have been a generous man had he not been handicapped by a deeply planted aversion to thanks of any description. His own gratitude had never been known to express itself by more than the simple words "Thank you"; and, amid a shower of neatly turned phrases, a hostess, somehow, usually remembered those formal words when others were forgotten. His generosity flowed in one channel only. To Lena, and to Lena alone, did he make presents. She, with that sweet womanly sympathy which was perhaps the most precious inheritance received from her mother, knew exactly how to thank her white-haired admirer for these gifts. In many cases her appreciation never showed· itself in words at all. A kiss, and a little touch of soft cool fingers upon the back of his corded hand—that was all at the time. Later on she would wear the gift, if it were jewelry—use it, if it were not ornamental—at the proper time and unostentatiously.

Charles Mistley was by no means ignorant of these traits in the character of Laurance Lowe, which the world naturally quoted against him with infinite gusto; and when, therefore, he received a curtly worded invitation to dine at a club, he knew that there was some reason for it.

The meal was ludicrously characteristic of the two men. No word was exchanged, directly, between them. Occasionally a mutual friend lounged up to their table with a nod of recognition, and made a remark to which both listened with grave attention, Charlie replying to it, while Lowe silently acquiesced. The old gentleman did not, however, do badly as regards the dinner, and the sailor did better—the waiter did best in the lift-cupboard. "Lowe's dinner-party" was a standing joke at that club for some weeks afterward.

After dinner they walked, by mutual and tacit consent, to Lowe's chambers in Adelphi Terrace. Here they found coffee awaiting them. The rooms were furnished with a comfort somewhat rigid in its simplicity, but a bright fire was burning in the grate, and the warm lamplight softened down the barest corners.

Charles Mistley knew that his companion had something on his mind, but was content to wait with a patience as enduring as that of Lowe himself. Old barriers are hard to break; the stones of an old wall are closely knit. Laurance Lowe was endeavoring to destroy a barrier which had grown harder and tougher as the years followed on. He made a little breach, but the barrier stood as firm as ever; when the moment came he failed, and retired into his stronghold of silence. He had fully intended to speak openly for once, but the old habit of self-suppression was too strong for him.

He motioned his guest to a seat, and drew forward a low armchair for himself. Then he pushed a box of cigars across the table, so that Charlie could help himself without moving. After they had been sitting for some time, during which neither had commenced to smoke, the host seemed suddenly to recollect the coffee, for he rose, and with slow, certain movements, entailing no unnecessary clink or contact of china, he poured out two cups of a fragrant brew, and set the quaint old coffee-pot down before the fire to keep warm. Lowe never smoked a manufactured cigarette, and he now proceeded to roll one, subsequently tucking in the stray ends of tobacco carefully with the point of a cedar-wood pencil.

He smoked meditatively for some moments, then, without looking toward his companion, he uttered the single word:

"Lena!"

Charles Mistley examined his cigar critically, and with much appreciation.

"Ye-es," he replied gravely.

Then Lowe made a herculean effort.

"I think," he said, "there is something wrong."

The young sailor's calm eyes were resting on his host's immovable face. He might as well have attempted to read the features of a sphinx.

"I have noticed it," he observed conversationally, "ever since I came back."

The ice was broken, the first word was said, and now it surely was easy enough to proceed. Only Englishmen could have failed so lamentably to take advantage of the situation. They actually continued smoking, and presently Charlie took a sip of coffee, which, slight though it may appear, as a mere incident, was enough to make matters worse.

"Monsieur Jacobi . . ." said Lowe suddenly. "Do you remember him?"

"Jacobi!" repeated the sailor thoughtfully. "Jacobi! There was a fellow of that name came one night to Mrs. Wright's about two years ago."

Lowe looked up. There was actually a gleam of life beneath his eyebrows.

"That is the man."

"I remember him. A slippery-looking fellow—to sleek for my taste."

Lowe nodded approval, and then said quietly:

"He is in it somewhere."

Charlie, completely puzzled, waited with extraordinary patience till the peculiar old gentleman should be pleased to vouchsafe further information. At length, after carefully depositing the ash of his cigarette in the fire, Lowe spoke again:

"He came that night . . . with the Baroness de Nantille."

"Yes—I remember her."

"Lena is now having singing-lessons with the Baroness."

Charlie felt convinced that his host was on the wrong track entirely, but refrained from saying so.

"But . . . Jacobi," he began. "is hardly the sort of man . . ."

Lowe stopped him with a little "sniff" of contempt and even derision, intended to convey his opinion of Monsieur Jacobi.

"I have watched," said the old fellow, "and . . . I know Lena pretty well. You will find that Jacobi is in it somewhere."

"But he never goes to Seymour Street!"

"No."

"Does she meet him at other houses?"

Lowe shook his head, and, leaning forward, took his coffee-cup from the mantelpiece. He emptied it at one long slow draught, and proceeded to make himself a second cigarette.

"The singing-lessons," he observed suggestively. After lighting the cigarette he handed the match to Charlie, who had not observed that he had allowed his cigar to go out.

"Then," said the young sailor, slowly and concisely, "the Baroness is in it also?"

Lowe nodded his head, and the ghost of a smile flickered across his face.

"That is how we will get at it," he said.

"Would it be of any use speaking to Lena herself?" asked Charlie, who was a lover of straightforward ways.

Lowe shrugged his shoulders, and continued smoking meditatively.

"Might try," he muttered doubtfully.

Young Mistley

At last Charlie lost patience. He threw his cigar into the fire, and, rising from his seat, stood in front of his host with his " able " arm resting on the mantelpiece.

" I wish," he said, without raising the level tones of his voice, but speaking rather hurriedly, " that you would tell me what you suspect, what you know, and what you wish to know. If we are to help each other, there must be no reticence between us. Of what has been going on during the last year I know absolutely nothing. Mrs. Wright's letters have rarely alluded to . . . Lena. The Colonel never wrote, Lena herself— rarely. My mother has been away in France. You, and you alone, are the only source of information that I have. I need hardly tell you that I am as uneasy about this matter as yourself. All I know is that Lena is different—all I suspect is that her mother is . . . no longer her confidante in everything."

Laurance Lowe looked slowly up into his companion's face, while the hand that held the cigarette shook a little.

" Seen that too ? " he said interrogatively. " All I know is that since she has been taking these lessons there has been something wrong. Before that she was anxious . . . about your brother. We have all been anxious; but now it is something more than anxiety."

" And what do you suspect ? "

" Seems to me that Jacobi has succeeded in establishing some influence over her. The girl is afraid of him."

" Lena goes to this woman's house for the lessons ? " asked Charlie.

" Yes."

" Could we not get that altered ? " suggested the sailor, whose ideas were quick, though his speech was slow.

Young Mistley

"Tried it."

" You *have* tried it; and who objected ? "

" Lena—piano or something."

" Did anyone make inquiries about the Baroness de Nantille before this arrangement was made ? " asked Charlie, who now turned and resumed his seat.

" Yes. She had a long and severe illness. Found, when she got better, that her property, which was all in Russia, had been confiscated, father banished, mother dead. Reduced circumstances, took to giving singing-lessons. She sings like an angel herself."

" And have you done anything about Jacobi ? "

" Lives by teaching violin—has many foreign friends. Eminently respectable; is supposed to be connected with several foreign political societies."

" Um—m—m ! In fact, he is a shady character," suggested the sailor.

" Damned swindler ! "

They sat and talked in the same aggravatingly " unfinished " manner until late into the night. As Lowe's theory gradually expanded under Charles Mistley's patient investigation, it assumed a greater appearance of likelihood. Little details, added suggestively here and there, spoke volumes for the keenness of the old gentleman's powers of observation.

Silent men are not always mental sluggards, and Laurance Lowe was far from being such. He had gradually accumulated evidence bit by bit, and therewith had built up a very neat theory, surprising Charlie with its accuracy and perfect sequence.

He argued that as Mrs. Wright was no wiser than themselves on the subject of Lena's mental trouble, it must consequently be the result of some influence of which she knew nothing. Such influence could only be brought to bear upon Lena during her visits to the house of the Baroness de Nantille. The deduction was ingenious, and Charlie began to feel that Laurance Lowe's theory was, after all, the right one.

"I think you and I can settle Jacobi," the old man said, as he shook hands that night with the young sailor.

It was not until some time later that Charles Mistley recollected that there had been no question of taking Mrs. Wright into their confidence. He wondered at this a little, and then, with characteristic *laisser-aller*, came to the conclusion that Laurance Lowe doubtless had his reasons for it.

CHAPTER XXX

A GRIM silent desert—a great level horizon, lifeless, waterless, hopeless. The sun, a scorching ball of fire, was now almost touching the unbroken line of sand, and yet the heat he gave forth was as strong, as parching, and terribly merciless as that of the hottest autumn noon in England.

It is easy to talk of desert and rolling prairie, but to realize these from even the most graphic description is impossible. To sit by a comfortable fire with friends around one, and to realize the awful loneliness of a desert, is beyond the most far-reaching imagination. The utter silence, the absence of created life, the terrible monotony which seems to speak of an unchangeableness extending over centuries—all these combine to act on the human brain as water acts upon a stone. The continual succession of cloudless mornings, cloudless noons, and cloudless nights is maddening in its serene beauty.

Each scrubby bush becomes at last an object of interest to the dazed traveller, something to be seen ahead, to be attained and left behind; and yet when it is passed, there is no change in the hopeless horizon.

Over the trackless plain, a traveller was plodding painfully. One hand held the bridle of a limping horse, and on the poor brute's back was huddled a human form.

Young Mistley

This sorry cavalcade was steering toward the setting sun, a little to the northward of it.

The man who led the horse was slightly above the medium height; a brown oval face all caked with sand and dirt; his short pointed beard was dull and dusty. The huge turban on his head overshadowed the upper part of his face, and from beneath its shade there looked forth a pair of eyes dark with sullen despair. For two months they had looked upon nought but this same hopeless waste of barren sand. His skin was brown and hard like leather. Immediately beneath his eyes on either cheek was a red patch, where, the sand and dirt having been washed away, the skin was of brilliant red traversed by tiny cracks. These were caused by the constant brushing away of tears slowly drawn from his eyes by the irritation of the finest grains of sand. His slight mustache —brushed straight to either side, after the manner of the Tartars—did not hide his lips, which were almost black and perfectly dry, like the skin of a dusty raisin.

The man walked with the mechanical swing of one who has been on the tramp for many months, and to whom walking is almost as easy as standing.

His foot-gear consisted of two pieces of untanned leather tied roughly over either instep; his wiry legs were bare, as he had looped his garment of soft, unbleached cotton above his knees for greater convenience in walking. His arms, exposed by wide, short sleeves, were brown and muscular; indeed, there was no flesh upon them, merely corded sinews.

As the sun touched the horizon he took from the folds of his dress a small compass, and noted the exact spot where the contact took place. Then he glanced at his companion, but made no remark.

Young Mistley

The man on horseback was of slighter build. He was all huddled up on the saddle, while his chin literally rested on his breast. His turban had come partly unrolled, and the end of it hung down over his face. Both hands grasped the high pommel of the Tartar saddle; his legs swung helplessly with each movement of the horse.

Since sunrise they had been on the march, and the horse, a mere skeleton with flapping ears and ungainly neck, showed fatigue more than the man walking at its side. Every now and then the poor brute stumbled forward as if about to drop from sheer weariness, and on each occasion the rider would slightly raise his head. For some hours perfect silence had fallen over the two men—their blackened lips were so hard and dry as to render articulation nearly impossible.

Suddenly the horse gave a great lurch forward, and, failing to recover himself, collapsed sideways with a piteous groan.

The man at its head dropped the bridle, and with marvellous rapidity slipped his arm round his companion's drooping body.

"Look out, Paul!" he exclaimed hoarsely in Russian.

The rider made no attempt to assist himself, and as the horse fell his full weight came upon his companion, who, however, managed to step back and keep free from the poor brute's dying kicks.

The man on horseback had actually been asleep, and as his companion laid him gently on the warm sand he slowly opened his heavy eyes.

"Little father," he murmured. The corners of his mouth were closed with a deposit of black sand, and his lips hardly moved. The other put aside the loose end of the turban-cloth, and exposed a fair, boyish face with

languishing blue eyes, and a jaw so square as to be almost
a deformity. The sun had burnt the fair skin in some
places, leaving others pale, the result being a fantastic
medley of browns, reds, and pinks.

"Paul!"

"Yes—little father."

"You are better for your sleep—is that not so?"
asked the other kindly.

But the younger man lay still, with his blue eyes half
closed. His mouth was so parched that he could scarcely
move his tongue.

"We will divide what water there is left," said the
elder man decisively. And he turned toward the prostrate horse.

From the saddle he detached a large gourd, which gave
forth a terribly hollow sound, and after some searching
in a loose bag that was suspended from his shoulder, he
found a small drinking-vessel, cunningly manufactured
from half a gourd.

He kept his back carefully turned toward his companion as, kneeling on the ground, he extracted the wooden
stopper.

Then the younger man painfully turned over on his
face, and, crawling along, stealthily approached. As
his companion elevated his arm to raise the gourd he
dragged himself forward, and watched the yellow water
trickle into the vessel with eyes devoid of human feeling—they were like the eyes of a wild beast in sight of
blood.

Slowly and deliberately the man poured all the water
into the little vessel—he appeared to have forgotten the
division of which he had spoken.

In setting down the gourd he glanced to one side, and

caught sight of his companion lying on the ground at his side, with agonized eyes fixed upon the water-vessel.

Then he turned, and for some seconds their eyes met; in one face was steady determination, in the other a wavering weakness, rendered terrible by the brute-like agony of the eyes.

"You drink your share first," said the younger man painfully.

"I do not want any. I . . . I am not thirsty." This with cracking lips and tongue as dry as leather.

The younger man attempted to raise himself, while the contortions of his discolored face were terrible to look upon.

"You drink your share first!" he repeated hoarsely.

"Will you drink it all?" The elder man gently inclined the drinking-cup so that the water glistened on the edge.

"*Will* you drink it all?" he repeated.

One precious drop fell on to the sand, and the dampness of it vanished instantaneously.

"Will you drink . . . it . . . all?"

Then he held the cup to his companion's lips and the water was gone.

He who did that deed to a dying man—beneath no gaze but that of his God—was Winyard Mistley. The young man was his servant.

Now he sat upon the sand and took his servant's head upon his knees. The water loosened the man's tongue.

"Little master," he said presently.

"Yes, Paul."

"I want you to promise something to a dying man."

Mistley made no answer; he gently moved Paul's head to a more comfortable position.

Young Mistley

"When I am dead," said the youth, "take your knife and cut the flesh from off my arm—you must do this—you must keep yourself alive to get home to England, and then you can tell them that Paul Maritch did not die in vain! You can tell the half-hearted ones that a true Nihilist died in joy, because he knew that his dead flesh was destined to keep you alive. You, the enemy of the Tyrant, the true friend of Holy Russia!"

Mistley could not conceal the look of horror that came into his eyes.

"If," he said, in his mumbling articulation, "I went home and told them that tale, every Englishman would turn away from me in horror, saying that it would have been a hundred times better to have left my bones to bleach in the Khivan desert."

The young Russian was half insensible; he could not hear the heavy gasping of the expiring horse a few yards away from him.

Mistley gently let the dying man's head drop on to the sand, and then he rose and stood beside the horse for some moments in silence. He raised his steadfast gray eyes to the heavens, now growing dull and of darker blue—he looked all round the level horizon. It seemed to him as if this were the whole world, and that he was alone in it; as if there was no world of civilization, of comfort, and of luxury.

"It may be brutal, but I think there is no sin in it," he murmured.

Then he knelt down on the sand, and with his knife he killed the horse.

Presently he cut out the tongue, and gave a mouthful of the warm flesh to his servant—he could not yet eat of it himself.

Young Mistley

The cooler air now revived Paul Maritch. He turned his head to where Mistley lay on the sand at his side.

The Englishman heard the movement, and crawled closer to him.

"It is coming . . . it is coming!" whispered the Russian.

Then Mistley roused himself.

"Paul, this is not like you," he said cheerfully, but it was a ghastly cheerfulness—"this is not like you. Where is your determination? Where is your hope? After a good long rest, we will move on; I am strong enough to help you. Who knows—we may see the river by sunrise to-morrow."

"I shall never see the sun rise again, little father."

"Nonsense, Paul! We will pull through yet. It is a strong combination—a Russian and an Englishman—so strong that we have always fought on different sides hitherto."

The Russian moistened his lips slowly and painfully with his tongue.

"Why did you take me?" he asked plaintively. "I was not good enough for you; I was not strong enough. For the last month I have been a burden to you instead of a help. I used to consider myself a strong man; but compared to your strength, to your energy, to your courage, I am as a fly. Ah, Mistley—the time has gone now for the nonsense of master and servant! You guessed my secret when you first offered to take me as guide, but you never guessed my real name. It seems strange, does it not, that the two men whose names are more hateful and more fearful to that . . . *devil* than the name of any other living man, should die side by side in the desert? Stoop low and I will whisper my name, for fear the heavens hear it. Do not start, for it is a name that curdles the blood of every honest man; and yet I have been honest. From first to last I have been honest. This is the last, and now, with the hand of Death upon me, I say, there is no God!"

"Hush, Paul! You need not tell me your name. I know who you are now."

"It is all very well for you in happy England," continued the other, "to say there is a God; for our country there is none."

"If you do not cease, I will go and leave you," said Mistley. To hear the rattle of the man's breath, as he gathered strength to utter these words, was a terrible experience.

"Mistley," whispered the dying man after a pause.

"Yes, Paul."

"If you live through this, never let them know that I am dead. Let the burden of my existence weigh on *his* mind. While *he* thinks I am alive, he will never know a moment's peace. Let this be my legacy to the man who made me what I am!"

Winyard Mistley crouched on the sand in silence. He had an Englishman's awkward shyness of mentioning the name of God in other sense than exclamatory, and yet he shivered to think that this man was really dying in his arms with blasphemy on his rigid lips.

Suddenly a sense of chilliness assailed him. Mechanically he touched the prostrate man's brow.

"Good . . . God . . . he is dead!"

Then he rose painfully to his feet. The silence of that great waste of desert was almost unbearable. Five men out of six would have gone mad in those first moments of realization. Winyard Mistley pressed his forehead

with his hands, now cold and damp. His stern eyes
slowly scanned the horizon—it was almost dark.   In the
sky, away to the east, was a shade of pearly-yellow.   This
was the soft promise of the moon yet below the horizon.
Mechanically the solitary man turned toward it.   Presently on the hard black line of the horizon there appeared
a fan-like glow of shimmering yellow, narrowing into
silver rays; then a tiny spark of light ever broadening.
With a flood of glory the great globe slowly mounted, till
its lower edge parted with the line of distant desert.

The scene was too majestic, too awful, and too lovely
for words.

It almost reconciled Mistley to the death which seemed
inevitable.

He turned and glanced at the prostrate form of Paul
Maritch, with its cold and relentless face turned silently
toward the God Whom he denied.

"If he could have lived a few moments longer to see
that, he would not have died with those words upon his
lips," he murmured vaguely.

Then his thoughts wandered away.   A rush of memories came over him, and sapped at his courage as running water saps at a stone pillar.

"If I could only think of something else," he muttered, pressing his weary temples.   "If I could only see
something else than her eyes . . ."

He slowly raised his face, and again scanned the hopeless desert around him.

Suddenly his gaze remained riveted on one spot to the
west of him.

"What is that?" he mumbled stupidly; "what *is*
that?"

Slowly, like a stricken tree, he collapsed, falling forward on his face, with his arms stretched across the dead body of Paul Maritch.

For an hour he lay thus. At last he recovered consciousness and awoke, as he had ever done from sleep, with every sense on the alert.

First he stood up and gazed fixedly to the west, along the white track of moonlight which extended to the very edge of the horizon; then he balanced himself on the dead body of the horse, and so increased his spread of vision. Across the broad line of light cast by the moon on the sand was a tiny silver streak.

"Yes, that is the river!" said Mistley. "My luck has not forsaken me, and his bad fortune has followed him to the very end!"

Mechanically Winyard Mistley scooped out a shallow grave, and gently laid therein the remains of his desperate companion, before he left the spot.

The peaceful moon looked down that night on the grim desert, and saw one of the finest and wholesomest sights to be seen on earth; ay, finer and wholesomer than the fairest woman ever seen. That sight was a brave man fighting doggedly, quietly and wittingly against odds so disproportionate as to render one sceptical regarding all things Providential.

CHAPTER XXXI

THE following season happened to be a gay one, and among the gayest was Lena Wright. She went out with her father and mother; she went out with her mother's sister —Lady Allron. She went anywhere, with anyone, and appeared to be suffering from an insatiable thirst for change and novelty. No number of dances tired her, no partner wearied her by dancing through from beginning to end.

The good dancers liked her because she danced beautifully, and never confessed to fatigue. She made a serious affair of it, as they did, and was not bored by silence; for the accomplished ones talk little when once the music has commenced—the smooth poetic motion, the quick obedience to their slightest signal, is enough for them. The bashful young men were devoted to her, for with them she was girlish and as unsophisticated as themselves. The staid and hopelessly selfish old bachelors admired her, because she laughed readily enough at their egotistical little jokes. And last of all, the matrons did not hate her, because, forsooth, her programme was at the disposal of the new-fledged youth with split gloves as heartily as if each had been the lion of the evening. She set her cap at no one, she was reliable and merry; and she appeared to like everyone, while in reality she was very near to despising them all with an impartial and large-minded contempt.

Young Mistley

Young ladies, however, did not take to her as a rule. They explained vaguely that they did not understand her, which in the ears of some cynical men amounted to a confession of inferiority. With them she was always sweet and kind, for Lena was of that self-reliant material which (brine it as you may), like mutton, refuses to be salted. She listened with an interested little smile to their vapid boasts of conquests made, of impressions created and hearts sore afflicted, but she never had similar experiences to relate.

There was one among the hard-working pleasure-seekers whom Lena did not despise. Indeed, she did not actually despise any of them; what she felt was more a sense of pity vaguely tempered with wonder that the clever and undoubtedly brilliant people around her should be content to fritter away their intellects in the unprofitable pursuit of pleasure. This one exception had no individual excuse. He was as frivolous, as objectless, and as lazy as any of them, but then Charlie, dear old Charlie, was different from other people. He could not be measured satisfactorily by the common standard.

The young sailor's club knew him no longer. His tailor received an order for a remarkably large suit of dress-clothes, of the latest material, constructed upon the newest principles. His huge Saxon frame was to be met with everywhere. It towered over one upon crowded stairs; it insinuated itself into the tiniest drawing-room, with that wonderful power of contraction which is so soon acquired in a crowded city.

Some weeks had elapsed since Laurance Lowe's dinner-party, and Charlie had not wasted his time. He had reassumed his old position in the Seymour Street household. The circle of visitors there had somewhat changed in his absence, as he soon discovered. This was the natural result of the Colonel's presence. Like all specialists, the old traveller was much sought after by his kind. Eastern authorities of every age and nationality sought him out, and with these rugged and sunburnt wanderers the Colonel loved to travel again over far-off deserts, comparing notes, asking and receiving hints. Gradually his house came to be recognized as the headquarters of the party designated "alarmist." Among these experts it soon became a semi-official secret that Winyard Mistley was "out there," and a few were taken into further confidence and allowed to share the Colonel's anxiety at his long silence. As Winyard's brother, Charlie found himself of some importance among these ancient luminaries of Eastern diplomacy. Thus he occupied a double post in the household. Firstly, as the Colonel's friend; secondly, as Lena's attendant knight wheresoever she might be pleased to go.

Through it all, like an undercurrent, ran the thread of his own diplomatic task. From Lena he had learnt nothing, but one important step had been made in the right direction. He had renewed his acquaintance with the Baroness de Nantille. She had even been invited to the Wrights' at his suggestion, upon which occasion he had with imperturbable calmness devoted himself to entertaining her, until he discovered that Lena was beginning to notice it. Laurance Lowe had been present on this occasion, as on others when the Baroness and Charlie were thrown together, and very little that passed was lost by him.

There were many drawing-rooms in London to which Mrs. Mistley and her sons had the *entrée*, and where they could be sure of a welcome; and now Charlie suddenly began to take advantage of this privilege. Wherever Lena went, he was sure to appear during the evening. At dull geographical and learned soirées he usually put in an appearance—very late, but by no means disturbed, for it had come to be an understood thing that Lena should accord a smiling *congé* to any bumptious and self-satisfied young explorer who might be by her side when the young sailor appeared.

These same young explorers (a growth of the present generation) afforded a fund of amusement to Lena and her family. They were so terribly prolific in print, and so lamentably dull in society. Their productions were so invariably more to the credit of the British bookbinding industry than to that of literature, and they were so desperately generous with presentation copies, duly signed with an inky flourish upon the fly-leaf. Such volumes were constantly arriving in Seymour Street, and Lena soon realized the fact that, though one may desire to see the author after having read a book, it is rarely satisfactory to read a work upon the strength of having met its author. In fact, she usually experienced a strong disinclination to cut the pages of a volume of which she had never heard until its writer had forced it under her notice. Unfortunately for the modern tribe of scribbling travellers, the human frame is so constructed that the size of a man's heart must remain a profound secret; and the ordinary observer is compelled to make his observations upon the basis of the frame itself. Now, most of these gentry are, by some humorous freak of Nature, endowed with a diminutive person; and Lena—a Northumbrian—sweet and tall herself, and accustomed to look up to men, could not succeed in making heroes of these mighty huntsmen (more accustomed to the smell of a proof-sheet than to the glorious odor of burnt powder), and withheld that admiration and respect to which they considered themselves fully entitled.

At balls Charles Mistley, who was nothing if not methodical, danced three times with Lena, and took Mrs. Wright down to supper. Then he rescued his mother, and went home to Bedford Place behind a very small cigar, which form of tobacco appears to be much affected by big men, as large pipes are by their smaller brethren.

Of course people talked about his devotion to Lena, adding to it or detracting from it according to the requirements of their purpose, as is the kindly custom of us all. The Colonel saw it, and shrugged his shoulders. Mrs. Wright saw it, and understood it not; but she watched more closely, and, strange to say, the pleasant friendship existing between her and the young sailor grew in warmth of mutual trust. Laurance Lowe saw it, and grew uneasy.

When anyone spoke to Charles Mistley on the subject, either with the bantering bluntness of a man or the dangerous innocence of a woman, he smiled his good-natured, lazy smile, which might mean much and usually meant nothing, leaving his questioner more puzzled than before.

If any woman took the trouble of placing Lena in such a position that some remark was absolutely necessary, she would say, "Oh yes, I like him *very* much," and then would continue the subject with an unconscious frankness which was vastly puzzling.

To the disinterested observer it would appear that these two young persons were drifting into something more than friendship; but the observations of that fabulous person are proverbially unreliable.

Young Mistley

No one knows better than the writer of these humble lines that a friendship—a perfectly *safe* friendship—cannot exist for long between young people of a different sex who are entirely unconnected by ties of blood. A man can be a true friend to the end of the chapter—to his female cousin. Beyond that the water is of uncertain depth, with shifting shoals and unmarked channels. Navigation thereon is dangerous—a collision would probably occur, resulting in serious damage to one or both vessels. Or one might run aground, while the other could only tack and wear and drift around, not daring to venture too close for fear of stranding on the same rock.

It would appear, however, that Lena and her large friend knew very well what they were about. At that time she needed someone, and the sailor seemed to slip naturally into the vacant place. They never overstepped the boundaries of friendship, and only once did they come near to so doing.

It came about one evening, and took them both a little by surprise. Lena, who made a point of watching the chaperons dance the Lancers, had no partner; and Charlie, who said he had not enough conversation for "that trying performance," came and sat beside her. They secured a pleasant corner, and for some time watched the dancers without speaking. In the set nearest to them was an engaged couple of youthful appearance. These two behaved after the manner of their kind; meeting, for instance, at the end of the ladies' chain as if the separation had been a matter of weary years.

Lena and her companion naturally observed this couple. Presently Charlie murmured vaguely:

"That sort of thing makes me feel inclined to cry."

Lena laughed gayly.

"Please don't," she said, with a great show of anxiety. "It might be embarrassing."

He laughed in his low, quiet way; and then, suddenly looking grave, he continued to watch the young couple lazily.

"I do not feel inclined to cry," continued Lena, in a graver tone; "but I should like to throw something at him—it is so weak and unmanly."

"I suppose we all pass through it . . ."

"It is to be hoped, for her sake, that he will pass through it pretty soon; and remember that he is a man, with a man's work to do."

"We . . . are severe," murmured Charlie innocently.

"Now confess," said Lena, suddenly facing him— "confess that your feelings are . . . contempt for him, and pity for her."

"Yes . . ." he answered slowly. "I suppose you are right—and yet . . ."

"And yet?"

"Perhaps I was once like that myself."

"Oh no!" she exclaimed with conviction.

"Who knows?" he said quietly.

There was something in the tone of his voice that made her turn to glance at his face. He was carelessly following the delicate tracery of flowers upon his programme with the atrocious pencil attached thereto. He contemplated his handiwork with his head upon one side for some moments, apparently with much satisfaction; then he looked up, and his calm eyes met hers with a little smile.

"I am dismal to-night," he said. "A brute of a

sailor-man gave me a strong cigar this afternoon, and strong cigars always make me dismal.''

But Lena failed to smile. She merely sat and looked at him speculatively. Charlie did not appear quite happy under her gentle scrutiny. By way of doing something, he leant toward her, and borrowed her fan, which he tried for some time to open the wrong way. While he was still attempting this dangerous feat, he continued:

''So you must please remember that it is not all natural density—it is partly cigar.''

Like most big men, he rarely smiled, and never frowned, which made it very difficult at times to say whether he spoke seriously or not.

''I wonder,'' said Lena speculatively . . . ''I *often* wonder why you so invariably try to misrepresent yourself—especially to me.''

He looked up with a twinkle of genuine amusement in his eyes.

''You think, I suppose, that it is my duty to make the best of a bad bargain.''

''*Is* it a bad bargain? ''

He shrugged his shoulders. With the fan he indicated the dancers before them.

''Give them all little slips of paper and programme pencils,'' he said. ''Take a ballot—good bargain or bad bargain—and what would the result be ? ''

She ignored this suggestion, and sat meditating for some moments.

''There is something,'' she said at length, ''wanting in your life. You do not look at things in a proper light. I think you want an object—something to be attained, something to try for, even if you fail.''

"Please," interrupted the young sailor, "do not look so serious—it is not worth your while."

"And," she continued, with a sudden change of manner, from grave to gay, "I know what it is."

"By George—do you? I am glad to hear it. Kindly prescribe at once."

"What you require," she said solemnly, "is someone very nice to fall in love with. I cannot think of anyone exactly suitable at the present moment, but . . . I will keep the matter before me."

"Is that all?" he asked in a tone expressive of great disappointment. "Your remedy is too simple to be of much use. Also, I have a strong argument against it—sailors should not marry, on principle. They should wait till they are old men, and then marry their housekeepers."

"Principles and generalities are to be avoided," observed Lena gravely.

"Well, if you do not approve of that argument, I can take up another. Suppose that you see in me an interesting young man with a story. Suppose I am a blighted being who has loved in vain, for whom life has no charms, existence no attraction. Suppose there is beneath this immaculate waistcoat a dried-up article which can never love again. . . . How about your object in life then?"

Lena did not reply at once. While watching the dancers, she was slowly opening and closing her fan. When she at length spoke, she deliberately ignored his bantering tone, and said gravely:

"I should be very sorry . . . to suppose all that."

"Why?"

"Because I should prefer to continue believing that you are different . . . from the rest."

With her glance she indicated a group of men idling near the door.

"It does not pay, in these days, to be different from the rest. Better pass through with the crowd."

"And," continued Lena, "it would not apply to you. If you really wanted a thing, I think you would get it—in an indifferent, lazy way."

Charles Mistley glanced up into her face, and then, slipping his programme into his waistcoat-pocket, he rose with a sudden access of energy and offered his arm.

"They have finished," he said in a matter-of-fact tone. "Let us stroll about and allow someone else to sit down."

CHAPTER XXXII

LAURANCE LOWE and Charles Mistley were not cursed with the conspirator's vice of too much talk and too little action. From the evening when they had first laid their heads together until some weeks afterward, no word passed between them relative to Lena or Monsieur Jacobi. The subject was by mutual understanding allowed to drop, though it was ever to the fore in either mind.

However, one evening when they were walking home together from what was modestly called a musical soirée, Charlie unearthed the subject. The evening had been a dull one. Lowe and his young companion had undoubtedly been sorely out of their element, and both knew that their presence at the entertainment was due to the fact that the Wrights had been there. Lena had sung once —beautifully and simply, as was her wont. And the Baroness de Nantille had obliged the assembled multitude three times. Her splendid voice had been greatly assisted by the artistic violin obbligato of Monsieur Jacobi.

"I did not get much farther on to-night," said the young sailor, as he stopped beneath a lamp-post to light his cigar.

Lowe, with his hands pushed deep into the pockets of a loose top-coat, and an ancient opera-hat tilted rather forward over his eyes, stopped also, and watched the delicate operation.

"Couldn't be expected," he said rather indistinctly, by reason of the cigarette between his lips.

"With Jacobi there, you mean?"

"Um—m."

"Did you observe that he took no notice of any of our party?"

"Overdid it."

"How?"

"We came in late," said Lowe. "It was unnatural not to look up."

They walked on, smoking pensively, and on the deserted pavement their steps rang out like the tread of one foot.

"I have followed up your hint," said Charlie; "and I think you are right—Jacobi is mixed up in it somewhere."

"Slippery customer," muttered Lowe.

"I have brought all my . . . irresistible . . . powers of fascination to bear upon the Baroness, but somehow I do not get on very rapidly. I cannot understand her—she is extremely changeable. At times she is most gracious, and then suddenly she seems to become distrustful. However, in one of her gracious moods she may make a mistake, some day, and then . . ."

Lowe took the cigarette from his lips, and after a pause he said:

"There is one way of . . . working it."

"Yes?"

"Make love to her."

"That is not much in my line of country," said the sailor, with rather an awkward laugh.

"Don't think you would find it difficult."

"What do you mean?" asked Charlie slowly.

"She would be quite ready."

The big sailor blushed—privately, to himself—a dull brick-red beneath the sunburn which he had not yet lost. He was rather fond of underrating himself; but this might after all explain one or two little peculiarities in the Baroness's manner toward himself. There was almost an apology conveyed in Lowe's voice when he spoke again.

"It's a beastly task to set a fellow, but . . . cannot do it myself, you know. We're in it now; we must go on, and . . . and Lena is worth it. I turn off here . . . g'night!"

Charles Mistley stared vacantly at the receding figure. How well he knew it! How familiar to him was every little trick of speech, every slow movement, every glance! There was no variety in Laurance Lowe; and as the young fellow stood watching the bent head and upright form, a strange sense of monotony came over him. The very words still ringing in his ears were such as the old man had used on a hundred previous occasions: "I turn off here . . . g'night." Simply stating the fact, and expressing no suggestion of regret that their ways should separate. Then the quick pressure of his waxen fingers, accompanied by a little forward inclination of the body. It was all so old . . . so desperately familiar. And yet how little . . . how pitifully little . . . did he know of the real man! The heart beneath that loosely-fitting coat, and the brain under the jaunty yet pathetic old opera-hat, were alike closed and illegible. Who could say what echoes of a bygone time, what shadows of a former existence, flitted through that fallow mind?

The forlorn old man, as he walked rapidly through the deserted streets, was a monument to the memory of Love, Hope, and Ambition—dead years ago, and buried.

Charlie was for a moment prompted to run after him, to walk with him, and conduct him safely to his own door, but he hesitated, and it was too late. The lone old fellow did not ask such little attentions; they would have surprised him, and probably he would prefer being left alone.

"I wonder," said the young sailor to himself, as he turned and walked quickly in the opposite direction, "I wonder if I will ever come to that!"

Laurance Lowe's cold-blooded suggestion bore rapid fruit. The following afternoon Charles Mistley called at the house where the Baroness de Nantille had for the time taken rooms. This was in an unfrequented street leading eastward from Portland Place. As the young sailor turned the corner into Duke Street, he descried the graceful figure of Monsieur Jacobi at the far end, going in the opposite direction. This caused him to slacken his pace so as to allow the violinist time to get round the corner before he rang the bell of number thirty-seven.

The Baroness was at home. Charles Mistley gave his name, and after a short delay was requested to step up-stairs. As he entered the drawing-room, she rose from a seat near the window to greet him, but did not advance a single step.

In deference to her foreign custom, the young Englishman bowed without offering his hand. He noticed that the Baroness was perfectly self-possessed, although very pale. Then he broke the momentary silence without displaying the least sign of embarrassment or hesitation:

"Miss Wright is not here?" he said quietly.

"No."

"But this is her day, is it not, madame?"

"No; she comes to me to-morrow."

"Ah—I have deranged you for nothing, then. I thought I would find Miss Wright here. I wished to tell her that I have received seats for a theatre to-night . . ."

He made a movement as if he would go, then he appeared to change his mind.

"I have never had an opportunity, madame," he said, "of expressing my sympathy. Since I had the pleasure of meeting you last year, you have had a great misfortune, I believe."

The Baroness bowed her beautiful head and resumed her seat with a peculiar smoothness of action, motioning her visitor to sit down at the same time.

"You are very kind," she said in a low voice, expressive of greater emotion than the occasion would seem to demand. "I have passed through certain misfortunes . . . too long to narrate even to such a patient listener as yourself."

Charlie had not accepted her invitation to seat himself. Instead of so doing he advanced toward the window, and was leaning against the woodwork, looking down at her.

"I was not aware," he said, "until just lately that you had the misfortune to be a Russian subject. Anyone of that nationality is interesting to me, as you are perhaps aware. My father was connected with Russia for many years, and now my brother . . . has followed in his footsteps."

Lower and lower the fair head was bent over the motionless hands, which lay upon her simple dress with a peculiar stillness; but the Baroness made no reply.

"But I do not wish to awaken disagreeable memories, madame; all I desire is to express my sympathy and my readiness to be of any service to you. It is the least an Englishman can do in his own country, which is not exactly renowned for its sympathy toward strangers."

The Baroness raised her head, but she did not look at him. She appeared to be studying the pattern of the dingy lace curtain. Her companion saw her eyelids quiver for a moment—then she spoke in her smooth monotone.

"Do not call me—'madame,'" she said. "I am not . . . madame. I took my mother's title for the sake of convenience, in London."

Ah, Mother Eve! How many neat little plots hast thou demolished! How often hast thou, by the sudden raising of thy restless tongue, upset the completest schemes ever woven by human brain!

Charles Mistley looked down at her without betraying the least sign of surprise; but he changed color slightly.

"That only makes your claim upon my services the stronger," he said, after a pause.

The Baroness bowed her head silently, and said:

"Monsieur, I have no claim upon your services. On the contrary, you are the last Englishman to whom I should apply in case I required assistance!"

"I do not understand . . ."

"You will do so, however, when I tell you that my real name is Marie Bakovitch."

"Marie . . . Bakovitch!" repeated the Englishman slowly—"Marie . . . Bakovitch!"

She raised her cold blue eyes to his, watching keenly the effect of the revelation she had just made.

"Then," she said, "your brother has told you?"

"No—Colonel Wright told me."

"And now do you understand why I can claim no disinterested service from you?"

"No," he said simply.

She laughed, a little short laugh that would have been harsh had her voice not been wonderfully melodious.

"You Englishmen—are so aggravatingly chivalrous," she said. "With us it is different—women are nearer to the men in Russia."

"I do not understand, mademoiselle," said the young sailor gravely, "why you have told me this."

"No?" She raised her eyes to his again. He would have been blind had he not understood what he read there. "It is a long story," she continued, "and . . . perhaps an old one. Also, it is not cheerful, for it is the story of a mistake."

"Tell it to me," he said quietly.

"Eighteen months ago, immediately after your brother left England, I had a long and serious illness. Through it I was nursed by my maid—a child of sixteen, assisted by my . . . friend, Ivan Meyer. When I recovered sufficiently to take an interest in life I learnt from him that he was impatiently awaiting the moment when he could leave me to return to Russia. There had been in my native town a reign of terror, and among the first to be arrested on suspicion was my father—a noted loyalist, a faithful Government servant. It is thus . . . monsieur . . . that Nihilists are made."

"Then," said the Englishman, "you have changed."

"Yes, I have changed."

"I am sorry for it."

"Why?"

"Because," said Charlie, "it brings you into contact with such men as Monsieur Jacobi."

Marie Bakovitch looked up sharply, but he avoided meeting her eyes.

"What do you know of Monsieur Jacobi?"

Charlie shrugged his broad shoulders contemptuously.

"Nothing, mademoiselle."

"But you *hate* him."

"Well . . . scarcely. I have never had the necessary energy to hate anyone yet. I do not like him."

"It is of Jacobi," continued the girl, "that I have to tell; it is against him that I must ask your help. Remember, I do not ask it for myself, for I do not fear him. It is for Lena Wright . . ."

Marie Bakovitch looked up somewhat suddenly. She met her companion's eyes, calm, impassive, and inscrutable as usual, fixed upon her face.

"Yes," he said; "go on."

"He is connected with several secret societies, political and otherwise. Notably the 'Brotherhood of Liberty,' of which he pretends to be the London chief. For some months he has been scheming to obtain money from Lena Wright for the purposes of the Brotherhood."

"I thought money would come in somewhere."

"Yes, all Jacobi's plots are connected with money sooner or later. He heard from sources unknown to me that she will be comparatively rich some day, and he has been endeavoring to persuade her to borrow this money; it is a large sum."

"You have not told me what hold he has over her."

"He has represented that the Brotherhood has agencies

and connections all over the world, and by these means
he could, with the aid of a certain sum of ready money,
obtain immediate information as to the safety, or otherwise, of your . . . brother Winyard. She . . . I think
. . . she . . .''

"Yes," said Charlie gravely, "I understand . . .
But how did he get to know of this? . . . he has surely
had no opportunity . . .''

"He learnt it from me."

"From you? You said just now that you did not fear
him."

"Not now. He can do nothing now—now that I . . .
that you . . .''

"Ah!" said the Englishman compassionately, "I
understand. He has been threatening you with the dis-
closure of your real name. You need not have feared
that, mademoiselle. No one except my brother could
have harmed you, and you have misjudged him if you
thought that he would do anything unmanly or . . .
cowardly!''

She sat before him on a low chair. Her face was hidden from him, and as he looked down upon her he could
only see the soft coils of flaxen hair and the white curve
of her neck. But he heard the long-drawn, sobbing
breath; he saw the quick rise of her shoulders. Assuredly he read these signs aright. No man with a tithe of
Charles Mistley's intelligence could have been so blind,
so cruelly blind, unless the blindness were intentional.

"It was not that, monsieur," she murmured, in little
more than a whisper.

He stood there motionless and strong as ever man was
created, but there passed across his face a momentary
twinge of real physical pain. Suddenly he roused him-

self with an effort, and said with a practical, matter-of-fact energy:

" Mademoiselle, we must waste no time. I am deeply grateful—more grateful than ever I can hope to express —for the confidence you have placed in me. You said just now that . . . Jacobi pretends to be the London chief of this Brotherhood; have you doubts about the truth of his assertion ? "

" Yes; I know that such a Society exists, and that its headquarters are in Rotterdam; but I believe Jacobi is no member of it. He has represented himself to be its chief, simply for the purpose of obtaining money. He has, in fact, deceived us all."

"Thank you. May I ask when you next assemble ? "

" To-morrow afternoon in this room, and Miss Wright is to be present as a probationary member—three o'clock is the hour."

"To-morrow at three. Thank you. You may leave everything to me, mademoiselle. I have a friend—Laurance Lowe—who is a journalist of some repute. He will doubtless know about this ' Brotherhood of Liberty '— the real one, I mean. I will endeavor to do everything in as quiet and . . . seamanlike . . . a manner as I can. I will see you to-morrow afternoon."

With a bow he left her, walking slowly as though allowing her time to call him back if she had so desired. But she remained motionless, and did not even return his formal salutation.

Through the open window came the sound of his firm footstep on the pavement below, dying away in the perspective of sound that travelled over the grimy roofs in one continuous roar of life from Oxford Street, and the neighboring busy haunts of men.

Young Mistley

The dull, smoky twilight came on apace. The red glow faded into purple, and imperceptibly assumed a neutral gray at last. Still Marie Bakovitch sat there with bowed head and lifeless eyes. No murmur of complaint passed her level lips, no sigh rose within her bosom. She merely sat there without appearing to think or reason—sat and endured with that strange, pathetic, *dumb* endurance which is the curse of the Slavonic race.

CHAPTER XXXIII

Lena's singing-lesson the following afternoon was interrupted by the arrival of Monsieur Jacobi. This gentleman was accompanied by his friend Mr. Ryan, a keen-eyed individual, who was ever ready to espouse the cause of the oppressed of every nationality, provided there was money to be made and little risk attaching. Presently a feeble-minded English lady of uncertain age arrived, and immediately behind her a mild-mannered German gentleman of short sight and unkempt hair.

This was the first time Lena had met the members of the Brotherhood of Liberty, and she was divided between an inclination to laugh and a desire to run away. But everybody was desperately serious. Monsieur Jacobi was suave and gentlemanly as usual, but not entirely at his ease. His hold over the Baroness de Nantille, as she was still called, had never been very secure, and he instinctively felt that it was slipping from him day by day. However, the man was possessed of a certain superficial courage—a type of bravery which shines in the presence of women, but goes no distance among men.

There was just enough mystery in the proceedings to content the English maiden lady and the short-sighted Teuton without unnecessarily aggravating the Baroness. When all were seated, not at a table, but round the room, without formality, Monsieur Jacobi began speaking:

Young Mistley

"I have considered it necessary," he said, "to call the London branch of this Brotherhood together, for the purpose of deciding a question of some importance. It is usual for myself and Secretary Ryan to decide such minor questions as may arise, but we feel that this is beyond our jurisdiction."

Here Monsieur Jacobi paused, and assumed a demeanor expressive of some hesitation in the choice of words necessary to proceed with a somewhat difficult task. The German gentleman took the opportunity of ejaculating "Goot!" which monosyllable was allowed to pass unnoticed. The English lady gazed admiringly with the weakest of eyes at the speaker, and rubbed her yellow hands nervously together. Secretary Ryan lay back in his chair, looking intensely business-like and practical. Lena began to feel that she was in what Charlie would call a "mess"; but, like her mother, she was endowed with a certain amount of pluck, and she waited patiently, glancing occasionally at the Baroness's scornful face.

"I need not tell you," continued Monsieur Jacobi, with some emotion, "that our movements are again hampered by the poverty of the Brotherhood. It is the old, sad story. The rich oppress us by their very riches. Against this demon we fight in vain. And yet, who can say that it *is* in vain? Is it for nothing that we work? Is it for nothing that those of us who possess certain means give what we have to the cause?"

"Goot!" observed the German, who was penniless.

"No; let us go on with our work, and hope that in the fulness of time—perhaps when none of us are left to witness it—the fruit may grow and ripen. It is enough for us to know that while assisting our poorer brethren, we are sowing the glorious seeds of liberty."

"Hear, hear!" said Secretary Ryan. He always said "hear, hear," after the word "liberty."

"And now—*now* at the moment when we are almost paralyzed by the want of funds, one among us has come forward willingly and nobly with open hands. My friends, are we to accept this generous gift? It is to answer this question that I have called you together. I do not desire to bias you in either direction. Heaven knows we want the money badly; we all know to what good use it will be put. But are we to lose sight of the fact that it must necessarily be obtained with some secrecy? Are we to overlook the possibility of misunderstanding, of misconception, that will hang over our own heads? My friends . . . I will say no more; my opinion must not be permitted to influence your decision."

"No, no," cried Ryan; "let us have your opinion."

Monsieur Jacobi hesitated for some time. He even succeeded in looking bashful. Lena glanced at the Baroness, and saw that her eyes were fixed on the door.

"Well . . ." began Jacobi. "If it is your wish I will speak. Now—listen to me——"

At this moment the door opened, and Charles Mistley entered the room, alone. In one comprehensive glance he took in the situation, noting the position of every person in the room. He closed the door, and stood with his back against it.

"No," he said imperturbably. "Listen to *me!*"

Jacobi half rose from his seat, and then sank back again with rather a sickly smile. Ryan made no movement whatever, but his unhealthy face assumed an ashen-gray. The maiden lady and the German sat gazing weakly at the stalwart intruder. Noiselessly the Baroness rose from her seat, and crossed the room to where Lena sat; and there she stood, waiting.

Lena felt that the whole situation was intensely funny from an observer's point of view; but unfortunately she was an actor in the comedy, which sadly altered the matter. However, Charles Mistley had too much tact to treat the affair jocosely. He looked gravely round him, and then spoke in a deliberately authoritative voice, which recalled to Lena's memory a half-forgotten remark of Laurance Lowe's, to the effect that Charlie was essentially a foul-weather sailor.

"I am sorry," he said, "to disturb matters, but . . . I think Monsieur Jacobi knows who I am. If he should require any explanation he knows where to find me . . ."

Jacobi shrugged his shoulders indifferently, while Ryan watched him furtively.

"Will you come with me now?" continued Mistley, addressing Lena.

There was a sad lack of dramatic effect about the whole affair. No one jumped to his feet and drew a firearm from his breast-pocket. There was no need for the sailor to assume a defiant attitude, and hurl back his assailants. In fact, the proceedings were decidedly tame. Charles Mistley not only succeeded in performing his task quietly and in a seamanlike manner, as he had promised, but went farther, and rendered the whole affair a lamentably dull incident. This is to be regretted; the loss, great though it may be to the world in general, is essentially one affecting the chronicler of these events. So much might have been made of it. What pictures might have been drawn of the huge mariner, barricaded by such movable pieces of furniture as he could lay hands on, standing in front of the trembling Lena, brandishing a chair over the muddled head of the short-sighted German! Bullets might have been made to bury themselves in the woodwork of the door, and . . . ah! glorious inspiration—Marie Bakovitch might effectively have been removed from the scene by the simple means of a revolver-bullet aimed at Charles Mistley's heart, but intercepted by her fair breast! The whole thing would have illustrated so well—what a chance for the artist commissioned with the design for a yellow-back!

The thought is a sad one; but Truth trims her lamp so well that the poorest writer must perforce keep to the path. The lives of most of us would not, it is to be feared, illustrate very well. Many of us would find it hard to provide a suitable and attractive incident for the cover. And, again, few of us are called upon to assist at the sudden demise of such persons as are hateful to us, or in our way, at the precise moment when such an event would wind up the second volume satisfactorily.

Nothing of a dramatic nature occurred. Lena rose from her seat, and crossing the room, she stood beside Charlie, experiencing a sudden sense of comfort and relief at the mere contact of his sleeve, which touched her shoulder.

"I do not know," said Charlie to the assembled Brotherhood, "and it is not my business to inquire, who is implicated in this swindle, and who among you are dupes; but it may be of some interest to you to learn that that man . . . there . . . Jacobi—is a common swindler. He is no more the London chief of the Brotherhood of Liberty than I am. Such a society exists, and I have been in communication with the authorities at its headquarters in Rotterdam. It has transpired that Jacobi was once a clerk in their office; and they are at present somewhat anxious for his address, with a view to the recovery of some funds which he, by mistake, removed from their cash-box, and omitted to restore. It is only fair to you, Monsieur Jacobi, to inform you that in the course of my inquiries I am afraid the Brotherhood must have learnt that you are in London."

Then he opened the door, and by way of intimating to Lena to pass out in front of him, he touched her arm slightly. It was not his habit to do this, as it is with some men. Not even with his mother did he ever indulge in such harmless familiarities. Lena noted the little touch, and somehow, to her, it said much that Charlie never allowed to appear in his intercourse with her. There was a sense of protection, a hint, as it were, of brotherly affection and reliability in this rare exhibition of feeling, slight though the indication of it might be.

At the head of the stairs he stopped.

"You will find Mr. Lowe down-stairs," he said. "I must go back and see after the Baroness. Walk on slowly toward Bedford Place; I will catch you up. My mother expects us all to afternoon tea, as arranged yesterday."

He watched her descend the stairs, and heard Laurance Lowe come forward to meet her; then he turned, and coolly reëntered the room where the so-called Brotherhood was still assembled.

With a vague feeling of unreality Lena passed out of the house with Laurance Lowe. Mechanically she noticed a sturdy, sailor-like man walking slowly past the house. This son of the Deep assumed such an exceedingly innocent air of exaggerated non-recognition at the sight of Laurance Lowe, that had Lena had her usual

keenness of observation at command, she could not have
failed to detect that he was connected with Charlie's seamanlike manœuvre.

Lowe said nothing for some minutes. He walked
slowly by the girl's side in unemotional silence. Before
they had gone many yards Lena stopped short.

"Has Charlie gone back," she said, with sudden realization of it all, "into . . . that room alone?"

"Yes," replied Lowe. "He will catch us up presently."

She made a little movement as if to retrace her footsteps.

"But . . . but," she exclaimed, "we cannot let him
do that! There are three men . . ."

"It is all right," said Lowe, walking on; "Charlie
knows the sort of men he has to deal with."

Nevertheless, he glanced back at the corner of the
street to see if Charlie had come out of the house yet.

They walked on together. There were a hundred
questions Lena wished to ask, but she was restrained by
a feeling of humiliation or shyness. Lowe appeared to
be in no hurry to explain matters. To judge from his
manner, it would appear that Lena had just come
from her singing-lesson. This method of slurring over
difficulties by silence is a terribly fascinating one, mistaken though it may be. It grows upon us as it had
grown upon Laurance Lowe; and, like any other habit,
the tendrils it throws out over the mind are stronger
than we believe.

Before they had gone far they heard a quick footstep
behind them, and Charles Mistley came to Lena's side.
They were in Portland Place, and as he joined them he
beckoned to the driver of a hansom-cab. There seemed

to be no question of Lowe getting into the cab with Lena. He nodded, and as he beckoned to a second driver, Charlie took his seat at Lena's side.

The young sailor began his explanation at once.

"Lena," he said, "only Lowe and myself know of this, and it will be better to keep the whole affair quiet for some time yet. Of course, it is not quite the right thing for you to keep it secret from your mother; but later . . . later, perhaps . . . when Win is home again, you can tell her all about it."

Lena turned slowly toward him. She was leaning back in the cab, while he sat forward with his gloved hands resting on the door. They were passing down Oxford Street, and the smoothness of the pavement rendered it unnecessary for her to raise her voice.

"When Win comes home!" she repeated wonderingly. "What has Win to do with it?"

She was fully convinced that whatever he might know, he could not have guessed at her motive for joining the Brotherhood of Liberty. *That*, at all events, was never to be disclosed. But Charles Mistley had provided for this.

"The Baroness de Nantille," he said, "is Marie Bakovitch!"

She seemed to be slowly forcing the realization of his words into her own mind. At the first thought it appeared to be an impossibility; but gradually, as she looked back over her acquaintanceship with the Baroness, the thing seemed possible, and finally she felt that there was no doubt about the truth of her companion's statement.

After a short pause Charlie continued:

"I have acted in the matter as I think Win himself

19   289

would have done. Of course, I do not pretend to know much of these diplomatic affairs, but . . . it seems to me, Lena . . . that nothing must be disclosed, even to the Colonel, just yet. By chance I learnt about Jacobi from the Baroness herself—some day I will tell you all about it. It is a long story to begin now. When I went back just now, she told me that Ivan Meyer, the man to whom she is . . . engaged—is coming to-morrow. She will write a note to you to-night, saying that she is leaving London suddenly, and cannot give you any more singing-lessons."

Then they drove on for some time without speaking. Presently Lena began to realize that all the events of the last half-hour were the result of forethought and deliberate organization. Every little mishap had been provided for, every moment had been utilized, and every action premeditated by the good-natured lazy sailor, who invariably maintained that he was the poorest organizer living.

She saw it all, and yet she could not begin to thank him. At last she spoke.

"How stupid I have been!" she said. "How idiotic and weak you must think me, Charlie!"

"No," he replied. "No . . . I think . . . well, it does not matter much what I think, because here we are in Bedford Place; and there is my respected mother at the window. It was arranged that I should bring you here from your singing-lesson—if you remember."

CHAPTER XXXIV

CHARLES MISTLEY never gave Lena the full account of his discovery of Jacobi's little plot. It is so easy to put off an explanation till a more convenient occasion, which somehow never arises. From Lowe she could learn nothing—explanation was not his forte.

And so the subject was shelved, partly with deliberate intention on the part of the young sailor, partly by the advent of a more momentous question. Jacobi disappeared, and never returned into Lena's life to wake up memories best left to sleep. Marie Bakovitch left England with Ivan Meyer. Some years later Mrs. Mistley heard of her in Paris, recognizing the beautiful Russian girl in a vivacious French description of the "ravishing" wife of a rising young artist. It would have been easy enough for the gay little Englishwoman to have made the acquaintance of the blonde belle of a Paris season had she desired to do so; but women are more charitably inclined toward each other than the world is generally pleased to suppose, and the mother of Winyard and Charles Mistley felt that it was better to avoid recalling to the mind of Madame Ivan Meyer the fact that she had once been called Marie Bakovitch.

On the day completing the eighteenth month after Winyard Mistley's departure there was a dinner-party at the house in Seymour Street. Any disinterested and

291

experienced matron, watching the arrival of the guests from between the laths of a venetian blind, would un-hesitatingly have prophesied a slow and wearisome even-ing for the guests at this entertainment. There were no ladies—"absolutely no ladies, my dear"—except Mrs. Mistley, Lena, and her mother.

The only young man was Charles Mistley, and he was handicapped by the presence of half a dozen veterans—white-haired old warriors, who were desperately attentive and vastly gallant to the ladies, more especially to Lena; sturdy old rolling-stones, with an inexhaustible fund of anecdotes, little calculated to entertain the fair. These old stagers, however, did weighty justice to the delicacies set before them, and were mightily pleased with the manner in which they each and severally entertained the ladies.

Mrs. Wright led the way to the drawing-room at the first opportunity, and the old fellows were left to pull down their waistcoats with a grave sense of satisfaction at the skilful manner in which they had kept up the spirits of the assembly.

It was rather a remarkable fact that, considering the previous hilarity, no sound of mirth travelled from the dining-room to the drawing-room in the lengthy interval that supervened before the gentlemen rose from the table.

When they at length trooped into the drawing-room, they found the two elder ladies sitting together near the fireplace, while Lena stood in the narrow window, taking advantage of the last rays of daylight to complete some dainty piece of needlework. Charles Mistley lounged across the room, and occupied in a masterly manner the remainder of that window.

"Spoiling your eyes?" he inquired indifferently.

"Yes," she replied.

The old men grouped themselves round the two elder ladies, and conversation was the immediate result. These two women of the world knew how to "take" their ancient admirers. They knew the style of conversation that interested them; they laughed readily at somewhat feeble old jokes. Thus these veteran actors acted to each other, knowing all the time that it could be but in vain. Mrs. Mistley knew that these travellers had been called together to discuss the probable fate of her son. The old men surely knew something of a parent's love; they must have known that this smiling, gray-haired woman was bearing with her such a weight of cruel suspense as only a woman could carry without sinking beneath the burden. And yet, forsooth, they talked of the "season," of Parliamentary reputations made and lost, and other matters of equal importance, throwing in their little jokes and helping each other cunningly with a ready chorus of meaningless laughter.

The fading light of the sunset was fully reflected on Lena's face as she stood in the recess of the tall window, working deftly. Charlie, leaning against the wall opposite to her, was looking at her absently. One would hardly have thought that he was noting the little painful droop of her eyelids when she ceased speaking. He had not the reputation of a keen observer.

His reflections were interrupted by the advent of Adonis, who solemnly crossed the room at this moment to pay his respects. He stooped and caressed the dog's rough head for some moments; then, without raising his eyes, he said:

"Lena."

"Yes."

The girl looked up from her work with her ready
smile, which had of late grown almost mechanical.

"At last—at *last* I am going to do something."

"To do something," she repeated, with ready interest.

"Yes. I have made a mighty resolution to be a hammer in future instead of an anvil."

"I am very glad," she said, in a more serious tone,
though still treating the matter lightly. "It is to be
hoped that it will prove beneficial to humanity."

"Do you know," he said, with sudden gravity, "that
you are looking desperately ill?"

She raised her eyes to his with a little defiant stare of
surprise.

"Are you going to study medicine?" she asked, returning to her needlework.

He made no pretence of smiling, and continued
quietly:

"You have a look about the eyes which, by some mysterious method, conveys to my slow brain the impression
that you dread waking up in the morning, and . . .
consequently wake up all the earlier."

She turned suddenly, and, placing both her hands on
the woodwork of the window, she looked between her
wrists into the quiet street. Her profile, pure and almost
painfully refined in its beauty, was all he could see. The
movement brought her closer to him, and once she swayed
a little to one side, so that her dress touched his sleeve.
He looked down at her gently, noting the slim straight-
ness of her figure, the firm curve of her lips. She was
very strong in her self-suppression; but compared to his,
her strength was as nothing.

"This atmosphere of suspense is killing you," he continued, in his monotonous voice. "It is all very well for

these old folks—they can stand it. Perhaps their senses
are a little duller than ours; but for us it is desperately
trying. I have felt it for some time . . . and . . . and
I have watched its effect upon you. It shows more than
you quite realize, I think. I am not a particularly sensitive fellow, or nervous, you know; and if I feel it, it
must be pretty bad."

"You make me feel quite interesting," she said, with
a brave little laugh, which, however, ceased abruptly,
and she closed her lips hurriedly.

He continued to look down at her gravely for some
moments; then he turned, and glanced out of the window
indifferently.

"Your left hand is trembling at the present moment,"
he said in a lower tone. "It may be—of course—that it
is resting on the nerve; but your mother is looking this
way . . . also mine."

She let her hand drop, almost impatiently, to her side.
Presently she resumed her work, and took no notice of
him for some moments.

"What has all this to do with your virtuous resolu-
tions?" she asked slowly and almost coldly.

"To-day is Tuesday," he replied; "on Friday I start
for Central Asia. I am going to seek Win."

She grew very pale; the color even left her lips.
Charlie continued to gaze out of the window. They
both looked remarkably bored.

"But he said that no one had to be sent before twenty-
one months—twelve weeks yet."

"Central Asia," replied Charlie, "does not belong to
Win. I can go there if I want to; I will risk disobeying
his instructions. The old gentlemen were rather difficult to deal with on that subject; but I succeeded at last

in convincing them that it was best for me to go. I have arranged about my leave of absence."

"Then," said she decisively, "you think there is something wrong?"

"Yes—Lena. I am afraid there is something wrong."

She was still working at the little silken trifle, through which the needle slipped at regular intervals.

"Tell me . . ." she whispered, "what you are afraid of . . . what you think has happened. Tell me if you have given up all . . . hope!"

"No, there is no question of giving up yet; there is every hope, every chance in his favor. Win is very tough; we are a tough race. I think he may have been delayed by a hundred mishaps, at which it is impossible to guess. When I am gone, Lena, it will be your task to . . . to keep my mother up to the mark. It is so much easier to be plucky when there are plucky people around one."

"I will try, Charlie," she said simply.

"And I will keep you posted up as to my whereabouts. If I miss him—if we pass each other on the way, you should be able to stop me somewhere; the Colonel is arranging all that. But—after all, if I wander about there, say, for a year or so, it does not matter much. A year more or less out of an idle life is of no great consequence."

He stopped, and looked down at her with his lazy, placid smile. Presently she looked up, and met his eyes.

"Yours is not an idle life, Charlie," she said. "I have realized that lately. I will never call you lazy again. It is only your manner."

"By the by," he said suddenly, as if recollecting himself, "I will leave this cross with you. It is the thing

Akryl bought from Win at Kizil Arvat. It is no good my taking it out there again. I will fasten it to your watch-chain. Allow me—no one is looking. It is all right!"

He made a movement as if to join the others. It was a silent suggestion that she should do the same; but she remained motionless, and for some reason he did not carry out his purpose.

"Charlie," she said, looking past him into the deserted street, "do you remember one night long ago . . . it was the first time that we danced so much together—the first time we found out . . . how well we . . . got on with each other?"

"Yes," he replied with a peculiar dull look upon his face. "Yes, I remember."

"You look now just as you looked then," she continued vaguely. "There is no change in your appearance; you are as big and strong and . . . and *reliable* as ever. Your manner is apparently the same. But there is a change somewhere—there is a change in you or in me. What is it—where is it—how is it, Charlie? Is it in you, or is it in me?"

"I expect," he suggested restlessly, "that it is in both. We are getting older, you see. People cannot grow older without changing a little, and it is generally supposed to be a change for the better."

"But—but this is not for the better."

"I believe," he said lightly, "that the whole thing is a creation of your own imagination. You admit that I am the same; I know that you are unaltered—where can the change be?"

"Yet—you must admit that there is a difference. Things are not as they used to be."

"It is the way of the world," he replied with a mirth-less laugh. "Things never are as they used to be. No —Lena, I admit nothing. There is an old gentleman opening the piano preparatory to asking you to sing. I must go and help him."

"I am *not* going to sing the 'Farewell' to-night," she said, as he moved away.

"No," he replied gravely. "Please don't!"

CHAPTER XXXV

So Charles Mistley tranquilly began his simple arrange-
ments for a journey he was destined never to take.

Suspense, like all mortal things, must have an end;
and for the watchers in Seymour Street the end was drawing near. It came at last, on the Thursday morning,
just twenty-four hours before the time fixed by Charlie
for his departure.

Lena was still in her room, although the punctual
breakfast-bell had been rung some minutes before. She
was in the act of fixing a little brooch at her throat, when
there was a hurried knock at the door, and the sound
of the Colonel's voice, vibrating with emotion, followed
instantaneously.

" Lena—Lena! "

" Yes, papa," she answered quietly enough. Then
she stood motionless with her back to the window, watching the door.

" May I come in, Lena ? "

" Yes! " She knew that there was news at last.

Then the door opened. For a moment Lena experienced a strong desire to laugh aloud. The Colonel
entered the room hastily; in one hand he flourished a
Submarine Telegraph form, in the other was the bread-
knife, with little scraps of brown paper adhering to its
edge.

Young Mistley

"Mistley is at Vienna!" he gasped. "He is at Vienna! Thank God for this!"

He threw the bread-knife upon the bed, and presently went there and rashly sat upon it.

"Yes," said Lena quietly. She was still engaged with her brooch, and now she turned to look into the glass.

"Lena," exclaimed her father, "do you hear me—do you understand? He is at Vienna—he is safe! Here is the telegram—they have just brought it!"

He held the paper toward her. She saw the action, and noted mechanically the slips of blue paper pasted on to the white telegram form. She remembered wishing with all her strength to step forward and take that paper; then there came a sudden blank—a sense of utter, boundless vacuity, and she found her mother's comforting arms around her.

At breakfast the telegram was discussed word by word. It was not entirely satisfactory upon closer investigation.

"Safe, but quite knocked up. Can you come to me? Tell mater and Charlie."

"'Can you come to me?' . . ." repeated Colonel Wright, with a fierce look in his eyes, as he swallowed a hasty breakfast. "Can I go to him? That is like Mistley. As if the fellow did not know . . . as if he didn't know! And yet he puts it like that; it is Mistley all through. You cannot tell whether the fellow means to be funny or pathetic, and somehow it is both."

Mrs. Wright made no reply. She merely laughed a low, gentle laugh, and behind the friendly covert of a large fern which stood upon the table a tear fell unseen upon a piece of fried bacon.

300

Presently Lena drove off to Bedford Place with the news. The morning was fresh and invigorating, with just a suspicion of autumnal sharpness in the clear atmosphere. Never had London appeared so fair to Lena— never had the world appeared so bright. The very drudges dusting the steps and black-leading the scrapers were not ordinary housemaids that morning. For them even life seemed to have its pleasures, its joys, and its consolation. The dust they caused to fly from overworked door-mats actually scintillated with gold.

The patient hansom-cab horse, with his flopping, nerveless ears, was worthy of all human sympathy—the very ordinary hansom flew through the rosy air with the speed of the sun-god's chariot.

Mrs. Mistley was standing with her back to the window, the *Times* in her hand, when Lena entered the room. The remains of breakfast upon the table showed that Charlie had already left the house. Mrs. Mistley turned her graceful white head somewhat sharply toward the door when the servant opened it. For a moment she looked at Lena with a sudden gleam of emotion in her calm gray eyes; then she laid aside the newspaper and advanced toward her.

"You have news!" she said, in her pretty, tainted English. "Lena, you have news; I can see it in your eyes!"

Lena had to stoop just a little to kiss the brave, steady lips.

"Yes," she replied, "I have news. Papa has sent me to say that Winyard is all right. He is in Vienna— here is a copy of the telegram."

Mrs. Mistley received the news cheerfully. She evinced no surprise, and was by no means demonstrative in her joy; in fact, it was hard to realize that she had ever felt a moment's anxiety. Lena expressed some surprise that Winyard should have telegraphed to her father instead of his own mother; but Mrs. Mistley thought nothing of it, explaining that Win knew her wandering ways.

"Charlie is out," she added; "buying a saddle or something. He has also gone to see the doctor to show his arm, which is as strong as the other now. I will leave a note for him, in case he should come in when I am out."

An hour after the receipt of Winyard's telegram Colonel Wright was at Charing Cross Station. Shortly before the departure of his train Mrs. Mistley and Lena arrived, accompanied by Adonis, who had now quite assumed the repose of manner characterizing a town dog.

It was arranged that if Winyard was seriously ill he should be taken to Seymour Street, which was quieter and more convenient for an invalid than Bedford Place. After a few days' rest the move to Broomhaugh could easily be accomplished.

All this was rapidly settled, and there were still three or four minutes to spare. They proceeded to walk up and down the broad platform somewhat restlessly amid the restless throng. To Colonel Wright this comfortable journey was nothing; he had secured a good seat, and there was no crowd, yet he was not at his ease. He felt compelled to break the silence, which was in reality by no means irksome to the ladies.

"There are," he hazarded, "many different sorts of courage. There is that of the soldier, which is emotional and strongly dependent on emulation; there is that of the sailor, which is perhaps of a higher order, though it is purely defensive; he repels danger and fights for his life. But highest of all there is the courage that needs no emulation, asks for none to share its dangers, faces solitude and continuous risk with steady intrepidity —surely this is the noblest courage . . ."

They turned and walked toward the engine again, Adonis meekly following with his left ear slightly elevated and his face expressive of dignified attention, for he loved the sound of the Colonel's voice.

" And," continued the old soldier, with a glance downward at the silent women on either side of him, both trim and straight and gracious, though one head was clad in soft, dry white hair—" And there is the wonderful courage of women who stay behind and wait . . . but that is different. I think . . . it comes to them direct from heaven."

When Charles Mistley called at Seymour Street later in the morning he was told that Colonel Wright had suddenly left home, but that the ladies were in.

The first person he saw on entering the room was his mother comfortably established with some needlework in her hands, as if she were one of the family. Some women have this pleasant way with them, knowing how to settle into any household—be it in joy or be it in sorrow—in a few minutes.

Mrs. Wright and Lena were standing near the window studying Bradshaw's " Railway Guide."

As soon as Mrs. Mistley caught sight of her son she rose, and, advancing toward him, took his hand, apparently forgetting that she had seen him only a few hours before. The action placed her rather cleverly between him and the two ladies, so that they could not well see his face.

" Charlie," she said quickly, " we have news of Win.

Young Mistley

I left a note for you at Bedford Place. The Colonel has gone to Vienna to bring him home, as he is knocked up."

The young sailor nodded his head gravely. Then he advanced toward Mrs. Wright, and shook hands silently with her and Lena. He was unusually awkward that morning, and looked very large and out of place in the dainty, womanly room. He stroked his chin with his strong brown hand almost nervously.

"I *am* glad," he said at length; "I *am* glad!"

Then he looked round the room rather helplessly. The chairs were ridiculously small and frail compared to his huge frame, and he made no attempt to sit down.

"I have just bought a very good saddle," he said suddenly, and without any apparent sequence of thought. "The man is altering it for me . . . I suppose I can countermand it now."

He smiled a little, and the ladies smiled sympathetically. The two elder women took an ardent interest in that saddle, just as they would have taken an interest in Digestive Bread or the death of Alcibiades, if Charlie had brought the subject under their notice.

Then they talked of Vienna and the journey there, praising the gifted Mr. Bradshaw, and abusing the German railways, until Charles Mistley took his temporary leave.

He wandered down Seymour Street in an absent-minded manner. Presently he came upon a little black-and-tan terrier sitting upon a doorstep, with its quivering spine pressed against the immovable door. He stopped before it, and the dog raised one paw as if to beg him to bring the bell, setting back its head, and looking up at him with pretty canine coquetry. Without thinking much of what he was doing, the sailor raised his hand and rang the bell; then he strode slowly on.

"I *am* glad," he murmured to himself; "yes, I *am* glad!"

After walking for some distance, he drew his watch from his pocket, and carried it for some time in his hand, as if to have it ready to look at as soon as he had finished with the thought then occupying his mind. He looked at the face of it for some moments without seeing the time; then he suddenly realized what he was doing.

"By George!" he exclaimed; "by George! I am in time for the alternative yet." And, calling a cab, he drove rapidly to the Admiralty.

20

CHAPTER XXXVI

THE three ladies were again sitting in the drawing-room in Seymour Street together. It was the Monday morning. Colonel Wright had telegraphed several times from Vienna and other towns on the homeward journey. The most important item in these messages had been that, despite medical advice, Winyard Mistley insisted upon coming home at once, and they might be expected at eleven o'clock on the Monday morning.

It was after eleven now. The ladies were working with a calmness which was perhaps slightly overdone. Adonis slept peacefully beside Mrs. Mistley's chair, upon a corner of her dress.

"These Continental trains are invariably late," observed Mrs. Wright, glancing at the clock upon the mantelpiece.

"Yes," was Mrs. Mistley's cheerful reply; "we can hardly expect them yet. Colonel Wright did wisely, I think, in suggesting that none of us should go to the station; there will be noise and fuss enough without my being there to agitate Win, and make him pretend that he is stronger than he really is. It is much better that Charlie should meet them."

"Where Charlie is," suggested Mrs. Wright, in a low voice, "there will be no fuss. He possesses the happy faculty of doing the right thing at the right moment, without appearing to know that he *is* doing it."

Young Mistley

"Yes," said Charlie's mother vaguely. She was about to say something more, but checked herself suddenly; and spreading her work out before her, she proceeded to smooth it out with deft fingers, patting it here and there, and tugging it cornerwise. While thus occupied, she spoke again, without looking up, in a light conversational tone.

"Do you know," she said, "I cannot quite realize that Win is ill. What ailments he has had have always come when . . . he was away . . . from me. I cannot picture to myself how he will take it; he has always been so well and hearty."

"According to papa's telegram, he is hearty still," said Lena gayly, as she carefully selected a thread of silk from a parti-colored tangle. "He telegraphed, 'Spirits high,' which sounds like a meteorological report."

"I think Win's spirits are proof against a good deal," replied Mrs. Mistley, with a glance toward Lena. It was a mere passing peep, but the little lady saw enough to convince her that the needle stood a very poor chance of being threaded just then.

At this moment the sound of approaching wheels broke upon them all. The vehicle audibly stopped at the door, and Adonis looked up sharply. Lena was still striving to get the silk somewhere near the eye of the needle.

Mrs. Mistley laid aside her work. She tried to do it as calmly and quietly as she could, but there was something dramatic even in her intense self-possession. She drew in a long uneven breath, and rose from her seat, looking toward the door.

Adonis stood at her side with his left ear on duty.

Already there were footsteps down-stairs in the hall. Then came a little laugh of one voice only, and Adonis literally shrieked at the sound of it. Like a battering-ram he sprang at the door, endeavoring to seize the handle in his strong teeth. He fell back and threw himself against the wood again. Then Mrs. Mistley opened the door.

On the threshold stood Winyard. The Colonel's arm was round him, and he had one hand on the old traveller's shoulder, for he could not stand alone.

Mrs. Mistley stood on tip-toe with an almost girlish grace, and Winyard's free arm went round her. No one spoke a word.

Then Mrs. Wright came forward and assisted him to a chair. As he sank into it she stooped and kissed him.

"Do not be too kind to me," he said, smiling. "I am rather weak, and kindness has been known to kill people, I believe."

He looked up to shake hands with Lena, and she saw that there were tears in his eyes.

Adonis was standing on his hind legs, with his fore-paws resting on the arm of the low chair. His faithful eyes were luminous with love, and he whined continuously with his square chin upraised.

At this moment Charlie entered the room. He was laden with sundry wraps and packages, which he set down absently upon a polished table.

"The return of the prodigal," he said cheerfully. "I *do* wish I liked cold veal!"

This brought Mrs. Wright's thoughts back to practical matters.

"Beef-tea!" she exclaimed. "You *must* have some beef-tea or some wine!"

Winyard pointed solemnly at the Colonel.

"Ask him," he said; "I know nothing about it. The

affair has lost all interest for me. He has taken charge
of the matter. I am not allowed to say what I like or
what I dislike—in fact, I am the bane of my own life! "

" Beef-tea," said Colonel Wright severely, as he drew
off his gloves. " Yes—beef-tea."

This was soon brought, and the whole party stood
round the sick man to see that he consumed it.

" And have you done all you wanted to do, Win ? "
asked Mrs. Mistley presently.

" Oh yes! " he replied breathlessly, between the sips.
" Won't you let me off the rest ?—I am getting down to
the sediment now! "

But Colonel Wright was not content with this laconic
account of his pupil's exploits.

" He has done that and more! " he said exultingly.
" He has done what no living man has done before him,
or could hope to do again. He has been right through
to Peshawur and back. He has mapped out every feasible route, noted the position of every well, and obtained
every imaginable item of information that the officer com-
manding a division could require. And that quite outside his own diplomatic work, which has been carried out
to the letter! "

Such was the home-coming of Winyard Mistley.

It was only by degrees that they extracted from him the
details of his perilous journey. How he escaped detec-
tion by the readiness of his wit. How, encompassed by
danger, treachery, and fanaticism on every side, he came
through it all by sheer self-reliance and intrepidity. How
he lay for months ill in a Turcoman tent, nursed and
tended by the simple nomads. How, time after time,
the combination seemed too strong for him to fight
against, and how his good fortune attended him to the

end. But all this had to be guessed at by his loving listeners. The story of that unique and wonderful journey was never fully told. Partly by aid of their own imaginations, partly by persistent questioning, they succeeded in putting together a more or less connected narrative; but Winyard's own account was decidedly unsatisfactory, as might well have been expected. A man cannot tell his own story advantageously. There was no one else to tell the tale of Winyard Mistley's achievement, and so it was never told. Far away, on the sands of the Khivan desert, out of the caravan route, in a trackless waste untrodden by the foot of man for years together, a few whitened bones, picked clean and scattered by the quarrelling vultures, lay beneath the gleaming sun, waiting the end of all things. This, and nothing more, was what remained of the young Englishman's daring companion during the greater part of his wonderful journey, and the story of it lay silent with those bones.

But if the record of the work was lost, the fruits were well preserved, and among these the Colonel spent many a busy day. The news of Winyard's return soon spread among the initiated, and the house in Seymour Street was besieged by visitors. The results of the journey were, however, kept strictly secret, only the Colonel and a few experts being allowed to assist the invalid in the work of putting them in order. Soon, however, the news leaked out, and questions were asked in Parliament, with the result of acquainting Russia with the fact that she had been beaten in her own favorite pastime of Eastern diplomacy. Article after article appeared in the Moscow papers, calling for further investigation into the carelessness of the avowed Russian agents in Afghanistan, who could give no details of the passage of this dangerous traveller through their midst. These writings, hot from the brain of one who, even as these lines are penned, is being mourned by the nation he served so well with pen and press, were issued with the view of learning more of the results of Winyard Mistley's observations; but in this object they failed. All that the world learnt was that the journey had been accomplished, whether alone or with companions, whether hasty and superficial or slow and searching, never transpired.

Day by day Winyard regained his strength, and the lines upon his face—lines speaking of hardship, hunger, thirst, and anxiety—began to disappear. They never quite left him, however, but remained there, signs of age upon a young face—silent testimonies of forgotten sufferings. His appearance had, at first, been rather a shock to all who remembered him as he was in former days. He was not pale, but the dull brownness of his face seemed only to accentuate the drawn and weary expression of his features; through all, however, and even when he could not stand unsupported, the brave, strong look never left his eyes.

It may have been by sheer force of will, but his boyish cheerfulness was as reliable as of old. He laughed at his own weakness and incapacity to walk alone; yet his laughter failed to detract from the pathos of the picture afforded by the Colonel assisting him to move about. He laughed at his own childish helplessness in the matter of cutting up his food, and audaciously handed his plate to Lena for assistance.

Altogether he was the most unsatisfactory convalescent imaginable, except that he made visible and rapid strides toward health. There was no demand for lowered tones and noiseless movements in his presence. Inquiries after his welfare were treated jocosely, and unless the medicine was administered with severity and regularity, he was only too ready to forget all about it.

CHAPTER XXXVII

A few days after Winyard Mistley's return to London, his brother Charlie went to Devonport. From there he wrote that he had been offered the *White Swallow* gunboat, destined for service in the Pacific Ocean. "Of course I have accepted," he wrote; and gave no particulars as to when the *White Swallow* was likely to sail, and of what duration her absence from England would probably be.

Mrs. Mistley, who was now established at Seymour Street previous to a move northward to Broomhaugh, received the letter at the breakfast-table. She read part of it aloud, and, as she folded it again, gave a little sigh of resignation.

"Such it is," she said, "to be the mother of a sailor and a soldier. They play Box and Cox to the end of the chapter. However, I suppose Charlie is to be congratulated. He is young to have command of a gunboat."

"With all his assumed laziness," observed the Colonel gravely, "Charlie will push his way upward through the ruck. He is a fine sailor, I am sure."

That same afternoon Mrs. Mistley and Mrs. Wright went out together, in order, they said, to have a quiet afternoon's shopping, as there were many things to be purchased and sent on to Broomhaugh. The mother and son had been nearly a week in Seymour Street, and there was now nothing to delay their departure for the north.

The Colonel, being left in charge of the invalid, proposed a drive in the Park, as the air was lovely and the sun not too warm. But Winyard languidly expressed a fear that he was not quite up to it, innocently ignoring the fact that he had walked down-stairs alone that morning. Then he lay back on his sofa and gently closed his eyes, as if composing himself to peaceful slumber.

Presently the Colonel left the room, treading noiselessly so as to avoid waking the sleeper. Shortly afterward the street-door closed with a smothered bang.

Lena was seated on a low chair near the window, the regular click of her needle acting as a lullaby to the sufferer. Soon, however, Winyard slowly unclosed one eye, then the other. The click of the needle continued. He turned slightly, and lay there watching her. He could scarcely have wished for a pleasanter picture to look upon than that fair English maiden, sitting with daintily bowed head and busy fingers—"on duty," as it were—quietly fulfilling her woman's mission. Like his brother, he noticed then that Lena was no longer the thoughtless merry girl whom he had known two years before. The same brave cheeriness was there, but it was less liable to the influence of circumstances; the same healthy power of enjoyment, but it was tempered by a greater thoughtfulness. Something in the curve of her closed lips, something perhaps in a newly acquired droop of the eyelids, reminded him of the bravest woman he had ever known; of one who, widowed, and the mother of wandering sons, had yet made her life a bright one, and by seeking to make others happy, had acquired the habit of happiness herself. What pen could hope to follow the thoughts passing

314

Young Mistley

through a man's brain? Winyard Mistley lay watching
Lena for about five minutes, but five pages of mine could
not tell a tithe of what was passing in his mind.

Presently he rose gravely from the sofa, and stood for
a moment by the mantelpiece, supporting himself with
both hands. His back was turned toward Lena, and on
the lean brown face reflected in the mirror—at which,
however, he never glanced—there was a strange restless
expression.

Contrary to her custom, Lena failed to look up. She
did not even ask him if there was anything he might require. Then he slowly turned and made his laborious
way across the room, assisting himself with one piece of
furniture after another. Somehow she forgot to offer
him her help; somehow he had no little pleasantry ready
to make her smile; and yet neither seemed to notice the
difference. She continued her work (the stitches were
unpicked later on, being of very peculiar construction),
and Mistley stood close at hand, looking down upon her
bent head.

There was a humble chair at her side, and into this he
lowered himself cautiously, after the manner of an old
man.

"Lena," he said, turning toward her with a hungering look in his eyes—"Lena, do you think that a man
can be sure of his own mind if the same thought has
never left it for nearly two years?"

She bowed her head lower over her work, still striving
to make the needle perform its right and proper func-
tion, but answered him no word.

He leant forward and took the work from her hands,
allowing it to fall to the ground. Then he quietly took
possession of those busy fingers.

315

"Answer me," he whispered—"answer me!"

"Yes . . . I think so," she replied at length.

"Through it all," he said eagerly—"through danger and through hope, through work, through sleep, through hunger, sickness, and success—there has been one thought in my brain. That thought . . . was . . . Lena—Lena . . . Lena!"

Still bending over her imprisoned hands, she swayed unconsciously toward him. Then, somehow, he found his arms were round her, though he had no recollection of placing them there.

*   *   *   *   *

Three weeks later, one afternoon as the sun began to throw a golden ray from west to east up the English Channel, a gunboat moved out into Plymouth Sound, and cast her anchor there. The *White Swallow* was ready for sea—"ready for anything," her young commander said. Deeply laden with coal for her long voyage, she was as taut, and trim, and sparkling as paint and polished brass could make her.

Already the strong individuality of the stalwart ruler was beginning to make itself discernible among the members of her company. The *White Swallow* was eminently a "quiet" ship. There was no shouting, no unnecessary blowing of boatswains' whistles. Everything seemed to fit into its place—every man into his duties. And yet she was not a gloomy ship, for every man looked forward to his six years' absence with serenity.

About an hour before she was due to sail, a boat put off from the Dockyard, and in a few minutes was alongside the gunboat. Seated in the stern of this small craft was Laurance Lowe. He climbed up the white ladder, and made his way aft with slow but assured steps.

Charles Mistley came forward to meet him, and they turned toward the quarter-deck together.

"It is very good of you to come," said the young sailor.

The old man did not appear to consider that this required an answer. He looked round him critically with a practised eye. It was not the first time that he had trodden the deck of a man-of-war, though his recollections of such dated back to the days of the Crimea. He loosened the old silk comforter that took the place of a top-coat on his spare frame, and said:

"You are ready?"

"Yes, we sail in half an hour."

The young sailor looked across the smooth water to where the land rose gently, green and tree-clad, toward the blue heights of Dartmoor. There was no shadow of fear in his clear eyes, no sign of flinching from the dreary years he knew he was facing. And thus they stood side by side, the old man whose voyage across the troubled sea was nearly over (he had made bad weather of it, beating up against a head wind all the way), and the young sailor—tall, stalwart, and almost painfully self-contained—who, like his companion, had met the stress at the very beginning of his journey.

They talked a little in their usual scrappy, unsatisfactory manner, and then Laurance Lowe beckoned to his boatman to haul up to the ladder.

He turned, and looked round the vessel once more; then he raised his solemn eyes to his companion's face. They were unusually wide open, and Charlie noted the pale blueness of the iris as he returned their gaze.

"I suppose," said the old man slowly, "I suppose"—and with a wave of his lean hand he designated the

317

vessel—"that you have got the object of your ambition now."

He finished his sentence with the shadow of a smile, which could only be seen in his eyes, for it did not move the white mustache or narrow beard.

Charlie did not reply at once. He turned to take some letters from the hand of a quarter-master, and waited till the man had left the quarter-deck before answering his companion's vague question.

"I think," he said at last, "that a man has two objects in his life. At least it is . . . it was . . . so with me."

Laurance Lowe waited silently for him to continue.

Charlie looked round his vessel almost critically.

"This is one," he said.

"Yes," murmured Lowe, standing in front of him, and looking up into his motionless face with lifeless eyes.

"And the other . . ." continued the sailor, slowly meeting his gaze. "And the other . . . I think you know what the other . . . was."

"Yes," said Lowe softly, as he held out his hand to say farewell. "Yes . . . I know. With me . . . it was her mother."

THE END